CHAMPION IMMORTAL:

Book Four in the Reject High Series

Brian Thompson

Great Nation Publishing, LLC
3828 Salem Road #56
Covington, GA 30016

www.authorbrianthompson.com
E-mail: brian@authorbrianthompson.com

This book is a work of fiction. Names, characters, places, and incidents are products of the author's imagination or are used in a fictitious situation. Any resemblances to actual events or persons, living or dead – are purely coincidental and beyond the intent of the editor.

Printed in the United States of America

ISBN: 978-0-9891056-6-8

Library of Congress Control Number: 2013936990

ACKNOWLEDGEMENTS

TO: My Lord and Savior Jesus Christ for the ideas used to build the Reject High world.

My wife and business partner Heather, and our two shareholders, Zae and Jaina. You three (and soon to be four) are the sweetest part of my life, and your sacrifices make all this possible. Thank you.

My father, Bradley, who suggested to me five years ago that I write a multi-book series in the first place, my mother, Barbara, for her continuous support and impromptu editing advice.

Thank you to the English teachers who changed my life: Kathy Walsh, Cindy Lutenbacher, Sue Posch, Linda Zatlin, Toni Salaam-Butz and Tim Askew.

To my editing partners, Jackie Rodriguez, who introduced me to the magic of the young adult fiction world, and Martha Brown and Jeff Hipps. First Mondays of the month are special because of you three.

My editor for the series, Mary Marvella Barfield. Thanks for your hard work. To my mentor, Tia McCollors, thank you for always having advice or an encouraging word for me.

My stepmother Debra, who is one of two people on the planet I know who would adopt a kid with anger issues like Jason. Thank you for letting me honor you and your unconditional love. To Phyllis Conway and the Lowe family for allowing me to use George Lowe's name and parts of his story to honor him. Also, to Christine Mayfield for inspiring Rhapsody, and Jeff and Diane Ransom – you may not be immortal, super-powered beings, but you are special to me.

Special thanks to my beta reading team, Bethany Allmon, Nakia Brown, Tamiko Bowman, LeAnne Hardeman, Crystal Kovacs, Anna Oliver, Valerie Strawmier, Adrienne Thompson, DeAnna Troupe, Brittany Watkins and especially Tiandria Cotton, Laura Almond, and Gina Johnston.

To Megan Boyd, LPC, Keith Clepper and Susan Kline for information and advice on how to write those with special needs like Jason and Michelle Hover for the physics lessons. Thank you, Kristi Liebel and Jenn Fetter, for sharing your stories about losing your mothers.

A posthumous thank you to Jennifer Reynolds, who educated me about *The Laundry List* and life as the child of an alcoholic.

To the people who have named or helped with characters over the past four novels, including: Beverly Cofer, Matt Criswell, Jennifer Grayauskie, Drew Helm, Seymone Jackson, Donna Mengel, Andreas and Susan Scherffel, and Theresa Ramsey.

Watch for a series of short stories that take place in the Reject High world, *Reject High Revisited: Tales from Between the Bells*, in spring, 2017.

This work is dedicated to the memory of Dorothy Meriweather and Virginia Meriweather

CHAPTER ONE

the band's breaking up

Instead of creating our science project, Rhapsody and I planned a getaway to Vegas. We'd catch dinner and a movie and spend the night. The perfect way to relax after six months of on and off crime fighting or so I thought.

Our friend Esteban asked to tag along. By ask, I mean *he begged me* to let him crash my date. His girlfriend, my ex, Sasha, had broken up with him *again*. I wished they'd never gotten together. Since I probably had something to do with this last split, I said yes.

The trip was almost a nine hour drive. Thanks to radioactive emeralds and the abilities they gave us, we flew there in under an hour. Rhapsody used her invisibility powers to make our trip impossible to track by radar. We'd arrived, eaten pizzas, and stood in line at the concession stand for drinks by the time Esteban met us.

"Ready guys?" A load of candy stuffed in his arms, he cracked an awkward smile. Sweat matted his brown bangs to his forehead and faint trails of green smoke drifted up from his shirt.

Why was he so friendly? Three months ago he *hated* me. Rhapsody was at my left, and I felt her scowling at the side of my face. Anything I said now would be an argument, and we'd gone a week without fighting. No sense in starting one.

We'd walked the long hallway together, gotten through the double doors, and had just settled into our cushioned seats when a fearsome *boom* shook the padded walls.

Groups of moviegoers dove onto the sticky floor and covered their heads. They thought it was an earthquake. Hopefully that's all it was, but knowing us, I knew better. Hair raised on the back of my neck. I hoped for the best.

Rhapsody must've sensed danger, too. She tapped my hand and pointed to the jagged crack in the ceiling. "Umm, Jason?"

My stomach dropped when I realized what she wanted to do.

Good thing I'd worn an armored bodysuit over my clothing. Installed in it was a cloaking device which I could activate or deactivate by pressing my palm. I did it and immediately the black suit became visible. Drawing its mask over my face, I flew up to the ceiling and pushed as much of it as I could back into place.

The structure creaked and moaned from the stress. A sizable chunk broke off and fell out of my reach toward the audience below. "Heads up!" I yelled into my mask's Bluetooth headset.

Rhapsody was already in place and used quantum tunneling – we called it "ghosting" – to make the debris intangible until it struck the floor. Once the shock of their almost death wore off, the people scrambled away before another tremor rattled the building.

The romantic comedy cut off, sending the theater into darkness. No one would notice me up here now, but it also meant they'd have trouble finding their way out. Rhapsody solved that problem when she screamed "Fire!"

Little chance of that, though even at this height the air did smell of burnt wire and insulation. Nobody stopped to ask questions. Using their cell phone lights as guides, they huddled together and moved out.

"Clear!" Esteban yelled. He and Rhapsody had uncloaked as well.

I zipped over to the theater aisle where Esteban and Rhapsody waited for me. Without my support, the ceiling thunderously caved in on the seats. Thick waves of dust and debris blew toward us in clouds.

"*Bomb,*" Esteban pointed toward the floor. "Not an earthquake a bomb. The blast came from beneath us."

Great. The one weekend we didn't want to save the planet and now *this.*

My heart jumped at my first thought: *terrorists.* The last big terrorist attack in America happened when I was four. I had just turned seventeen last September.

"It's our fault," I said out loud. "They wouldn't have gotten past the terrorism alert system if..."

"No time to point fingers, Cap." She put a hand on my shoulder. "You wanna help? Let's help."

"Cap" was short for "Captain Obvious," a nickname Rhapsody had given me on our first day together at Reject High. But she was wrong this time. *Dead wrong.* Obviously it *was* our fault. The solar storm we'd created last year had ravaged electrical systems across the globe.

Telecommunications went in and out. Whoever had detonated the bomb had exploited that. We were to blame. I didn't see another person responsible.

"All right," I said.

We sprinted into the hallway to assess the damage. In the background, white lights blinked and the emergency alarms screeched loud and often. The rushing, screaming masses looked like bloody rugby scrums. Parents struggled to protect their children.

Esteban surveyed the destruction. "I could've stayed at home for all this."

He told the truth. The rolling brownouts in our town meant situations could turn upside down at any time. I wondered what was taking so long to repair the damaged electrical grid. The solar storm had happened in May, 2013. This was March, 2014. Nearly ten months had passed. Were the power grids nationwide that bad off?

"Let's go to work," I said.

Rhapsody bounced on her toes and flapped her hands. Were there a cigarette anywhere nearby or half trampled on the floor, she'd have smoked it. "What's the plan?"

For a long time my therapy revolved around one question. "What's the responsible action here, Jason Champion?" Susan, my therapist, wanted me to think before acting, which was hard for an ADHD kid like me. We *had* to help. Doing nothing or running away wasn't an option. Not since Rhapsody gave me the emerald she'd found in the basement of Reject High.

My skin tingled. *Too much pressure. Have to think. What would Sasha say? She should be doing this.* Since she'd left our team, I'd figured out everything on my own. *I wish I could pick her brain right now.*

We had to hurry, so I winged it. "Okay...okay...well, at least it's different this time."

"No Selby, no Sasha. Fine." Esteban cleared his throat. "People are going to die if we don't move. Make the call."

Esteban's teleportation power could get us to the center of the action the fastest. It didn't take a master tactician to figure that out. I pointed at his chest. "Get us to the lobby. *Now.*"

He teleported the three of us behind the concession stand. In front of it a sea of men, women, and children scrambled to exit the building. The beige walls decorated with huge coming attraction posters were intact, except for in the far corner. There, the structure had crumbled like a waterfall of solid concrete. Since the distance from the theater to the lobby was short, my body adjusted pretty quickly to the shift. Teleporting made me feel like I was drunk with a stomach full of food.

"There!" I pointed out the falling structure to Rhapsody. The billowing gray dust and smoke would make this even more difficult. "Umm...Esteban and I are going into the basement. You should get as many of them out as you can!"

"Done!" she yelled back before vanishing into thin air.

I took a deep breath seconds before the next round of teleporting. Esteban could only take us somewhere he'd been before or could see. With the theater on the third floor and a five level garage beneath us, we had seven stories to go. Each time we went in and out it made me nauseous. *Why didn't he do them all at once?*

When we made it to the first level of the parking lot, I steadied myself on the solid flooring and patted my cramping stomach. "Sorry," I whispered to it.

Esteban and I pressed the outside of our gloves to key our suits' lighting mechanisms. A purplish glow lit up around us. We were standing near the blast's flower blossom-shaped epicenter. The explosion had spread remnants of destroyed vehicles to the lot's cratered surface. My tense muscles relaxed. *No bodies.*

Passengers trapped in their cars rolled down their windows and screamed "Help!" At the sight of us, several of them stopped to look. To them, *we'd* caused the damage. Bloggers and news media outlets called us "vigilantes," like we'd harm them. We stayed invisible when possible, but sometimes we just couldn't.

I noticed that several of the support columns had cracked, but the one closest to where the bomb detonated was rubble. The ceiling held, for the most part, but if we didn't stabilize it soon, it would crush the survivors.

"What do we do?" Esteban repeated himself as if asking the same question six times in a row would encourage me to think faster.

"Get them out! I'll do what I can down here."

He nodded. Green teleportation puffs of smoke popped all across the level. I choked on the stench of leaking fluids and a rotten egg odor. I'd never noticed Esteban's power carried a scent before.

Looking up, I saw a spot where I could at least keep the structure from caving in. By instinct, I flew to the top of the parking deck, and this time I braced it with my back. Soon after, a huge chunk of the concrete roof demolished a black PT Cruiser and its driver. Turning my head, I swallowed hard and pretended the crunching I'd heard was metal and broken glass and not the snap of human bones.

I'd seen death strike many times before, but it hadn't gotten any easier to watch. Blinking away the stinging tears in my eyes, I shouted "Hurry up!"

The copper cabling overhead bent and then finally gave. Heavy concrete fragments fell onto occupied cars. I swooped around the garage level and tried to stall the imminent collapse. A blinding headache raged across my brain from the wails and blinking headlights of car alarms. I had to concentrate – if I lost it, even for a second, my powers might fizzle out. More people would die.

The blast point. With that one spot for me to focus on, the sound around me faded away.

When Esteban had rescued the survivors, he disappeared to the next level of the parking garage. That's when I noticed movement in the shadows.

Someone is down here. I waved my hand in his direction. "Run! Get out!"

Right before I was going to fly over to it, the shadow assumed a human shape. I hovered in the air. "What are you doing? Get out!"

The person casting it never appeared. Fantastic, *another* dead body.

Sweat dribbled into my eyes. I'd been hallucinating. I closed my eyes and reopened them. The shadow was gone and the garage continued to implode. I'd imagined it. That's all. It's what tends to happen when you have PTSD and don't sleep.

I'd been concentrating so hard. *Had Esteban said anything? Were he and Rhapsody in trouble?*

A giant hole opened in the ceiling. Rows of cars skidded down and plunged down onto my level. *Were there any survivors left?*

"Rhapsody!" I shouted over the collisions. My voice sounded way higher and shriller than I wanted it to. "What's your 20?"

"Shopping level!" she shouted back out-of-breath. "What's all that noise?"

Because I was unsure of how many people remained, I couldn't leave, even if it was only one. I could still save him. "Garage! Now!"

"In a minute!" she shouted back. "Little busy here."

With scarlet emerald radiation in my body, I could harness telekinetic energy. I tried stopping the destruction with my mind and lost some altitude doing it. "Okay. That didn't work," I said to myself while the chaos continued. "Help me!"

She didn't answer. Was she hurt, or pissed at me, frustrated, or on her way? I don't translate female silences well at all, and she'd had a lot lately. Down here, she could be a big help. She'd gotten my powers plus hers by drinking a potion made of my blood and an aquamarine. Good thing her blood was AB negative like mine. We'd hypothesized it was the reason the transfer hadn't killed her.

"Rhapsody!" *Please, God, let her answer.* "Esteban! Say something!"

Neither of them did. My throat tightened. I was on my own.

Huge slabs of concrete smashed over my head and fell to the ground. The construction could be blocking my Bluetooth signal. Or he'd passed out from teleporting so much. Adrenaline kick-started our powers and made us tired and hungrier than newborn babies. After all this, whether we wanted to or not, we'd have to eat a lot of food.

I closed my eyes, thinking it would help me center my thoughts. Instead, I sensed someone standing underneath me. *Who's crazy enough to stay in a collapsing structure besides us?* I looked down and saw a man about twenty years old or so, with curled dark hair and tanned skin. Because of the dust and falling debris I couldn't get a clear look at his face. Dressed head to toe in black, he held a wicked looking knife with a gray metal handle in his left hand. Its blade was an off-white color, shiny and smooth.

Goshenite. One look at it, and I knew that it could kill me.

I wanted to land but couldn't. He had a scarlet emerald on him. My ADHD prevented him from reading my mind or controlling my actions. He could freeze me, which was what he was doing. Cars continued to plummet down and pile on each other. Everything about this guy, plus the tightness in my gut, said *terrorist.* He was the deliveryman. I had to stop him or we'd never find out who he was working with.

He stared at me. *Is he one of us?* He had to be. *What does he want?* I memorized his facial features. Then he *changed* them. He was a shape-shifter.

With wavy red hair and a fair complexion, he looked like Taylor. She was the last person with shape-shifting abilities I'd met, but she was dead. A second later, he morphed into a teenage black girl. Did she or he go to North High with us? That wasn't possible. I refused to believe I'd been attending school with an assassin for months.

"Who are you?" I mumbled, unable to move my tongue.

She flipped the knife by the blade and tossed it at my chest. I closed my eyes and grunted, expecting to feel sharpness plunge through my skin. The knife froze in place – its tip touched me right above the heart. She waved her hand and it dropped back into her palm.

"I've got your attention, and I've seen enough," she said before waving goodbye. "We'll be in touch."

She disappeared behind a stack of smashed vehicles. The stiff way she cocked her hand when she waved made me think it might've been the same person who had seen Rhapsody and me fly away to Xobai last year. But that person was *male and alone for all we knew.* This girl was a female and had a partner. *Who?* David King, who we stopped from destroying the planet, was dead.

A large section of the fractured ceiling yawned and caved. Vehicles slapped together and smashed into one another like expensive cymbals. The collisions were deafening. *What's Rhapsody hollering over my earpiece?*

"Get out, Jason!" I finally understood between all the curse words.

Eyeing the yellow exit arrows painted on the ground, I gathered my remaining strength and flew out of the parking garage. The entire structure folded behind me, sending shockwaves through the air. I'd exited so fast that I didn't bother to swerve away from the storefront boutique across the street from me.

I crashed through the glass display, tumbled across the floor, and rolled to a stop in front of the dressing rooms. Surrounded by mannequins, shattered glass, and knocked over display carousels, I laid the back of my head against the carpeted floor and exhaled. Once again we'd make the news. We'd be vigilantes who caused millions of dollars in damage. No one would know we'd saved hundreds or maybe even thousands of people. All our lives, somebody has been calling us screw-ups. It might as well be telecast to the world, I guess.

Rhapsody stepped over my body, leaned over, and brushed her hair behind her ears. She'd dyed it all black except for a few streaks that she'd colored fire engine red. She'd pierced her left nostril and lost some weight, which I mentioned all the time. Her tired smile showed the same exhaustion I felt.

"I signaled *drag bunt*," she shouted over the store's security alarm. She extended her hand, and I grabbed it to help me stand. "You slid for home plate! That's what I get for pulling you off the bench to pinch hit."

It was funny, but I didn't want to encourage her by laughing. We turned our heads at the chopping of helicopter blades outside. "Where's Esteban?" I asked with a little too much irritation in my voice. *The cops will be here in a minute.* "We've gotta get back home like yesterday."

Rhapsody shrugged. "Tell me something I don't know, Dude. He's off being emotional and pouting somewhere, I guess. You got enough gas to get out of here?"

"Not even. Maybe a block or two, but that's it. You?"

"Same," she said. "I'm so tired I'm lucky to know my name."

We jogged past the displays of high end clothing to the rear of the boutique. Using the employee entrance, we found ourselves at the rear of the commercial lot. Fire trucks, policemen, and ambulances roared down the Las Vegas strip and flocked to the scene. They painted the sky a kaleidoscope of white, red, and blue lights. A sick feeling crept into my body as we looked over the boutique building. The Multiplex Grande teetered like a flaming unstable house of cards.

We scrambled to the side of the lot. Policemen in black uniforms constructed a blockade. "Get back!" one said, coughing from the rancid fumes. Towers of water streamed toward the out-of-control inferno. They did nothing to quench the smoke rising in black wavering pillars. It reminded me of the hospital fire last year.

We'd evacuated many of the people from the lower levels. What about the three stories of shopping above them? How may had we gotten out? *Did they get out or were they way past screwed?* The lead weight in my heart answered me. *People died.* "This is bad," I thought out loud.

Rhapsody added, "Definitely not good."

Even I knew this was worse than facing our worst enemies. They all were gone. David King earned death instead of immortality, and Selby didn't have a hunter's knife to stab anyone. This large-scale destruction was in a different class of crap storm. *Hundreds of people* could still be inside the complex, crushed and incinerated.

Weakened to exhaustion, all we could do was stand by and watch the building fold, collapse on itself, and spill onto the street below.

My shoulders sagged. *What good are these powers if we still couldn't rescue everyone?* The fatality number wouldn't be released for *weeks.* Stuff like this was the reason I begged Susan to prescribe me sleeping pills. She did it out of pity, but it was all I could do to stay sane.

Rhapsody kept something in her nightstand, an object to get her peace. She'd excuse herself to another room to use it and say, "Don't follow me. Don't listen at the door, either." *What could it be, drugs?* Though the suspense nearly killed me, whenever I spent the night at her apartment, I didn't snoop in there or ask. I drugged myself to sleep. Who was I to criticize whatever she did to get rest? As long as she wasn't burying bodies or sneaking off with another guy, should I care?

But I cared, and we'd fought about it more than once. Didn't make her stop, though.

We flew away as far as we could push ourselves to go. I sent Esteban a text message to let him know we'd be eating about a mile up the strip in a nondescript burger joint. We peered through the glass door and saw no movement. Of course, with a possible terrorist plot, the place had been locked up and long deserted. There'd still be enough food around for us to eat our fill.

"C'mon," Rhapsody said with a hint of sadness. "You know we have to."

She ghosted us through the door and kept us invisible. We unplugged the security cameras. Thanks to the millions in cash the Collective had stored in their bunker, we had money to burn. I stuck a $100 bill underneath the cash register and plugged up the grill and fryers. Then I cooked eighteen burgers and four full baskets of frozen French fries. Our stomachs growled like they were arguing with one another. The sizzle of cooking meat and popping oil stoked my hunger even worse. Rhapsody's, too. I could tell by the weary lines on her face.

"What happened back there?" She stared into her Coke as I managed the grill. "Why'd you stay in there so long?"

The strong aroma of sizzling beef rising from the flat grill was intoxicating, so much so that I ignored her question, and she didn't press me for details.

Once the burgers were no longer red, I slapped American cheese onto the patties and stacked them in threes onto buns – two for me, two for Rhapsody, and two for Esteban. Usually, I liked to cook, but anytime I used my powers I hated anything and everything related to food. I appreciated the fact that I could breathe, but I didn't take joy in it. That's how it was with food now.

Taste was a function of it being on my tongue and swallowing kept me functioning. It's one of the things that sucks about being superhuman.

We dug into our food while waiting for Esteban, finishing our first triple burger at almost the same time. I ate a handful of fries.

"Remind you of something?" she asked me with the toy of the month in her hand. At the center of the toy medallion was a shiny blue jewel that resembled an aquamarine.

For her, it was a joke. Radioactive aquamarines brought back the dead. I'd used one to resurrect my mother. Taylor, who wanted my blood to make her boss immortal, had one, too.

Rhapsody patted me on the back. "Jason," she said to me with concern in her voice. "Crap!"

She probably thought I was going through a rage blackout. Not quite.

The room grew sweltering hot, and it turned red as the walls sagged and collapsed. My brain swelled and pressed against my skull. I waved my hands and tried to catch my breath. No good. I couldn't breathe.

I heard an explosion like the ones during the solar storm, and I dove for cover underneath a table. More bombs, one after the other. "He's coming!" I shouted.

King was back. His wiry body grew ten feet tall. A stalk of wild black and gray hair topped his head and his mustache grew out into a long ragged beard. He stalked toward me with his eyes glowing red. The white walls lit on fire and slid down to the floor like melting chocolate.

He hissed my name, his lips wet with drool and blood, *my blood.* "Mr. Championnnn."

I covered my ears with my hands. "Go away." *Where's Rhapsody?* I couldn't hear or see her. Like almost everybody else in my life, had she finally abandoned me, too? I figured it was only a matter of time.

How much time has passed? Everything had returned to normal except for me. My pulse raced. Sweat drenched my body. I was hugging the fragment of a table. I'd clutched the center bar so hard that I'd broken it. The chairs set on top of it had fallen to the ground. Rhapsody knelt beside me with tears flowing from her face down onto her bodysuit.

Esteban stood next to us. *How long has he been here?* Long enough to see me disintegrate, I figured.

"Finished freaking out?" he asked me as I stood up and faced him. "It's been a long night."

Rhapsody dried her tears and rubbed my shoulders. "He has PTSD, fool. Obviously."

When she called him a "fool" Esteban raised an eyebrow. "So what? Remember, I grew up in Everwood. Blood central. You live in the hood – gang fights, drive bys -- bullets flying. Suck it up. We all have PTSD."

She rubbed her temples. "Speak for yourself. You don't do *this.*"

"Nevermind that," I said, still catching my breath. "Why'd you go dark back there?"

Still simmering from Rhapsody's name calling, he bristled. "I didn't *go dark.* Signal went bad. Remember the cell grid we trashed? And it happens in a concrete garage, you know."

"Her signal got through, though."

He shot back, "You got out, didn't you?"

Esteban's comments and tone were sharp, like he felt something he didn't say. He had been dating Sasha, and I was her first love. According to Rhapsody, the fact that Sasha and I dated meant Esteban and I and she and Sasha could *never* be friends for long. Sasha's New Year's Eve party was proof she was right. He thought Sasha had cheated on him with me, and she hadn't...until the end when we kissed.

Heat built up in my face. "I almost *didn't* get out, waiting for your signal."

"I told you, the concrete knocked the Bluetooth out." His skin flushed a light shade of red. "What did you want me to do? You're *invincible*, remember? You can take care of yourself. The whole building could've fallen on you and you'd have been fine."

I wasn't sure he was right about the immortality, but I wasn't positive he was wrong, either. My grip tightened on the edge of the table.

Rhapsody must've noticed my anger building. "We're supposed to be a team."

"A *four-man team*." He pointed at us. "You two. *You're* a team. My partner is at home resting from what you let Selby do to her."

His accusation lit a fire inside my belly. "I didn't let Selby do anything. She volunteered."

"Volunteered, huh? And you signed her up. I thought *you* made all the calls, *Captain*."

The corner of the metal table snapped off in my tense fingers. I dropped it and brushed its silver debris off of my gloves. A tense silence. I stared at Esteban. He glowered back. I didn't have to imagine what he really wanted to say. I'd read minds so often these days it was second nature, almost involuntary.

Sasha's injuries played into their relationship, and she broke up with him because of the mood swings from her medication. They got back together.

Sex was against doctor's orders. He thought it was a lie and Sasha wanted to be with me instead.

Man, he's insecure. I halfway *pitied* him. He remembered everything Rhapsody had said about not pining after someone who didn't want him. He thought he still had a fighting chance.

I should've apologized for reading Esteban's mind, but I didn't. My actions must've shown in my expression.

Esteban's face sparked with realization and he vanished in a column of green smoke.

Rhapsody had watched the whole thing play out and stayed silent, which was the right thing to do. She returned to her food and popped a fry into her mouth.

"What?" I asked her. During the argument her eyes never left me.

"Nothing, Ringo," she said, still chewing. "Paul and John are gone. I guess this was our Abbey Road."

CHAPTER TWO

rhapsody's still jealous

We'd eaten and had drunk our fill when a series of emergency texts chirped on our phones.

NTAS ALERT UNTIL 2 AM PST 3/14/15. RESTRICTED AIRSPACE. INBOUND FLIGHTS REROUTED. OUTBOUND FLIGHTS POSTPONED. ALL RESIDENTS SHOULD STAY AT HOME OR THEIR PLACE OF BUSINESS UNTIL FURTHER NOTICE.

Rhapsody and I cursed at the same time. Nevada had issued a National Terrorism Advisory System alert. Statewide lockdown. A week long!

They suspected other bombings. Had the chick bombed someplace else we missed?

"Guess we're stuck here for a while," I said, letting out a small belch into a napkin. "Not like we were going home tonight anyway."

"Yeah, about that...our hotel room has a pull-out couch, but I didn't think we'd actually have a guest." Rhapsody downed the rest of her soda. "I told you before I'm bicycle, not tricycle. C'mon, Cap. I got all pretty for our date, straightened my hair, went to Vicki's and everything. Esteban shows up...tell him to kick rocks."

I knew it and hated I'd ruined the evening by letting him tag along. I hadn't even thought about ruining my date by inviting Esteban, not until he called me from the underground fortress. "You should've heard him. Drinking beer, watching surveillance tapes. I thought he might do something…Sasha broke up with him. Again."

She swiveled on her stool. "And? They'll get back together. I talked him through Christmas, New Year's -- they made up around MLK Day. It'll happen."

"He went on and on about Julio and Luis, too."

"Oh."

Six months ago, his brothers drank a solution of my blood to become immortal, and they disappeared. I'd bet money their bodies had rejected it and they were dead.

"I think he blames me," I said.

Rhapsody didn't agree or disagree – she knew I had a point, but she didn't want to admit it. The three of them were triplets. Even if it wasn't my fault, he could've blamed me. After Mom's first death I understood how losing a family member could do crazy things to your life.

My chest tingled when I thought about them. "Do you think they're still out there?"

She munched on a fry and didn't answer right away. We continued chewing while the overhead lights buzzed. Thank God no one on the strip had noticed us in here. "I'd have to see their bodies to think they weren't."

No thanks. I've seen enough corpses for a lifetime.

Rhapsody deserved to know about my shadowy visitor in the parking lot. It's not like things could get any worse.

I swiveled on my padded stool and confessed everything I'd seen. "I saw a shape shifter in the garage. I think it was the same person who saw us flying to Xobai." I swallowed hard and said the rest. "He...she had a wicked goshenite blade."

Her eyes bulged. "What? How do you know it's the same person?"

That's part of the problem with shape-shifters. "I don't. He shifted shapes to Taylor and some girl. How should I know? He can imitate anybody. Maybe I'm hoping."

"And he didn't kill you." Rhapsody's face tightened. "Too weird to process."

How would we find him anyway? For starters, we'd have to use white prisms – goshenite – against him and he...she...had access to a stash of it. Thankfully, Rhapsody and I had goshenite radiation in our blood. Using it against everyone we knew wouldn't make much sense. There had to be a better way, but we couldn't figure it out on exhausted brains.

"Think," she said with a mouthful of burger.

"I am thinking."

Still chewing, she said, "Well, can you remember anything else?"

The bomber had looked at me like I should know him. "He said he'd be back, but even with a week-long no-fly order, I don't know how he'll find us before we get out of here."

Sasha had rigged our phone signals to ping across cell towers, so no one but she could find us. With time the bomber might be able to locate us within a few miles. Staying put for a night was risky, but the best we could do under the circumstances. Two against one were better odds. Three if we could convince Sasha to come back.,

"We'll wait it out tonight and hitch our way home tomorrow."

Rhapsody's lips formed a smile. "All right. Let's get to the hotel, then."

We ghosted through the restaurant door. I almost wished we hadn't. The dimly lit streets were a jigsaw puzzle of bumper-to-bumper parked vehicles. The police couldn't clear the gridlock of unmanned cars. Tow trucks couldn't get through. People ran to their destinations with screaming children in their arms. It looked like an action scene from a disaster movie.

We stood there, mesmerized by the chaos in the cool night air. I surveyed the scene, thinking of the best way to help out. There wasn't one. We'd have to lift and carry each car, truck, and SUV in sight to a safe parking spot. That would take hours and put us in a difficult position. Cars floating through thin air would make everyone freak out.

"Yeah, Dude." Rhapsody sighed. "Let the cops figure this one out."

Invisible, we flew to the outer edge of the strip and landed at the hotel. From the outside, "Camelot" looked like a low budget place to stay with a five-star name. Ten or twelve stories with outside balconies, a heated pool and Jacuzzi – I wondered if there was a knight's round table inside or a fake Holy Grail.

Considering the cluster of shady-looking people in the parking lot, I doubted it.

About twenty Hispanic and black men in basketball jerseys stood in the handicap parking spaces. Three women – two Hispanic and one white – sat on the hoods of tricked-out cars painted yellow with blue racing stripes. The men smoked and looked at us.

We took the sidewalk. As worn out as I was, I might actually sleep without taking pills.

When we were halfway to the lobby, a guy wearing a Miami Heat jersey had the bright idea to step into our path. I gave him an audience, only because I needed a good laugh.

"Hey, baby girl, what room you in?" he asked us while stroking his thin beard.

At first, I wanted to laugh. Then he kept talking and my chest burned.

"I'll come up to your room in a little while. You can ditch young buck here and give me a…"

Before he could finish, I grabbed the guy by the throat and lifted him off the ground. "What's that? Speak up. I can't hear you over the choking."

However, I did hear the click of guns and the snap of opening switchblades. The red and yellow neon "Camelot" sign shined light on the weapons his friends drew on us.

"Put him down," said the one in the throwback Lakers jersey. His voice wavered. "Do it."

His threat would've been an impressive display if we weren't bulletproof.

"No," I said.

I'd been bullied for most of my life. Kids picked on me because of my height and build. Before my mom died and I started having rage blackouts, I got beat up a lot. After I started raging, I got lucky every once in a while and knocked out a couple guys that way. Then I got a reputation as the crazy black kid. Not the greatest way to become known, but it beat being a human punching bag.

It felt good not to be the bullied one for a change. I squeezed his neck until he squealed like a girl.

"Under radar, remember?" Rhapsody said loud enough for me to hear. "Put him down. Please."

I glanced at his buddies, the ones with guns aimed at me. They wouldn't shoot – they might accidentally hit him. That's what they were thinking. Their thoughts popped into my head as if they were my own.

"Please don't hurt him."

A girl stood near the front of the crowd with her hands balled up at her face. I frightened her.

I lowered my arm. The guy fell to his knee and coughed, his hands at his throat. His girlfriend rushed to his side and stroked his back. Then the men put their weapons away in awe at what this scrawny kid under six feet tall could do. Rhapsody's stare bore holes into my face. She could've stopped me. Why didn't she?

We walked unmolested through the cigar cloud and into the red carpeted lobby. No one bothered to follow us. They knew this wasn't natural. I'd overpowered a man two times my size by lifting him three feet into the air. I had to be on performance-enhancing drugs, steroids, or something.

We approached the dark brown wooden desk. "Reservation for Ruby Martinez," she said to the front desk clerk. I stood at her side, but she completely ignored me.

"Of course, Ms. Martinez. We've been expecting you." His slicked-back hair and gentle smile did little to calm my nerves. He slid two black keycards to us. Rhapsody showed him our fake IDs and paid for the room in cash – an untraceable transaction. Rhapsody strutted toward the elevator without me.

"We'll be checking out early in the morning," I said and slid him an extra fifty dollars across the counter. "Make sure no one disturbs us."

He took the bills and smiled. "Of course," he said with a wide grin. "Enjoy your stay."

By the time I reached the gray elevator, she'd pressed "12" and didn't hold the doors for me. I managed to make it through before they shut.

Rhapsody flashed her hands at her sides. "What was that about?"

"I don't do something to protect you, I'm a punk. Now, when I do, there's a problem?"

She crossed my arms. "Nobody said you're a punk."

That's what you think. "Guys like that don't snitch, especially when it makes them look that bad."

She pointed at me and said something in Spanish I didn't understand. "None of that had to do with protecting me, and you know it. It was all about you and your male ego pumped up on superpowers."

I put my hand at my forehead. We didn't need to have this conversation right now, but I felt helpless to stop it. "I've been beaten up my entire life," I said. "Words and fists. Think what you want about me. I'm not getting pushed around anymore. Neither are my loved ones."

The argument ended there.

Soon the bell dinged for the Camelot penthouse. I didn't know what to expect from it except that it might look less shabby than the rest of the place. We yawned and walked down the short white hallway to our room – number 1200. I used my key to open the room and went in first. Not because I wasn't a gentleman, but I hated bad surprises and I'd rather take one head on first. Those guys from the parking lot could've trailed us or taken the stairs and gotten into our room somehow.

I flicked on the light for the foyer. Beige shag carpeting and matching walls, off-white baseboards. The glass bathroom door's hinges creaked as I pushed it open and searched the inside. Nothing looked out of the ordinary. The drinking tumblers were clean with a cover on them. I saw a high-powered blow drier mounted on the wall. Rhapsody would use it after showering.

She'd gone ahead of me into the bedroom and started undressing. She took off her armored suit, hung it on the clothing bar, and uncovered the desk lamp to move it close to the closet. Our suits were solar powered, but we'd found strong artificial light did the trick, too.

I stepped out of my suit and hung it up next to hers. We'd have to sleep with lights on so that the suits wouldn't run out of power when we needed them. No problem.

I had my sleeping pills in my pocket with my Adderall. I'd get no less than six hours sleep. The clock said 2:45 a.m. By eight o'clock, I'd be ready for a big breakfast and a nine hour car ride home.

With her suit now in the closet, Rhapsody wore distressed black jeans with a metal chain belt and a lacy black bra. Her face softened. She might not totally understand my reasons for doing things, but she'd forgiven me for the parking lot. "Need a shower," she said. "There's room in there for both of us."

Ever since the court emancipated her from her absent mother, she'd insisted on showering alone. I should've jumped at this chance. "Nah, take your time," I said.

A simple scrub down wasn't all she offered. Even I knew that. "C'mon. I'll wash my hair later."

"I smell like smoke and old food. Nobody wants to be around that."

She bit her lip. "I might. I like old food."

I smiled but politely declined again. "I'll pass."

She said, "Okay," and disappeared behind the door. Soon I heard the sprinkle of water into the bathtub. The metal shower rings slid across the bar. She wouldn't be out for at least ten minutes, fifteen to twenty if she washed her hair.

I peeled the damp Raiders t-shirt off my chest and sat on the king-sized bed in my undershirt, white mesh shorts, and socks. The air conditioner cycled on. The cool air felt good on my skin. For the first time in a while I felt sleepy. Thanks to the hot atmosphere and the parking lot bombing, I needed to take a shower, too. That's the major reason I didn't want to hop in with Rhapsody. It would've been functional washing first, which wasn't attractive, at least to me.

I didn't know if I could wait and stay awake until she finished, though. I laid back on the right side of the bed against the billowy pillows. I'd been dozing off when my phone rang. The caller ID registered "unknown." Thinking it might be my stepmom Debra calling to check on me, I answered it. "Hey."

"You all right?"

My heart jumped. Sasha. I took a deep breath. I needed to hear that voice. "Hey," I said after eyeing the bathroom door.

For a few seconds, I concentrated on removing Rhapsody's powers so she'd appear if she were eavesdropping. I hadn't expected Sasha to call me this late. Especially considering what Rhapsody and I might've been doing at this hour had the Multiplex not exploded.

"Why're you up? It's three in the morning."

"Bomb in Vegas?" Her words slurred a little. She might be tired or on a new medication. "You two can't die, but Esteban can and he's not answering my calls. Debrief. Now."

She did that Rhapsody rapid-talking nervous thing. I told the story without the details of the shape-shifting bomber to keep the conversation short. "We're fine," I said. "He's fine. He's not answering because he's teleporting back without us. GPS him and you'll see."

"Oh." Her voice kicked up an octave. "Oh. I'll ping him then. Sorry to interrupt you."

I waved my hand. "No. We'll talk tomorrow night."

"Oh…tomorrow?" She hung on the "tomorrow" at the end of her sentence, swallowing whatever else she was going to say.

"What?"

"I just…"

I could tell she had to tell me something important. "Spit it out."

"I thought you…"

Whatever it was, she wouldn't say. The water in the shower abruptly stopped and I hung up.

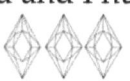

After sleeping until eight a.m. we woke up to the sound of knocking. Rhapsody awoke next to me and turned us invisible. I got out of bed and levitated to the front door so my footsteps wouldn't be audible. I'd hung a "do not disturb" sign on the doorknob last night, and floated the front desk clerk fifty dollars to make sure this did not happen.

The bomber. I became aware of my heart and its quickened pace. What if the bomber tracked us down, or the guy from last night came for revenge? Was there an explosive device on the other side? He'd said he'd "be in touch" – code for he'd kill me later?

Peering through the eyehole, I saw a short maid look at the "do not disturb" sign. She rolled her eyes and moved her cleaning cart to the next room. Simple mistake.

"She's gone," I relaxed and drifted to the floor.

Rhapsody rubbed her eyes. "Good."

I turned into the bathroom and washed up. Rhapsody did the same after I'd finished. We spent enough time in her apartment to be official roommates. She insisted we not see each other doing stuff like peeing or brushing teeth. "It's to keep the mystery in us," she'd say.

As we got dressed, I turned on the television to see the news. A mixed anchor team of a young black woman and an older white man delivered the latest news on the terrorist bombing.

They cut to a scene of the collapsed Multiplex. It looked like a giant robot had stomped a hole in the middle of it and set it on fire. Twisted metal, broken glass, and shattered concrete littered the street. If the structure had stopped burning, it had done so recently. Trails of white smoke drifted from the wreckage and headed skyward. Bystanders surrounded the cordoned-off area taking pictures and holding vigils for people presumed dead.

"To this point, authorities have not tallied fatalities or released the names of those still missing, but information is forthcoming," said the male anchor. "Stay tuned for updates."

That's all I needed to hear about it. Every station I found had ongoing coverage of the disaster except the cartoon channel, so I stopped flipping there. Rhapsody stopped fastening her suit when she saw the animated characters and heard their squeaky voices. Saying nothing else, she shrugged and finished getting dressed.

The Camelot had a continental breakfast of muffins and pastries, juice, coffee, milk and cereal. There were eggs, but from the consistency of them, they had to be powdered. We loaded up enough food on our plates to be polite to the other people in line. This would satisfy us unless we used our powers.

Just our luck, the breakfast area television played twenty-four-hour news channel coverage of the terrorist event. The president would comment on the events in the next hour.

Halfway through a chocolate chip muffin, Rhapsody swallowed a bite, took a sip of orange juice, and asked, "What's on your mind?"

I popped a piece of sausage into my mouth. "What do you mean?"

"You were...distracted...this morning."

"Uhh."

She dropped her fork onto her plate. "Uhh? That's it? I deserve a better answer than that."

Thoughts run through my brain nonstop all the time, mine or someone else's. She knew that. "I don't know."

Lips pursed, she folded her hands and asked, "Were you thinking about Sasha the whole time we were...?"

I pounded my fist at my breastbone to stop myself from coughing up my apple juice and Adderall. I'd hidden last night's phone call from her because of this. According to Rhapsody, her beef with Sasha "goes way deeper" than me.

Once I stopped hacking, I answered her. "Are you serious right now?"

"Don't even." She pointed at me. "Were you?"

"No. You know that."

Her eyebrows scrunched together. She doubted me. "But she called, right? What did she say? Or was she singing Lauryn Hill to you again?"

Her accusation pissed me off, but I played it cool and drank my juice. I took pills so I didn't have to have Sasha sing me to sleep. "She proclaimed her undying love to me."

Rhapsody's face blanched. She set her muffin down onto her plate. "That's not funny."

"You eavesdropping on private conversations isn't funny either. Tell me what I said since you were listening."

"I heard you talking in a low voice to someone, so I guessed it was her. At least I didn't read your mind. And you know she gets under my skin." Rhapsody hid her shaking hands on her lap underneath the table.

"Because you let her," I shot back. "For someone who demands privacy when she sneaks out of the room, it's a pretty hypocritical thing to do."

She threw her napkin down. "Truth? I call Esteban and talk to him when I can't talk to you."

The revelation stabbed my heart – she's confiding in another dude. "Why?"

Her eyes moistened. "It turns out, I need a friend, too. One I'm not sharing my space with 24/7. For real, he's a sounding board – that's it. Once stuff gets out of my head, talked out, I can sleep. But your sounding board – she's the hottest, smartest girl in school."

She didn't have to be around me so much if it was a problem. I rolled my eyes.

"Please just tell me what she said, what she really said."

I thought Rhapsody had ghosted through the wall and listened to everything I'd said, when in reality, she'd heard nothing except the tone of my voice. We'd fought a dozen times over her invisibility and intangibility powers and how she used them. I laughed the first time she appeared through a wall in the shower, but afterwards it made me think she was always around, even when she wasn't. The worst part? I couldn't tell one way or another unless I sapped her powers or she revealed herself.

"Debrief." I reached under the table and grabbed her hands. "Esteban wasn't answering his cell. She heard about what happened and knew we were here. That's all."

Instantly, her shoulders relaxed. "That's it?"

Sasha was about to say something more, but since she hadn't, I'd been telling the truth. "Yes."

"Sorry."

Things were still mega-weird, but we finished breakfast and headed outside. The sun shone down on us. There wasn't a cloud in sight. I wanted to mask up to shield my eyes from the brightness, but its voice distorter would make it difficult to talk to other people. Because of the terrorist alert, no traffic left the deserted strip. Hitchhiking would be impossible this way.

We'd found the best way to hitchhike – ghost through a tractor trailer with dry contents and stay there. Truck drivers stopped when necessary and only checked their cargo when they unloaded it. That way, Rhapsody could rest without having to keep us invisible.

Rhapsody drew close to me and placed her hand on my chest. She rested there for a minute. Laying her hand on me was her way of saying sorry again without saying sorry. "So, Plan B?"

Thinking for a quick moment, I only came up with two scenarios. "A commercial plane would take hours. Bus and train would take half a day. Or we risk it and fly back."

Rhapsody's lips curled into a sly grin. "I vote for risking it. We'll be back before noon."

"Yeah," I agreed. "If we don't get shot at in the process."

Together, we made our way out to the edge of the strip. "We stay low, then, mix up our speed," she said. "It's 600 miles or so. We won't break the sound barrier. They'll never see us."

I wished we could've done this last night, but flying in the dark made me sleepy. Plus, Sasha hadn't perfected a night vision goggle design yet, so we'd have been flying blind. Soaring high enough to avoid birds, low enough to dodge airplanes and jets while changing speeds to stay off radar was hard enough to do when we could see, much less when we couldn't.

"Ready?" she asked me before vanishing in front of my eyes.

Taking off at the same time, we sped up the dusty, unlit strip about fifty to sixty feet above the roadway – high enough not to hit concrete bridges and green and silver highway distance markers. The roadways were empty, except for highway patrolmen, who were there to enforce the statewide curfew.

Going home this way might've been a bad idea. The sky, clear and blue, bore not one cloud. Nothing masked the sound of our travel. By the time Nevada noticed it, we'd be home and on land. Besides, the military's concern should be with things entering the state at high speeds, not leaving it.

My fear went away as soon as we zoomed past the state line.

"We're home," I sighed with relief and dialed down my speed. "Slowing down over here."

"Starving over here," Rhapsody said. "Pudgy Burger? You can invite someone if you want."

I smiled beneath my mask. "I thought you were bicycle, not tricycle?"

"Invite them both. Shape-shifting bombers equals a four-person job."

"Pit stop to check in with the parental. Come with me?"

"Sure."

We flew back to the two floor tan Victorian house Debra and I had rented in the Heights. With Aunt Dee deciding to stay east, I had my own bedroom again. We could've bought it outright, but my lawyer father advised against it. He called it "unwanted attention."

"The IRS will wonder how a postal worker on disability pay owns a $300,000 house with no debt or mortgage," he'd said.

He had a point. Debra had endured enough because of me.

Touching down in front of the stained wooden post fence, we stayed invisible and walked through the thick emerald green backyard on the approach to the back of the house. When we reached the steel back door, I took out my keys and felt around until I could slide them one by one into the many brass locks. Above us, a camera whirred and swiveled back and forth.

Debra couldn't see us through the monitor it connected to, but she had to have known I was here. Nobody else had five different keys, other than the landlord. The locks, the security system – she had even bought a handgun, loaded it with goshenite, and learned how to shoot it. I could protect us, but I wasn't always around. Security had never been an issue for us before. Not like this.

As soon as we opened the door, the security alarm said "back door open." Debra called out from the living room, "Welcome home. Hi Rhapsody."

Her snapped neck had healed, but for the most part, she was still broken. She endured nightmares and had her own bouts with PTSD. I tried my best to make things right. If I went out to save the world, or I stayed home with her and watched cable television, nothing seemed to make it better.

"I know, I'm a terrible stepson and I should've called."

"Yeah, you should've, but you didn't. That's the point."

The gruff voice belonged to our landlord, Tucker Freeman. He was a former gunnery sergeant in the military – a "do everything I say the way I say it" type. Muscular, with thick shoulders and an olive complexion, he might be black or half-black or not even black at all. I could never tell his ethnicity. Nothing gave it away. Every once in a while his accent sounded Northern. Our house was his rental property, and he preferred to do maintenance work himself. "Builds character," he'd say.

Since Debra stayed home all the time, he always found something to fix in the house. So they became friendly.

"They're totally dating," Rhapsody kept telling me.

Debra hadn't dated since divorcing my father years ago. As a matter of fact, I didn't even recall Debra ever talking to or about another man in a romantic way.

Freeman didn't know about my double life, but he had it in for me whenever I saw him. Showing him respect didn't work. We mixed like water and electricity. I'm the man of the house, not him. He thinks he's a guy for me to reckon with.

Socket wrench in hand, he stood up and secured his black baseball cap on his head. It had "Desert Shield" on the bill with an American flag. "Answer me when I'm talking to you, Son."

"Ray Champion is my father," I said. "I pay you for this space, not for your opinion."

Debra eased to a standing position beside her chair. "Jason!" She wore a flowing blue sundress, not her usual pajamas. Her short, natural hair was neatly brushed into place and her lips shined a little.

"Lipstick? You're wearing lipstick for this clown?"

Half laughing, Freeman approached me, intent to show me I knew nothing about nothing. "You pay me? You? With what job? Your stepmom gives me her disability and the crumbs 'Ray Champion', your father, tosses her. She uses the rest to put food in your ungrateful mouth."

The truth stabbed at my heart. Debra had shared too much with him. Though I'd never said not to tell our business, it felt like she'd betrayed my trust. The back of my neck grew hot. "Did she tell you she refused child support in the divorce, Tucker, or did she leave that part out?"

I saw worry in Rhapsody's eyes. She thought I'd do to him what I'd done to the guy at Camelot. Then we'd have to explain the whole superpower thing and hope he didn't turn us in to the authorities.

Debra's chocolate skin tinted a shade of red. "Now Tucker, Jason, hold on a second."

"I'm sorry, Debra, I just..." He tossed up his hands. "He comes and goes as he pleases and talks to you how he wants -- he doesn't understand the sacrifices you've made for him."

Freeman was a jerk, but he did care about my stepmom.

The burning in my chest ebbed away the more I thought about how he cared for her. Making me an obedient robot was part of that.

With hands up, I apologized before he got too close for comfort. "I'm sorry."

"I'm sorry, Sir," he said back to me.

Rhapsody's eyes met mine. Hot barbed wire lined my insides. He'd pushed me too far – he wanted me to react, but I wouldn't do it. I gritted my teeth and repeated. "I'm sorry. Sir."

My apology stopped him in his tracks. I'd insulted him, cracked jokes to his face and behind his back. Since we signed our lease, I'd never apologized to him or called him "sir."

"All right then, young man." Satisfied, he turned around and returned to securing bolts on the staircase.

Debra waved Rhapsody and me to the kitchen. "C'mon," she said. "You two could use a Debra Brown world famous fruit smoothie."

She dropped fresh strawberries, blueberries, bananas and crushed ice into the blender. Rhapsody and I couldn't help but wonder about her desire to mix fruit at this moment. After flying 600 miles we could both use a cold beverage, but why now?

Debra pressed the high speed option and spoke clearly so that we could read her lips over the grinding and whipping. Now I got it – Freeman couldn't hear us because of the blender.

"You can't go off at the mouth like that, Jason," she warned me.

I felt my face twist with disgust. "Like you told him about Ray and how he thinks we pay for things, and all that other stuff? And are you dating him?"

She looked down. I had to study her lip movements to understand her over the high speed grinding. "Not the point. He was asking questions. I had to answer enough to throw him off the trail. And though it's none of your business, he brought over takeout once and that's it."

From her point-of-view, it made sense. Besides, she had to talk to someone. Aunt Dee lived three-thousand miles away, and if I wasn't off at school, I was with Rhapsody, on the phone with Sasha, or preventing a disaster. "Tell him what he needs to know," I said. "No more. Please."

"Fair enough." Without a pause, she jumped into her real question. "Did you have anything to do with that bombing in Las Vegas last night?" she asked us. "Weren't you there?"

My stepmom had long since given up policing how Rhapsody and I spent our time. The heliodor in my blood made me unable to have kids, but it didn't ease her worrying about me bringing home a super-powered grandchild. Not like she could've kept us in town when we could fly to other continents if we felt like it.

"Yes."

Rhapsody wagged her thumb at both of us. "We were on evacuation duty."

Debra patted her heart. "No wonder you smell like smoke. Thank God you're okay."

We explained the rest of the story— that another super being or "beings" were out there. The brief joy she'd shown at our arrival disappeared. She wasn't sure we were safe anymore.

Neither were we.

CHAPTER THREE

first breakup's the charm

Pudgy Burger used to be my favorite spot to eat. Not much had changed inside of the white and red-tiled walls from my childhood up until now. The fire engine red padded chairs and booths were the same. Employees wore the white shirts and pants and red aprons they always had. The food was still top notch.

But we'd eaten here so much over the past half year that we'd almost come to hate it. The waiters and waitresses knew us by name. In fact, they fought over serving us. We tipped well, and with all the food we ordered, our bills ended up close to $200 every time. That's a whole lot of money for a friendly and inexpensive restaurant.

"Hey," said a perky blonde hostess our age. Her hazel eyes showed a glint of recognition. She might've gone to North High with us, or she could be a new employee. Either way, she didn't know our names and hadn't heard of our eating legend here. "Booth or table?"

"Booth," I said holding up four fingers. "There'll be four of us. You can seat us now. They'll be popping in at any minute."

She grabbed four laminated menus and led us to an open booth. An elderly couple occupied our usual table and they were in no hurry to leave. That disappointed me. My father Ray, my mom Anna and I used to sit in that booth. I looked at them long enough for Rhapsody to notice me.

"Next time, Babe." Rhapsody laid her hand on my shoulder.

I'd told her what it meant to me. One time when we came here we'd sat in my favorite booth. The morning sun had been shining into Rhapsody's face. "Can we move?" she'd asked me.

I'd told her about my family's time there. In response, she'd slid her food across the table and joined me on my side to avoid the sun.

While waiting for Sasha and Esteban to appear, we sat and ordered Sprites. Unless she let Esteban teleport her, which I doubted she would, Sasha would drive her purple Cougar rag top convertible from the other side of town. She'd take the longest to arrive. Considering that, there were no guarantees that Esteban would even show his face.

I had sent him a text message from home and he hadn't answered. "I don't get it," I said. "I told him we were meeting here, the four of us. The text went through, so…"

Rhapsody took out her phone and typed out a message. *"There,"* she said after sending it. "He'll be here with bells on."

"How do you know?"

She showed me the text. "Pudgy Burgers on deck. Sasha's comin. U shld tell her how u feel."

Had she just sabotaged the whole meeting? "You're not serious."

"Totally. The sooner he breaks up with her, the better. The way she treats him...she doesn't deserve him. Maybe Selby but not him."

I felt a little offended for my ex and for myself. Selby almost killed me and Sasha. *He's a murderer.* Besides, Rhapsody's tone of voice made it sound like she actually cared about this situation more than she should.

"How do you know? You want them to fight?"

"No worries. They'll break up for good and we can all get on with our lives."

It was hard to tell when Rhapsody was genuine concerning Sasha. *Was she doing it for Esteban's good? Because she wanted to hurt Sasha?* Unsure of what her motives were, I let it pass, only because I didn't have a better plan in mind to get him here.

After fifteen minutes of slurping soda and awkward small talk, we flagged down our waitress and put in orders. Rhapsody ordered Esteban two half pounders medium well with extra pickles and a double order of fries. I thought Sasha would want a chicken salad since she'd given up red meat, so I ordered her one. If they didn't like their food then they should've been here.

"I hate that we missed Mass this morning," she said as the waitress left.

We had been attending church services together pretty often, like she had promised my mother she would. Debra wasn't crazy about the fact I worshipped in a Catholic congregation, but at least I was going and staying awake. The service was about an hour.   The priest said things about God and I understood him. The choir sang gospel songs, so it felt natural. Except when they took communion. I don't share cups with *anybody*.

"Sorry," I said. "Next week?"

"No worries." She smiled. "There's a six o'clock service tonight. Catch that one?"

The NCAA college basketball tournament's first round started tonight, so I made a conscious effort to keep my shoulders from dropping. "Okay."

With nothing else to say to each other for now, I took out my cell phone. The restaurant's free Wi-Fi had a strong signal. I internet surfed to pass the time. Rhapsody did, too. I'd been so caught up in checking game scores that I hadn't seen Sasha walk up to our table.

"Is there room for me here?" She smiled while touching my arm.

Her outfit was simple for a girl with supermodel looks. She wore a pair of dark blue skinny jeans, knee high tan boots, and a red and black plaid flannel with a black tank top underneath. She'd pulled her hair into a ponytail and had a little makeup on. The dark purple Zara Hristoff bag on her shoulder matched her car. It was a Christmas present from her dad, Wesley. She'd gotten straight A's for the thousandth time in her life. I was lucky to get Cs.

I scooted over, and Sasha sat next to me. Rhapsody shot me a look. This jealousy with Sasha was past annoying. It wasn't like she'd offer to sit with her. We had important things to discuss, Sasha sitting next to

Esteban was an invitation for them to fight the whole time.

"Esteban's coming." Rhapsody pointed at Sasha with confidence. "He wants to talk to you later."

The announcement shocked Sasha. She shifted her position on the booth seat and crossed her arms. "I'll believe it when I see it. So now, tell me everything."

It took a few minutes but we recounted everything from our individual perspectives. Rhapsody described how she'd ghosted waves of people through the crumbling theater to safety. My version was way shorter.

"I held up the building and I saw the bomber," I said. "He's a shape-shifter, like Taylor."

Sasha pointed at me and took her old Geiger counter watch out of her handbag. The straps were brand new. She put it in my hands and brushed her finger against my skin. A spark of static electricity popped between us.

"I thought about that since we talked. I calibrated this to detect .13 rads, which is how much radiation your body used to take in from the prisms per minute."

I felt my face tighten. "What's a 'rad' again?" I asked her while I attached the watch to my wrist.

"Unit measure for absorbed radiation. Right now, if you emitted a tick higher than .13 rads per day, you'd give radiation poisoning to anyone who came near you. When the source crystals blew up, you gave off 10 krad. We had to wear containment suits to feed and bathe you."

That was a sobering thought. I'd been a living, breathing, *naked* nuclear accident. I didn't care to relive my coma any more than that. "We can find him with *this?*"

Sasha nodded. "In theory."

"It'll detect *anyone* wearing a prism, won't it?" Rhapsody tapped her chewed fingernails against the metal table. "That's the theoretical part. We could catch the wrong guy."

The Geiger counter watches clicked when radiation was present. We had used them to track the source crystals, which didn't exist anymore. All that remained was a vial of radioactive fluid that we didn't know what to do with so we kept it hidden in case it might prove valuable. Rhapsody didn't wear a prism and neither did I, but because of my blood, it would click around us. Esteban wore one, so we'd have to get around that somehow.

Besides him, only seven hundred people on the planet had blood able to metabolize high proton radiation into superpowers. I doubt if any of them had crystals.

She reinforced my logic. "There aren't that many of us. The odds aren't high."

Soon our food arrived. We started eating after Sasha said a prayer and Rhapsody and I did the Catholic cross thing.

"You converted?" Sasha asked me with surprise.

I shoved a fry into my mouth and shook my head. "Not officially," I mumbled.

Rhapsody smiled a knowing grin. "I told Anna I'd keep him in church. Promised her, actually."

Sasha stirred her salad around with her fork.

Everything tasted good, but I had just eaten two pretty huge burgers last night. For ten minutes or so nobody talked. The clink of Sasha's fork against her bowl was about the only sound coming from our table. Believe it or not, at this point, I was kind of tired of fried food. That meant a lot coming from me. Plus, I couldn't sit in my favorite booth.

Sasha jabbed at her salad, and she occasionally ate a bite. I was curious how the surgeries had affected her. I'd called her once a week to see how she was doing, but she wouldn't talk about her injuries or the incident at all. Her mother Joyce had taken a sabbatical from work, and she hovered over Sasha so much that we never got to chat for long.

The extra plates on the table belonged to Esteban. Sasha glanced at them every few minutes with regret. I wondered who was responsible for this break up. Sasha would blame herself, but since her accident he'd been overbearing. It takes two to make a relationship go bad – at least that's what Debra says.

Near the end of the meal, dessert came, followed by the bill. Sasha had our waitress bag up Esteban's food. I guessed she planned to take it to him and apologize or something.

"Get me Rhapsody's Geiger watch, and I'll modify it before school tomorrow," Sasha said to me. "Or, I've already calibrated another one. Come over and I'll give it to you."

Rhapsody waved her hand in a "don't-worry-about-it" motion. "*I'll* drop mine by."

"Thanks," I said to her. I was in no rush to go over to Sasha's house. Joyce and I didn't have the best history in the world.

I had just gotten a spoonful of apple pie a la mode into my mouth when Rhapsody changed the subject. "What's the plan for finding this wacko, Cap? It's not like we can fly over the whole planet with the watch and wait for it to click. Anything giving off .13 rads could set it off."

I knew that. Sasha was a better strategist than I was, but Rhapsody wouldn't ask her for input. Thank God she was here to give it anyway.

"He'll find us," I said. "I guess until then we do what we normally do."

"Nothing you do is *normal,* Jason," Sasha said. "If you want my opinion, normal is the exact *opposite* of what you want to do. It's..."

I cut her off. "Wait, what? You think we should use our powers in public?"

"Bad idea Girl Genius." Rhapsody shook her head. "Remember Chicago?"

She cleaned off her mouth with a napkin. "Right, but listen. King derailed a train to kill us. This guy set off a bomb in a populated area that you *happened* to be in. He could've known you were there. If he didn't..."

I jumped in. "He did it to draw our attention."

"...because he figured you wouldn't let innocent people die if you could have done something about it. At least you're responsible and predictable 'vigilantes'."

It made sense. Even Rhapsody had to admit that. She hadn't rolled her eyes while Sasha explained. She was considering it. We had to use masks to hide our identities, but it was still a heck of a risk to operate in public.

I paid the bill and the three of us left the restaurant through the front doors. Like I thought, Rhapsody's text didn't pay off, after all. Esteban had ditched us. We'd have to do without him *and* Sasha, which sucked.

Maybe I could at least change her mind. "Hey," I said to Rhapsody. "Let me catch up with you in a few at your place."

She knew I wanted to talk to Sasha. *Alone.* Her face turned with disapproval. She backed behind the brick wall, turned invisible, and took off into the sky without a word.

Sasha stared at the spot where Rhapsody had flown away. "It's like that?"

I tried to make humor out of the situation. "All day, every day and twice on Sundays."

We walked from the sidewalk surrounding the building into the parking lot. Sasha keyed her car alarm and it chirped. "Flying visibly in broad daylight is a bad look. Let me give you a ride. You'll need the extra time to come up with reasons why I should suit up and join you."

I rounded the car, opened the passenger side door, and I got in. The off-white interior made me self-conscious. I might be dirty or my scaly armor might destroy it.

Trying not to move much, I said, "You still have the new car smell."

"I know, right?" She started the engine and backed out of her spot. "I don't do anything in here but drive. No eating, no coffee, no makeup. Don't worry, I wouldn't have invited you in if I thought you'd do any permanent damage."

That made me relax a bit. "Okay. Hey, what about Esteban's food? Want me to go get it?"

She paused for a moment then said, "If he wanted it he could've come and gotten it himself."

I said nothing else about it. She'd changed her mind.

The car's steering column responded with the slightest movement from Sasha's hands on the wheel. After a turn or two we zoomed onto the highway. The engine roared and shifted into fifth gear before it resumed its customary humming. I wanted to test the top shelf sound system, but Sasha and I hadn't talked at length in months, and the drive to my house wasn't far.

"You live in the Heights, now, right?" she asked me. "Peters' old neighborhood?"

"1210 Pine Street, yup."

Her parents had made her swear not to visit me, so she hadn't visited the house's physical address. We passed a turnoff for Morgan and Madison's steakhouse. The exit for the Heights was three miles ahead.

"How's Debra doing there by herself?"

I made sure to leave out Freeman. "She's getting there. Rehab's tough and she's been on disability now. Aunt Dee still has Zachary visiting out east until Debra gets a little better. She misses him."

"How old is he now?"

I did the mental math. "He'll be three in three months. You know, Debra asks about you all the time."

Sasha stared straight ahead. "Does she?"

I pressed forward. "She'll see you drop me off and want to know how you've been. So give me something to tell her."

"I'm fine Jason."

After reading Esteban's mind, I knew that wasn't the truth. "She won't believe that."

"Then make her believe it." Sasha paused. She'd noticed the level of force in her voice. "I know she won't. But the truth is too hard for me sometimes."

I let it be. "What makes you think I want you to join us?" I asked her.

She opened the flip down case above her and took out a pair of rounded sunglasses. "Because I know you. You *think* you need me."

"We do," I said. "I suck at making good plans."

She put the sunglasses on. "You saved thousands of people last night. That's a good plan."

I was aware of that, but there had to have been a better way to do it, and she would have known. She always knew.

I excused it away. "Luck and instincts."

"Sometimes, that's what makes a strategy work."

She was right but I couldn't take full credit for it, could I?

"We're friends?" she asked me out of the blue.

I didn't know how to answer that question. Do friends kiss on New Year's Eve? There always *something* going on between us. Rhapsody must have sensed it, too, which is why she hated it when Sasha and I were alone.

"I thought so. We're not?"

Traffic slowed down for a stretch. A stream of cars shifted from our lane to the right. Ahead, a traffic sign blinked a warning that one lane was open ahead.

While we waited for an opening, Sasha turned toward me and looked me straight in the face. "Then why don't you say something when Rhapsody treats me like crap? I wouldn't let my man make nasty comments to you."

I looked into her brown eyes. *Why don't I say something? Maybe I don't know what to say? Or I don't think it was a big deal?* "You're right," I said. "I don't know. That's the truth."

She huffed at my answer and switched lanes. The car ride was silent for a few awkward minutes until she turned off for my exit. At this rate of speed, I'd be home in minutes.

"If we're *friends,*" she said finally, "you should have my back."

I shrugged. "I thought you two were getting along."

"Tolerance and 'getting along' are two different things."

I accepted that I was the common denominator between the two of them. Rhapsody hung out with the Goth/punk rocker crowd and Sasha allied herself with the smart kids. I kind of floated around wherever. Had it not been for me, they never would have talked to each other.

Rhapsody's problem was Sasha still loved me. "We'll break up," she'd said to me, "and you'll get back together with her."

I wouldn't say that was untrue and I couldn't say it was true. Our old mentor, Courtney Stafford, was the one who could predict the future, tell me how this would turn out. But she was dead.

Sasha pulled into the Heights subdivision and I gave her directions to Pine Street. The water restriction must have lifted. Many of the residents had turned on their sprinkler systems or hand-watered their lawn. Freeman, hose in hand, was one of them.

"It's this one," I said, pointing to the ebony wood structure to our right. "Pull around back, though? That's my landlord on the grass."

She wheeled past the house without slowing down. "Not a fan?"

I repeated what she'd said. "Friendliness and 'getting along' are two different things."

Her car stopped at the back of our house and she cut the engine. The distant hum of lawn mowers let me know we were alone for the most part. I sucked at reading signals, but this one was pretty straightforward. She wanted to talk some more.

I unbuckled my seat belt and gave her a brief hug, careful not to hurt her. "Thanks for the ride."

As I came back to my side of the car, I saw her wince from pain. She rearranged something tight-fitting beneath her shirt on the left side – where Selby had stabbed her.

"Oh God, are you okay? I'm sorry."

She drew in a few deep breaths. "Yeah," she said. "Scar tissue's a little tender today. It's okay. You didn't know."

I repositioned myself in her seat to face her. I should've known. Three months ago she couldn't hug me at all. "Why don't you wear your prism?"

The radioactive prisms healed our injuries and slowed down the aging process. Sasha wouldn't be in pain at all and she'd be able to clone herself.

She smiled and looked down at her abdomen. "I'm the biggest idiot in the world for wanting to recover the natural way, huh? I've thought that myself a couple times."

I wanted to agree but didn't.

"Eventually I'd have to take off the prism anyway, when I turned eighteen," she said. "And then what? I'd be right back here. Might as well cut out the middleman."

"So you wouldn't stay this way?"

Sasha folded her hands on her lap. "What, *super?* In the right situation I would."

Curious, I had to know the rest. "If you didn't, why wouldn't you?"

"I want to *love,*" Sasha blurted out. "I want to love and be loved, and grow old, and when it's all over, I want to die when I'm supposed to. I want to get married, have kids, and not have to defend the planet when some maniac tries to blow it up again."

I'd never thought about it that way. If I wanted marriage, I'd have to be with Rhapsody or another girl with powers. We couldn't have children – not with heliodor radiation in our blood – and who knows when I'd finally die?

"Today, I actually *tasted* my salad, Jason. I eat regular-sized meals and like them all. I feel pain, but I also feel *human*, too. Yeah, I'm gonna die one day, but not anytime soon. You promised."

Back at her beach house I'd sworn to keep her alive. She was right about food, too. Thinking back, I couldn't remember the last meal I actually enjoyed. Maybe my birthday dinner in Xobai? Those crab cakes were delicious and not at all fishy.

"You said 'maybe'. Why would you wear a prism again? What would have to happen?"

She didn't answer, but instead she patted my left hand on my lap, leaned over, and gave me a kiss on the cheek. The electricity again. She pulled back, and it wasn't static this time. The stickiness of her lip gloss lingered on my cheek. Everything in my body from my heart down to my stomach glowed with heat. Our eyes met. Her lips never looked as full and perfect to me as they did now.

Sasha's face drifted toward mine. *She's going to kiss me?* My mind raced – I had to stop this. When I was with her, I'd kissed Rhapsody, and vice versa. It wasn't fair to either of them. *Why does Sasha have this effect on me?* I couldn't regulate it or control my attraction toward her. Rhapsody knew that.

Her perfume was intoxicating. I was stupid. All this was inevitable. I hated that for all the strength I had, I couldn't overcome the temptation of a beautiful girl.

"Are we doing this?" she asked me.

"We *can't*," I said, not even convincing myself.

Our mouths were so close that the front of my lips brushed against hers. Sasha repeated my words, but she almost said it with a lilt at the end like a question. "We *can't?*"

Right as we barely kissed, a green cloud yanked me out of the car. I landed face down on macadam. Esteban stood in front of me with his fists clenched and his chest heaving. Next, he sent me on top of the roof of a nearby house and then to the highest limb of a tree before returning me to the street, face first.

I had enough presence of mind to turn off the cloaking of my suit. However I couldn't pull my mask down. Another couple teleports and I'd throw up anyway.

"You weren't happy with me. All right." His voice rattled with anger. He focused his voice behind me where Sasha was. "Cheat with anybody. Not *him.*"

Esteban teleported me again. For a split second I saw nothing but a swirling cloud of green dust, like a bottle of green paint had detonated around me. I found myself back in the exact same spot I'd left. He did this two or three more times. I fell to my knees. Esteban knew he couldn't beat me hand-to-hand, so he used his powers against me. Lack of concentration meant I couldn't fight back, and he knew that.

I groaned. The world spun in my eyes. Right when my thoughts unscrambled a bit, he sent me out and back in again. I coughed up spit and fell on my side with motion sickness. It was the worst feeling. My insides quivered with spasms.

"Stop it!" Sasha yelled at him. "We were *talking!* We weren't doing anything."

He walked over to me and cursed. I could see the white toes of his sneakers. "Rhapsody was right the whole time about you two," he said. "It wasn't your meds, the injuries, mood swings, whatever between us. It was always *him.* Wasn't it?"

Her silence was as much of a "yes" as she'd admit to.

"I haven't been fair to you, either of you," she said. "I'm sorry."

He'd stopped teleporting me long enough for me to catch my breath. We were in the middle of a neighborhood street. Good thing the Heights had quiet pockets. None of the area kids were outside, but that didn't mean no one had watched or filmed us on a cell phone camera and broadcast it.

This had to end quickly. Whatever it took.

"Six months of this on and off bull…and that's all I get from you? 'Sorry'?"

Sasha's boots clicked against the pavement. Closer. I wished she would get to safety and let me figure this out. The last time she'd gotten involved, she'd almost bled out. Esteban was right. When she got stabbed I blinked when it counted. Maybe I should've killed Selby and not brainwashed him instead.

I couldn't let that happen again. I'd promised her I'd keep her alive.

The throbbing in my brain and body slowed down. I was beginning to feel like myself again. In another few seconds I'd blindside him before he could teleport away. "Go," I groaned, waving my right hand at her.

"I couldn't get him out of my *heart*, Esteban," she said with a bit of sorrow. "Blame me, not him. He's my first love. You never forget."

Esteban was usually harmless. Not so much with superpowers. He grunted and cursed. "I wanted to be your second, maybe your *last*," he finally admitted. "If you had let me. Stop covering for him. It's *all* him."

Interesting view of history. I put my hands on the street. My calf muscles tensed with anticipation. Before I could launch myself toward him, he stretched out his hands to teleport me. I closed my eyes and hoped he'd send me someplace nice like a white sandy beach or something.

Seconds later I was still on the street. He'd tried to move me and couldn't. He was frozen. *Did I do that?* No, it wasn't me. And Sasha didn't have a prism.

That left one person.

I gathered myself and got to my feet. He stared straight ahead. I turned around. Behind me, Rhapsody stood next to Sasha.

"You've had your fun." She crossed her arms. "Enough."

Sasha touched Esteban's palm to uncloak his suit. When it appeared, she unzipped his armor and removed his green prism necklace. Instantly his skin lost a bit of its color and a healed-over bullet wound scar appeared on his bare chest. His superhuman abilities had left him.

She held her arm out to hand the necklace to Rhapsody. Instead of taking it, she turned her back on us and walked away. Esteban unfroze and panted.

I snatched his necklace from Sasha and crushed it to dust in my palm. The fragments sparked and fell from my hand as I brushed them onto the street. The moment Sasha and I had shared came to mind. There was no way for me to tell whether Rhapsody had seen the "almost kiss."

Turns out, it didn't matter. I knew what would happen next.

Sasha parted her lips. She said something to me, but I didn't hear it. It was like someone had pressed the mute and slow buttons on my life. I guessed it was something to the tune of, "Go. We'll talk later."

I'd let Sasha deal with Esteban. I had to go after Rhapsody.

She was talking to herself in Spanish and angrily waving her hands as she continued to walk away. She wanted to talk about it. Otherwise, she'd be in the sky by now.

"Rhapsody, wait..." I called after her.

She whipped around and slapped me. The smack of her hand against my skin caused shockwaves that shattered the windows of the parked cars lining the streets and driveways. Afterward, she cursed and favored her hand like she'd sprained it.

I stretched my jaw and pretended to feel it. Now wasn't the time to boast my invulnerability.

Tears flooded her reddened eyes. "I knew it, you know? I warned Esteban, I did. Told him to set his watch. It would happen. I trusted you *again*, and you cheated on me, *again*. With *her*? *Why?*"

"I didn't. . ."

She pointed her left index finger in my face. "I'm not enough for you? I haven't given you *everything*? My heart, my body…it wasn't enough? You call me crazy, like I'm insecure for no reason. This is the reason. I can't trust you!"

I tried to protest, but she showed me her phone. On it was a video clip of Sasha and me in the car from a few minutes ago that she had filmed. From the perspective of the rear window we did kiss. The distance between our heads was so small that even if I told her we really hadn't she wouldn't have believed it. No matter what I did or said, I was going to lose this battle.

I grabbed her wrist. "There's somebody after us. We can't do this now."

Her eyes darted. "Don't change the subject! We *have* to do this now."

She cursed at me and tried to shake loose. She was so angry she might've been able to throw me into the next county if she had tried hard enough. I could feel the fire, the conflict within her. A small part of her kept her from doing it, from leaving. She *wanted* to give me another chance.

"Believe it or not, I did not just kiss Sasha. I didn't. You can ask her if you want."

I'd said the wrong thing. Her resistance gained momentum. "It's the same old story, Jason. I wouldn't have to ask anyone…if I could just believe my boyfriend who says he loves me, who's *supposed* to love me."

What Sasha said was true for me, too. I couldn't get her out of my heart if I tried. "I *do* love you," I said, my hands at my sides. "That's never changed."

Rhapsody dabbed away her tears with her fingers. "Not with your whole heart. You love her, too. That's never changed, either. And it's not good enough for me. I deserve better than that."

I didn't need her to say it. This was the end, and I'd have to cut Sasha one hundred percent out of my life to make our relationship work. Both of us knew I couldn't do that.

"Goodbye, Jason," she said before disappearing into thin air.

A sense of loss weighed inside of me. For the first time in a while, I was totally alone.

CHAPTER FOUR

we meet a legacy

I waited for Freeman's dusty white pickup truck to pull away so I could go home without a "responsibility" lecture. That left me plenty of time to sit and stew. *Rhapsody broke up with me.* I kicked the curb. A section of concrete shattered around my foot. *Should I try changing her mind?*

My therapist would use a kind of therapy called EMDR to urge me to talk about it. I'd use the safe word before that happened. During one session I'd torn her danger room door off its hinges and chucked it into the ocean – thus the safe word. She wouldn't press the issue if I used it.

Once I set all the locks and keyed the intruder alarm, Debra relaxed. We'd glued down a layer of crushed goshenite around each entry point for emergencies. Push come to shove, Debra could use it to depower a super being. Most times she kept her distance from the doors. Too much exposure caused incurable bone cancer, like it had with Mom, Rhapsody's father, George, and now my father, Ray. I'd given him goshenite to protect himself and it made him so paranoid he'd overused it.

Debra busied herself in the kitchen by washing dishes. Meanwhile, I went to the living room and plopped down into a black leather recliner I'd bought for myself. It was extra comfortable with heated back and leg massagers. I switched both of them on low. Since I couldn't turn my powers off all the way anymore, many things other people do to relax, like massages, didn't work on me. But the whirring sound of the metal up and down my body was soothing. I groaned and tilted the seat back. The air smelled like garlic chicken. That must be tonight's dinner.

I drifted off to sleep. A gentle tap on my shoulder woke me. Debra handed me a steaming hot Superman travel mug – her idea of a joke.

"Looked like you could use a cup," she said.

I sniffed its contents before looking inside. Coffee with caramel creamer and an insane amount of sugar. The thought of caffeine made me a little too excited. "Thanks, Mom."

Every time I called her "Mom" it brought a smile to her face. Truthfully it had been a long time coming. After my real mother Anna died, came back to life, and died again, calling Debra by a name she'd earned with me seemed natural.

"All right." She eased into her leather recliner beside mine and exhaled. "What did Rhapsody do this time?"

I flipped my hands on the armrests. "Broke up with me."

"Over Sasha," she said, way too nonchalant for me.

"Yeah." The fact that she knew the reason didn't even concern me. Anyone could've figured that out.

I flipped the mug's top and took a long sip. The caramel scent coming from it intoxicated me.

"Bummer."

Turning my body to face her, I said, "That's all you've got? *Bummer?*"

Debra had turned on her back and leg massagers and didn't say anything for a minute. Usually she had a wise word for everything, even if she borrowed it from the Bible. *Is she thinking about what to say?* I stared over at her. She'd closed her eyes as the heated metal balls traveled up and down her back in cycles. *Did her pain meds kick in? Is she sleeping?*

Finally, she spoke. "I sure do appreciate this chair, Jason, except I can't use it on my bionic neck. Which means the place I could use it the most, I can't use it."

"What?"

"I digress. You do so much for so many people and they never know it," she said. "Six months ago I almost didn't get to tell you. Thank you for rescuing me and saving my life."

"You've thanked me a hundred times since then," I replied. "I'm the one who got you injured in the first place. King wouldn't have come for you if it wasn't for me. Aunt Dee and Zachary would be here, if it wasn't for me. I just don't see why I'm so important to everyone."

She missed her other son, and so did I, but it was better for him to stay in Philadelphia while Debra recuperated. "You're so close to becoming a man...but you're *seventeen years old,*" she said, blinking away a tear. "You don't give yourself enough room to screw up every once in a while. Even the best capes have a bad day. You're no different."

"Capes" are her nickname for those of us with unnatural abilities. I looked down at my feet. "Yeah, well, when I have a bad day, people get hurt. Killed. And I need to be able to protect you."

She continued to stare ahead and talk into open space. "That's true of everybody in the world, including us non-superhero types. Life doesn't come with a road map, Son. And you do protect me, but only God can be everywhere at once."

While that may or may not have been true, it didn't do anything to make me feel better. Since I'd helped save the world, making me feel better about my mistakes had grown to be my stepmother's specialty.

"My fault with Rhapsody, too," I said, my fists balled up at my temples. "Can't get Sasha out of my head,"

"You mean your *heart*?" she corrected me. "Maybe you're not supposed to."

"What's that supposed to mean?"

"You keep getting drawn back to Sasha for a reason. Maybe that's the relationship you need to explore instead of trying to get back together with Rhapsody. You know, between trying to find the sociopath from the Multiplex garage and what he wants."

"So you think I should be with Sasha?" I asked her. "My mom liked Rhapsody."

Debra looked me in the eye. "Anna Champion was a good woman, but nobody is right one hundred percent of the time. I've known both these girls for almost a year…"

"And?"

"…and this mom likes them both. But if I had to choose…"

She let the end of her sentence linger as she rose from her chair. I wanted to question her further, but her preference was clear. In a way, I'd always known.

Sunlight shone on my eyes from a crack in the blinds. I bought blackout shades for this reason, but they must have fallen down or something. Rubbing the sleep from my eyes, I squinted at the yellow aura. My blackout shades had worked, but that was no six a.m. sun shining through them.

I was late for school.

I stripped my clothes off, hopped into the shower, and did just enough washing so that I wouldn't smell the rest of the day. I got dressed, stepped into my armored suit and turned on the cloaking. Even with all the rushing, no way I'd make the bus. Today was A-track, meaning I had an hour-and-a-half of biology with Rhapsody as my lab partner. Debra was still asleep. If I flew north and ate a good breakfast at McKelvey's Diner, she wouldn't know the difference. Con my homeroom teacher to mark me present? Most definitely. But I didn't want to miss my opportunity to catch our terrorist.

Debra's voice cracked. "Want me to drive you?"

Driving was a no go after her neck surgery. What she meant was, "I don't want you to fly and get caught."

I tossed my backpack over my shoulder. "I texted Sasha. She's going to pick me up."

The bedsprings shifted. *Did she buy my lie?* "From the other side of I-48 with rush hour traffic? Morning bell rings in twenty minutes. You'll *both* be late."

"She has less tardy slips than I do. I'll see you later, Mom."

"Love you."

"Love you too." I planted a kiss on her cheek.

I fled out of the door after setting the alarm. Once I was standing in the backyard, far from Debra's bedroom window, I phoned Sasha.

"Hey," I said to her through my suit's earpiece.

"Good morning," she said with a little extra bounce. "What's up?"

"Need a ride."

She clicked her teeth. "Stuck in bus traffic, Cap, but I'm almost at North. It's a miracle *I'm* on time."

"So, let's ditch." I suggested we go to her favorite diner. "Come get me and we'll hit up breakfast at McKelvey's. You can get those fruity pancakes you like."

"Love to…" she said. "Well played, by the way. But I can't miss any more seat time. Neither can you. And we have a psycho goon to catch."

Did she say "we"? Did she mean "we"? Is she wearing a prism? "They can't be monitoring the skies that hard anyway, right?" I thought out loud. "Know a spot where I can land?"

"That's my boy." I could hear her smile. "Behind the football practice field's announcer booth. Give me ten. I'll park and meet you there."

"Done." I hung up my cell and pocketed my phone inside my suit.

From behind a tree in our yard I lifted off and arrived behind North High in a minute flat. I checked to make sure the cloaking device. White leather Jordan shoes, black denim shorts, and a gray knitted V-neck shirt. Good – my outfit was visible. I leaned against the whitewashed announcer's booth and listened to music while I waited.

Almost exactly ten minutes later, I saw Sasha approach from the side of the red brick main building. I sprinted to meet her. She wore a black catsuit and a short orange suede jacket. Regular sneakers covered her feet, which was out of the ordinary for her. Usually it had to be something with a heel or some kind of sandal. In her hand was a white fast food bag.

"Hey." She presented the bag to me. "You don't have long to eat this."

Taking it from her, I dug inside. On top was a black fork and a breakfast bowl from a takeout joint not too far from the school. Eggs, potatoes, onions, sausage – it smelled *so good.* By instinct, I did the Catholic cross thing and started eating.

"I thought you hadn't converted," she said.

"Haven't," I mumbled between bites. "Thanks. How did you know?"

She flashed a smile. "Simple math. You were late, so you couldn't have eaten yet, and it was on the way for me. You need your energy."

I'd eaten the first bowl before she finished her sentence. A second one waited at the bottom of the bag, along with a hot cinnamon roll. I tossed the empty bowl into a nearby blue can. I held out the second bowl to her. "There's an extra fork in here. "Want some?"

"It's for you," she said. "I ate at home."

Soon I'd scarfed down the food in the second bowl. I bit into the cinnamon roll, a warm lump of cinnamon sugary goodness. I had barely slowed down enough to taste the breakfast bowls, but they'd stopped my stomach from rumbling.

I disposed of the trash. Sasha then gave me a recalibrated Geiger counter watch and a tall bottle of orange juice. I strapped the watch to my wrist. If its display was correct, the late bell would ring in about sixty seconds. Unless I flew us to our homeroom's window, Ms. Burbank would mark us both tardy.

I pointed to the school. "You said you can't be late." I took a swig of juice. "If you run, maybe she won't make you go to the office and get a pass."

"I won't have to. Neither will you."

It took a second for me to realize what had just happened. I was talking to *Original Sasha*, her base clone, and her analytical side. She'd sent a Clone Sasha, her emotional clone, inside for homeroom. Original Sasha handed me a tardy slip. I didn't recognize the signature, but it had today's date and 7:25 AM, which gave me an extra ten minutes to get to class.

"Tell her you were with the track coach, talking about joining the team. Tryouts are this week and today was the last sign up day."

I almost choked on my juice. "Ms. Burbank wouldn't believe that. She's seen me run. I'm slower than Selby is."

"Well, she's never seen you throw a discus."

Original Sasha had a point. Anyone who'd attended North High the past year or so knew of my legend. I'd raged and beat up a football player way bigger than me.

Yup, muscular football player Selby got beat up by a skinny black kid. He would never live that down here, even if he tried.

The bell rang when we were halfway up the beige and brown staircase on the way to homeroom. She paused on the second to last step.

"I have French III after homeroom," she said. It looked weird to watch her feel around her neck and pull an invisible mask over her face. "If you find out anything after that, text me."

The science hall was a floor above the foreign language classes. I didn't know how much help she'd be that far away. "All right," I said, putting my mask on as well.

As soon as I approached Ms. Burbank's classroom, I wondered how Sasha would absorb her clone. In a moment of misdirection, her clone opened the door while my hand was still on the handle. Then, Original Sasha vanished from next to me and somehow combined with her clone inside of the room. Usually, the clones went in to the original. My mouth dropped. *A new power? How long has she been able to do that?*

I gave my note to Ms. Burbank. She mumbled something nasty about the track coaches and changed my attendance to present instead of tardy on her computer. My forged note ended up in the trash can. Right when I was about to sit, the bell rang to dismiss to first period.

"Walk me to the stairs?" Sasha asked me with a devilish smile. Her con had worked. Of course it had. She'd strategized the crap out of what had just happened.

She'd bought me breakfast, so it was the least I could've done. "Okay."

We turned into the hallway. Standing there, hands in shorts' pockets, was a chubby redhead I'd grown to hate –Selby. He stared into a glass display case, where there was a map of Walsh and a Future Farmers preservation award from last November. Funny. Had it not been for us, Walsh would have been a smoking crater instead of a town.

Sasha elbowed me and pointed. "Focus up."

Selby wasn't just standing there. He was a *statue,* mesmerized by the pictures of grain and grass.

I moved closer to him. Sasha understood to keep her distance. The last time they'd been that close to each other he'd skewered her with a hunting knife.

While the crowds rushed by, Selby's eyes glazed over. I could tell by his reflection in the glass. He wasn't looking at the blue jacketed students but what was *behind* them. The field resembled the location of the secret fortress where he'd been brainwashed.

Is he remembering something?

"You're going to be late, dude," I said, trying to sound cavalier and casual.

Selby's lips trembled. "Something important about that place. You've been there. So has Rhapsody, Sasha, and that Mexican kid she's dating. I know it."

One of the many things I'd erased from his brain was the fortress' location. I hadn't touched his recollection of Walsh, the town itself. My mistake.

"Yeah, there is. We won!" I said, pointing at the multiple blue ribbons. "FFA! Woo hoo."

"I should remember more," he muttered. "Why don't I? Wait! I think...why were we there?"

He winced, like something sharp had struck him, and he punched the sides of his head. A drop of blood fell from his nose onto his stained white practice jersey.

Sasha and I exchanged worried glances.

With my hand at his back, I pushed him to walk in the opposite direction of the photo display. "Have the nurse check you out, Dude. Might be a concussion thing."

"Concussion," he slurred. "Right."

He wandered forward like a red-haired zombie in search of lost memories to consume. Should I follow him? Feed him a new memory? No. We'd have to drug him like last time to make it stick.

"He's gone into a trance like that every day since they put up the display," she told me. "Been late to first period so much they threatened to suspend him for tardies."

I shook my head. "How come I didn't notice it before?"

Sasha pivoted and turned me around by the shoulders. Through the crowd, we saw the bright red streaks in Rhapsody's hair and her black and white "Sarcasm is only one service I offer" sweatshirt.

"You were always going in a different direction than he was," she said.

That made sense. I didn't realize how much I'd been into Rhapsody not to pay attention.

She squeezed my elbow and handed me another Geiger counter. "Wait until I'm a good yard or two away to listen for the clicks to double up."

After we parted company, I made it to Biology just in time. Rhapsody sat at our usual black-topped wooden table, chin in her hand. She scooted her stool away from me once I arrived.

"Hey," she said, disinterested in whatever I had to say.

"Sasha just gave me this. Put it on."

Rhapsody cocked an eyebrow. "Your voice..." She leaned in while strapping her Geiger counter to her wrist. "You suited up? Why? Did you see him?"

"Not yet. So we can communicate."

She knew I didn't mean Esteban, and we hadn't talked since she left me on the street, so I could only be talking about one person.

Her voice strained with displeasure. "Oh."

"Mask up, just in case. Lower the volume on your watch."

After a lot of eye rolling, she put on the hood of her sweatshirt and her mask at the same time. Then she removed her hood. It was a good cover.

I twisted the volume button on my Geiger counter. "Sasha said the clicks will be on top of each other when we find him."

"I got it," she said.

Ms. Cofer rambled on about something having to do with the human skeleton and bone density, I think. I zoned in and out of the lecture, and her game on the Activboard didn't help. When she turned off the lights to brighten the board's display, Rhapsody passed me a folded note on yellow notebook paper.

Come over later to talk?

I didn't know what to make of it. Maybe she did want to *talk*. An invitation to her apartment after school usually meant we wouldn't be talking much. I gave her a half smile.

"Excuse me, Ms. Cofer?" someone asked from the back row. North High didn't have a large Asian population, so the hard accent surprised me. "Can I go to the bathroom?"

Must be a new girl. She didn't know her rule, and Ms. Cofer only had one: "as long as it don't get me fired." She literally said that to all her students, and she still had a job. No matter what the circumstances were, if it fulfilled her rule, it was okay to do.

"You. New girl." She gestured her board pen to the back of the room. "Must be a transfer. What's your name? I don't know how to pronounce it. Ah-mah…"

"Amauri," she said. "Amauri Camuto."

My heart stopped.

Rhapsody slapped at my hand at the sick practical joke. Whoever was pulling it knew information they shouldn't have. Anyone acquainted with the real Amauri Camuto would have had to have been more than a hundred years old. All the Collective members were dead except for Jeff Peters. He wasn't a shape-shifter. Plus, he would've *chased* a young girl not pretended to be one.

We turned to face the rear of the room. In the dim light it was impossible to tell where this guy pretending to be a girl was or the origin of the voice. I wasn't hearing things because Rhapsody and Ms. Cofer had heard them, too.

My breaths shortened. The cooling system in my suit kept my sweating at bay. I got ready to move. Since we sat in alphabetical order front to back, we were in the middle of the room. Rhapsody couldn't turn us invisible without revealing herself. We'd have to wait for our chance.

Ms. Cofer leaned forward and pushed her square glasses up her nose bridge. "I have one rule, Amauri. As long as it don't get me fired. You told me where you were going. Go."

As "Amauri" walked closer to the front of the room, our Geiger counter watches clicked at an extra fast clip. He had a prism or prisms.

"Is that coming from you two, that clicking?" Ms. Cofer asked us. "Turn those off or go out in the hall and get rid of them. They're annoying."

"Okay," we said at the same time.

We rushed into the hallway and turned off our cloaking. The shape-shifter was still out there. Waiting. He wore clothes styled like the Amauri Camuto we knew – black-rimmed glasses, hair pulled into a ponytail, white button down shirt with black pants and shoes. Except he wasn't completely Asian – his skin was as dark as mine maybe a shade or two darker.

He was the bomber.

Hands at his sides, he stared at us as if he expected us to do something. The Geiger counters on our wrists clicked so fast my head hurt.

"Any news?" Sasha asked through our mask Bluetooth headsets.

I whispered, "You could say that. Get up here right now."

"He's there?"

Rhapsody said with force, "He, she, it, shim, whatever. Get up here."

If he had a prism on I could take away his powers. I concentrated and watched for a reaction. He didn't change forms, which meant he was truly a she.

Her lips curled with a wicked grin. She wagged her index finger back and forth and clicked her tongue against her teeth. "Aww…you almost had me."

She took off running down the empty hallway. It sounded like she was laughing at us as she fled.

We gave chase. Rhapsody pulled me by the arm to the right and ghosted us through the busy classrooms – whiteboards, armchair desks, office supplies. As we ran she made the walls to our left intangible so we could see our enemy. We passed through hordes of moving bodies to cut her off as she turned the corner. We stepped into her path.

Her appearance changed before our eyes.

"*Rana.*" She'd morphed into Rhapsody's father George. The voice was weak, raspy – exactly like *his*. In a hospital gown and thin black slippers, she resembled him in his last days.

Her hesitation was enough time for the shape-shifter to get another good head start. She bolted for the stairwell. Rhapsody didn't move.

"C'mon!" I yelled. I could've picked her up, but that wouldn't have helped my speed.

I could hear the heels of the shape-shifter's shoes tapping down the steps until suddenly they weren't. A student resource officer must have seen her running. There was a struggle, the sick sound of slashed skin, and the slump of a heavy body weight to the floor.

The shape-shifter wasn't on the bad end of that fight.

I forced the lump in my throat down and helped Rhapsody to her feet.

"Can you?" I asked her and looked at the floor.

Blinking the tears from her eyes, she said "Yeah."

She dropped us through the building's structure onto the next level. A scream sounded from behind us. I whipped around and saw an Indian girl with a long black braid. One of her hands covered her mouth. She pointed the other in our direction.

The shape-shifter appeared in front of us, holding the guard's pistol in one hand and the bloody goshenite knife in the other. She sprinted toward the nearest exit door. When we turned the corner, Sasha was waiting for us.

"Amauri" whirled around and fired at us. I put on the brakes and almost fell. A bullet hit me in the shoulder, ricocheted off, and cracked a window. Rhapsody ghosted the other three bullets, which passed through her and Sasha. Terrible screams tore through the classroom walls into the hallways. They'd imagined the worst.

"Attention, students," said Principal Allen Rush's voice over the PA system. "We are in a hard lockdown.

Teachers, follow your procedures and await further instructions."

We'd caught a break. A hard lockdown meant no students would be around to get hurt. Chasing the shape-shifter became a lot easier.

The more we ran, the more the girls pulled ahead of me. I could fly faster than I could run, but controlling my direction around tight corners would be impossible.

Esteban could've helped in this situation, but who knew where he was?

"I've got an idea," Sasha said.

Immediately she split into nine clones. Groups of two split off and fled in four different directions. Original Sasha stayed with us.

"You two, go up and give us an idea where this is heading," she said.

"I *can't,*" Rhapsody said.

Had the George imitation rattled her too much? "Why not?" I asked, out of breath.

Hands on her hips, she delivered the news. "I can't fly anymore. Strength is gone, too."

"What? How?"

Original Sasha waved. "No time for theories. Take her with you and find her."

I grabbed Rhapsody. Together we ghosted through the ceiling, insulation, pipes, and steel beams and soared into the open blue sky. I circled the building's perimeter.

"There!" Rhapsody pointed at a white and black dot bee-lining for the parking lot.

Blue, red and white lights flashed on the main road. *Cops.* Whichever way we wanted this to go, we had to make it quick, or time would make the decisions for us.

"Eyes on her heading for the student parking lot," I told everyone listening. "Going in."

"Copy that," said one of the Sasha clones.

In a flash, we landed in front of the shape-shifter. She stumbled to a halt. Soon Sasha's clones met us, too. Breathless, the terrorist held her hands up in surrender, the gun still in her right hand.

"You got me," she said. "Bullets don't work on the two of you."

"But goshenite knives do. Hand it over."

Her eyes rolled and then she focused squarely on me. "Strip search me and find it, Jason."

Rhapsody hissed. "She's trying to get me to kill her."

Too quick for us to react, "Amauri" turned and emptied her magazine at Sasha's clones. One by one they fell. Kevlar lined the body suits and protected us, but would Sasha's cloned versions hold up? I wasn't sure. There was no way to tell either way from this distance.

Check on Sasha or keep the shape-shifter in custody? I had to decide. For unknown reasons, Rhapsody didn't have super-strength anymore. She couldn't hold our captive alone.

"Sasha?" I yelled into my microphone. "Sasha!"

She didn't respond.

I grabbed "Amauri" by her throat and lifted her off of her feet. "If she's dead or even injured," I said between my teeth, "I'll kill you myself."

She shape shifted into Debra, which forced me to ease the pressure on her neck.

"You're not a killer, *Son*," she said. "You hesitate. Think too much."

No one had ever accused me of thinking too much before. "Shut up."

"No," she said. "You *want* me to talk. I like this game. I'm only here because I *want* to be. You're here because I know how to pluck your strings."

Thinking about what I'd done to King, I said, "I'm too dangerous of an enemy to have."

She rubbed her neck and coughed twice. "Oh, I *know* that, but if you wanted to kill me you'd have done it. Maybe I haven't pushed you far enough. I wonder…what would do the trick? What would unravel you?"

Rhapsody's voice rang out with a warning. "Ca-ap…running outta time here."

With a swift chop to the front of the shape-shifter's throat, I'd damaged her larynx. She thrashed her arms. At least I wouldn't have to hear her talking for a while.

While Rhapsody stood guard, I sprinted through the grass over to the Sasha clones and checked them for injury. The bullets had not penetrated the armor.

Is she this bad a shot, or are we being played?

The police closed in, yelling "Freeze!" with guns drawn. They'd seen us "vigilantes" on the news, thought we were hostile, and treated us as such.

"Sasha, what's your 20?" I asked her.

She finally answered in a whisper. "See that fourth police car on the grass?"

I gazed through the suit visor's shielding. Many police officers crowded around in a circle. They had arrested her. *Not like I want them to, but why haven't they unmasked her?*

"I'd wave, but, you know, handcuffs and Miranda rights and stuff. Plus, I've got a migraine."

When Sasha split, her base clone – the analytical side – was the one who stayed in control. I didn't know it had a sense of humor. "There are three clones over here," I told her. "Combine with them. And bring your handcuffs with you?"

"What for?" she asked me. "Do I wanna know?"

"Seriously?"

"Gotcha," she said in response.

Sasha recombined with her clones and disappeared right in front of the cops' eyes.

The next thing I knew, a caravan of policemen patrolled the grass and formed a twenty-yard wide perimeter around us. They coordinated their approach, closing in a couple steps at a time, weapons drawn. They yelled confusing commands: "Get down!" "Hands where we can see them!" "Freeze!" We had to move to do any of those.

Sasha and Rhapsody stood within arms' reach. Amauri lay at my feet.

"All right," Sasha said, putting her hand in mine. "You promised me a flight?"

I gathered the girls, slung "Amauri" over my shoulder and blasted off.

CHAPTER FIVE

drama in a cornfield

Minutes later we landed softly in Traveller – a small town just outside the middle of nowhere. A perfect place to interrogate the shape-shifter *any way we needed to*. Scraping her memories for clues wouldn't be fun, but I'd do it. Not like it'd hurt her.

I let go of the girls. Both of them stretched and groaned. "Are you hurt?" I asked them as they stretched out.

"Little bit." Sasha shook out her hands. "Ease up on the Kung Fu grip next time."

At least I didn't drop them. "Sorry."

Being super strong, I had to constantly control myself around regular people. A little too happy, upset, or angry and I'd crush someone bones or destroy property. I'd damaged a lot in my time, but I drew the line at human bones.

Rhapsody winced and rubbed circulation back into her arms. It was the first time I'd seen her so vulnerable in a long time. The last time we'd saved the world she'd almost died doing it. Taking a dose of my blood mixed with an aquamarine had saved her life and given her powers like mine. I couldn't have hurt her back then. We had had a few laughs fighting each other. Then it turned into us hooking up and we almost knocked over a radio control tower.

"Amauri" was still unconscious and draped over my shoulder. I hated to even think "Amauri Camuto" was her name, especially after watching the real one hemorrhage to death. She disgusted me, but she had what we needed.

In front of us was the abandoned insane asylum where Margaret King had died the first and second time. There was a Ryan Cain-sized hole in the front door. I laughed thinking about throwing him through it.

I kicked away shards of the wooden doorframe. "C'mon," I called to the girls.

The front yard's tall green weeds made a soft bed for her body. I laid her down. When she woke I'd interrogate the crap out of her. Rounding the side, we heard squeaking squirrels or mice running up and down the pitch of the roof. The place was spooky, and I don't even scare that easily.

In the cemetery behind the house, David King had used an aquamarine to resurrect his wife. Together, he'd planned for them to rule the planet. He'd get rid of anyone in his way to get what he wanted and his motives disgusted her. Rejected and distraught, he'd murdered her, too.

Before he did, Margaret had said two words to me, "Champion Immortal." I'd thought about it ever since.

"Creepy Guantanamo you picked here, Cap," Rhapsody said about the house.

Usually I ignored her snark, but I couldn't let that one pass. *What did she expect?* The last time we took someone outside of our circle to the fortress we'd regretted it.

"No one will look for us here if things get messy ..."

"Messy?" Sasha interrupted. "I thought when she said Guantanamo she was joking. You're gonna torture her?"

I raised my voice. "Can we debate superhero ethics later? She's a *terrorist.* She's not gonna write us a confession or give us information if we say 'please'."

Sasha crossed her arms. "You want to go into her brain? Leave me out of it."

Ever since she'd ventured inside a policeman's mind and accidentally killed him she'd hung up her mind reading badge.

"Fine," I said. I'd do almost anything to get to the bottom of all this.

I didn't have to open the front gate – Ryan's body had crushed it half a year ago. Good. I didn't need the horror movie sound effects. Even without them, bumps formed on the back of my neck. Neither of the girls said anything, either. The crunch of unraked leaves and snapping twigs let me know the girls trailed behind me.

Sasha rushed up my left side and held her hand at my chest. I stopped walking and looked at her.

Rhapsody shrugged, her thoughts ringing in my head. *What's going on? Why are we stopping?*

She tilted her head toward the back of the house and held up her index finger. She wanted me to listen. Only then did I hear it. A *clunk* of metal. Dirt landing. Clunk, dirt landing again. My muscles tightened.

Digging. *Are they putting something in or taking something out?*

After a massive solar storm in the 1800's called "the Carrington event," twelve people banded together. Calling themselves a collective, six of them swore to protect the source of our powers. The ones who hadn't made it were buried in the place's backyard.

Once King died, Sasha came up with the idea to scatter their graves across the US.

"Whoever you're looking for, you won't find them here," I said as I approached.

The gravedigger kept pausing to catch his breath – signs of an older man. He wiped his brow with the sleeve of his denim shirt. I don't know if he heard me or not, but if he did, he continued heaving with passion. This was personal.

I took a step forward and my Geiger counter watch double clicked. My heart skipped a beat as I steeled myself, ready to fight.

"Mr. Champion."

He addressed me without breaking his digging rhythm.

That's when I knew who we were dealing with. Jeff Peters – our former Earth Science teacher and the last living member of the Collective. Besides King, he was the only person to call me Mr. Champion. Every time I heard either of them say it my shoulders tensed.

I gently laid the shape-shifter on the grass. Rhapsody and Sasha flanked me. After all, though he'd helped us save the world, this man had also tried to kill us.

I figured he must be digging up his wife, Diane. On his request, her grave was the only one we'd promised not to touch after King died. I'd thought about moving it anyway, but I hadn't.

He was hardly the picture of sanity, and the last time a Collective member raised someone from the dead the world had almost ended. *What will keep him from doing the same thing?*

Peters' head was covered with a thick mane of gray hair. His eyebrows and ragged beard had turned white, and wrinkles covered his damp face. His blue denim shirt was stained with large circles of sweat. The muscles beneath his khaki pants tensed as he bent his legs and tossed a mound of dry earth to the side. The clods of dirt smelled like stale rain water.

"Give me a hand?" He sounded sincere, like he actually *wanted* me there. "Took you long enough."

He was expecting us? I checked my phone. Peters had sent me a text message to meet him here seven minutes ago. I stood at his side and he handed me a shovel.

Peters pulled an aquamarine and heliodor necklace from beneath his shirt. "You know, the aquamarine has to be closer for it to work."

Yeah, I knew all about that. He'd dropped a radioactive aquamarine onto her body. The power of the other stones was one way -- we soaked up the radiation, and it gave us abilities. This stone was reciprocal. Their prisms linked two people together, and they'd share a life force and powers. Peters had to be close to two hundred years old. Whatever life he'd have left with her, it wouldn't be long.

"How long?" I asked him.

He'd die soon after resurrecting Diane and he knew it. "Once I bring her back, you'll never see us again."

It would be the end of an era. He, Courtney Stafford, Solomon Hughes, and the real Amauri Camuto were more or less mentors to us. Half of the time we were unsure of their motives and then, when we knew what they were after, we disagreed with them more. But when we needed someone to turn to, for better or worse, one of them had always been there. After this, it would be up to us.

"They were all leverage." He spoke, only pausing to dig. "That's all family members are. Leverage. Weight. Better not to have any. David threatened…to destroy their bodies so we couldn't bring them back. He made us do…*things.*"

In a twisted, psychotic mind, I imagined what those "things" might be. Like planting source crystals under buildings so people either die or get superpowers.

He continued shoveling. "One hundred fifty-five years." After a tired heave, he added, "I dug this grave myself."

Sasha's face flushed with sympathy for him. And here I assumed he liked young girls for the obvious reasons. Through all he'd done, he'd never dealt with his grief.

The wrinkles in his face deepened. I'd never seen this side of him. For a long time I'd thought he and the other Collective members didn't or couldn't experience emotions.

Peters stuck his shovel into the ground. He brushed the back of his hand across his moist, bearded mouth. "Who is *she?* Where did she come from?"

I'd heard Peters ask with interest about a good looking girl's identity, but that's not what he was doing. He pointed to the shape-shifter. "Who are you?"

She maneuvered her legs through her handcuffed wrists and got to her knees. With her hands now in front of her, she stood to her feet. Her thin braids had come loose from their ponytail, and they hung down beside her face.

"Amauri," she said through her teeth. I imagined the others had to read her lips like I had done.

Rhapsody stepped back and readied to fight her. Maybe I should've done the same.

"She's dead. Who are you *really?*" Peters asked her again.

The thing with shape shifters was you could never be sure of what they were capable of doing or becoming. It was a mind trip to see dead people you cared about being mimicked on a living canvas. "My protector named me Kai."

Circling the mound of dirt he'd made, Peters faced Kai nose-to-nose. He eyed her from head to toe. She did not back down like I thought she might.

"And who's your protector?" he asked.

Kai sucked her teeth. "My mother. I've heard I have her eyes," she said for no specific reason. "Don't you think so?"

Peters' eyes bulged. "Who's your birth mother?"

Amauri leaned close to Peters' right ear. I read her mind to understand what she was saying. *"Possible,"* she'd said. "C'mon, Walking Dead. You know the truth."

Holy crap!

She's Camuto and Hughes' daughter!

My heart raced. *Was that true?* Heliodor radiation made us sterile, didn't it? At least that's what Ryan Cain said. *Ryan Cain,* the reason I'd gotten sent to Reject High in the first place. *Of course he lied.*

If we can still have kids, then...

Rhapsody grabbed my forearm. No matter what Kai said, she was saying Rhapsody and I weren't going to be a set of superhuman teenage parents.

Sasha shrank back. She'd figured it out, too. She'd wished I had been with her first instead of Rhapsody. It was written across her mind and her drooping face.

Peters said something to Kai a few syllables long. At that moment, he blocked me from reading his thoughts and hers. How'd he do that?

Her eyes rolled around her head as if she wasn't sure how to answer him. Then, "Yes."

Returning to the mound of dirt he'd created, Peters uttered a primal yell and snapped the shovel handle in half over his knee. He tossed the fragments into the feet-deep hole he'd dug and walked away.

"Peters!" Rhapsody continued to call after him, but it was no use. When he reached the edge of the backyard, he kicked a hole in the fence and stepped over the bent metal.

"He's such a diva," Rhapsody sighed as she walked away. "I'm on it. Hold it down here."

I signaled we'd hold our prisoner.

"Enough games." Sasha turned to Kai. "What'd you say to him?"

She jingled her handcuffs and looked at Sasha. "All right, all right. Take these decorative wrist ornaments off, and I'll fill out a membership form to your little freaks' club, okay?"

This was what I meant by questioning getting messy. "I can take what I want from you," I told her.

She bit her lip. Not in an innocent way either. "I'll give it up. Buy me a nice dinner first and sweet talk me."

I concentrated and waded through her consciousness. Most of the live action scenes I saw were fractured shards of unconnected subjects. In one she was kissing a guy whose face I couldn't see. Then I saw her in a gray-walled basement tweaking the bomb that took down the Multiplex. In front of her lay the unconscious bloody body of a security officer. At her workstation, a blurry black and white picture that looked like Hughes and Camuto as mid twenty-somethings.

Another scene in her mind showed her eating a salad in the crowded food court of the Multiplex after she had planted the bomb. Her cell phone rang with a particular jingle I couldn't forget, and she answered it.

"Yeah?" she'd asked the person on the other line.

"This better work, Kai," said a male voice. "Or---"

Still chewing, she'd interrupted him, "It'll work. You'll have it."

Whether I stopped reading her mind or she forced me out, my mind reading session cut short. I found myself being shaken by the shoulders.

"Jason!" Sasha screamed into my face. "Wake up!"

I blinked and moved my lips to answer her and say that I was fine, but nothing came out of my mouth.

Streams of blood dripped down my nostrils and onto my lips. Nothing hurt, but my brain did feel kind of numb on the right side and in the front.

Sasha pinched my nose until I had the presence of mind to do it for myself. "Told you it was a bad idea."

She spoke from experience. Our prisoner Kai lay in a shivering heap on a bed of weeds at our feet. Without touching her pale skin, I could tell it was freezing cold like mine. *Did I damage myself? Her?* I'd erased entire sections of Selby's memory, and he was no dumber than normal. She wore a heliodor prism, so any damage I could've done wasn't permanent.

I recovered first, and I carried Kai's body over my shoulder. We caught up with Rhapsody down the grassy hill about fifty yards away or so. She'd found Peters in a cornfield.

He glanced at me then Rhapsody and recognized what we'd found out.

"How did this happen?" she asked Peters.

With a twisted smile, he responded, "Well, when a man loves a woman, he…"

Sasha shoved him. "How many illegitimate homicidal super-powered kids exist, Peters? You have a couple dozen 'legacies' yourself, right?"

He dug his hands into his pockets and rolled his fingers around. He wasn't thinking about it. He was deciding whether or not to tell us the truth. "You're going to lecture me on the benefits of safe sex and contraception? *You?*"

"How many?" I asked him.

"Two living. That I know about."

That answer pissed us all off. He'd been with half of North America's twenty-something female population – of course he didn't know for sure.

I flung Kai to the ground and called him a couple of names I'd been saving for a special occasion. "How long have you known about the other one?"

He sighed. "The prisms affect us on at least a biological level. We've studied ourselves for a century. There's always the possibility we didn't know everything and they'd survive. We didn't think…"

Rhapsody blurted out, "That's the problem with you, all of you. You don't think about anyone but yourselves. How many kids are out there?"

He scratched his head. "Less than ten, I'd guess. They weren't supposed to be *any*. We've outlived all our relatives and loved ones. You expected us to be monogamous?"

The casual way he talked about it all…it was awful. I thought of my little brother, Zachary, who would turn three this year. Some woman out there could've had a son his age or younger whom she had to bury because his of radiation in his blood. How many had died like that? *Dozens? Hundreds?* Had the Collective killed them? Why had so few of them survived? Was that even the case?

There were too many questions to ask Peters at once, and he was the one person alive to answer them. Would he even tell us the truth without sparing the important details? No, if it didn't serve him or his purposes.

Hands on hips, Sasha sneered. "Making babies you know will die young is *sociopathic*."

Peters scratched his beard. "You think you're so *different*, better than me. Tell me, what's the difference but a moment and an iota of genetic material? You're a naïve child."

"Who the –"

"You haven't lived long enough to fill a 140-character message with wisdom, any of you. Your judgment means *nothing* to me."

Rhapsody glanced down at Kai's stirring body. "What about *her* judgment? What's the over/under on her target being Peters, Girl Genius?"

Sasha put her finger at her lips. "Blow up the Multiplex to target *him?* She might've not known the Collective was dead. Not sure it's that simple. What's Jason's part in it?"

I didn't think I had anything to do with it. "She's working with a dude."

Kai groaned and rolled over onto her back. Sasha, Rhapsody, Peters, and I formed a circle around her. I took the lead and suppressed her powers to keep her from shape-shifting.

Spitting the braided hair out of her mouth, she said, "I have to know, Jason. Did you like it? Being inside of me?"

The way she asked me made both my ex-girlfriends uncomfortable. Peters smirked. Their styles were similar – ridiculous with plenty of inappropriate innuendo.

"We know your secret," Peters said to her.

Kai rolled her eyes at him and spoke into my mind. "Wasn't a secret, if you think about it," she said. "It's not even what you wanted to know about me. Ask. Anything you want."

Going into someone's mind felt like a violation every time I did it, like watching them shower on camera. I'd broken into lockers, safes, and buildings before. Making the leap from objects to brains was something different, though, even if I was invited to do it.

"What do you want from me?" I asked her.

She grinned. *"Everything."*

The scent of growing corn and the March breeze faded away from my senses. I didn't notice the sun's brightness or the cool interior of my body suit. Peters, Rhapsody, and Sasha disappeared. All that remained were Kai and me alone in the cornfield.

My next question was more specific. "Who are you working with?"

Kai now stood in front of me and her mouth was moving along with her words. It was hard to tell whether this scene was reality or the reality going on in her brain.

"Meet with us," she said. "Tomorrow. Midnight. You'll know where."

Her cuffs dropped to the ground in an emerald cloud. She was gone.

CHAPTER SIX

my dad says goodbye

I still haven't gotten the hang of doing the right thing, but a part of me wanted to figure it out. *I'm so done being a screw up.* Right now, everyone around me pointed fingers and accused me as if I'm the one who gave Kai teleportation powers.

"Didn't see *that* coming," Rhapsody said.

I shrugged. *Me neither.*

"Prepare for every eventuality." Peters shook his fists and spoke at us with so much force that spit particles flew out of his mouth. "She's the child of a shape-shifter *and* a teleporter. A monkey with fine motor skills could've figured out the powers could be hereditary. Just inexcusable."

I pointed my finger at him. "Not all of this is on me. Camuto never shape-shifted in front of us. I'm not a strategist."

Strategist was Sasha's role on the team, but she hadn't played it for months. Still, she didn't take it as an insult or me throwing her under the bus.

"What are you talking about? There's no way he or any of us could've known her powers were hereditary," she said. "Play Monday morning quarterback, but you could've told us."

Peters scoffed at the idea. "You *knew* coming in that Hughes was a teleporter. He should've suppressed *all* of her powers. Shape-shifting has a manipulative nature, not an aggressive one."

My cell phone rang in my pocket. I let it go to voicemail.

"Manipulation *is* aggression," Rhapsody said. Kai had turned into her dead father and it had frozen Rhapsody stiff. Now, she'd gotten so fired up that a pencil-thick vein in her neck bulged. "Let her shape-shift into Diane and see how you react."

That shut him up on the spot. Arms behind his back, he clasped his wrists. We watched him pace a circular pattern in the high stalks of weeds.

Is this how he thinks out a problem? I hope he finished obsessing sometime soon. Outside of the swishing of the weeds, the silence drove me nuts. My cell phone chirped, indicating that I had a phone message. I'd check it soon.

Baring my teeth, I screamed, "What're we supposed to do now?"

He stopped in front of me and flashed a smile as if his refusal to answer questions broke my resolve. "Assuming the two of you discussed this in the privacy of your own minds...when is the meet-cute with the other immortal?"

For once, neither of my ex-girlfriends were suspicious of me talking to another girl. *"Tomorrow."* I crossed my arms. "I don't know where, but I'll look for the evite. And I'm not immortal, by the way."

He laughed. "You're not? Okay, if you say so. You *are* going though, right?"

Rhapsody held her hand out. "Hold up. What did Whack Job say to you, Peters?"

I tried reading Peters' mind, but he'd erected a mental wall to block me again. "None of your business," he said to us before casting a glance my way. "Especially not yours. You have *one job*. Go to the meeting, and come back alive."

I'd had enough. Whenever stuff went down he spared hoarded important details. "I'm not doing that Collective-isn't-telling-me thing. You owe us. We're all you have left."

Peters brushed his hands through his hair. "No. You're not."

He'd spent almost two hundred years piling money, drinking, and spending time with young women. What else had he done worth mentioning?

"*Leverage*." Sasha looked sure of what she'd said. "She threatened his daughter's life."

His wrinkled cheeks drooped. "My *son*. And see, Mr. Champion, she didn't have to read my mind to figure it out. She's useful. Keep her around and you might get to be adults after all."

They *could* have children. We could have children. Whatever powers each parent had, they transferred over to their kids. Kai and her partner targeted *me*? Why?

A headache blazed in my sinuses near my temples. The constant text messages coming through on my phone didn't help. Instead of crushing my phone to my chest, I unzipped my suit and looked at its display.

"What's so freaking important?" I asked out loud as I read the messages from Julia, my other stepmother. Sasha leaned over to see for herself.

"Ray," she said.

I fastened my suit and took to the sky at supersonic speed.

◇◇◇

The house was an hour's drive away but I got there in no time, landing on the back lawn in plain sight. *Who cares who saw me?* Ever second counted. Ray and I had our differences, but my remaining birth parent wouldn't die without me by his side.

Julia opened the door beneath the wooden deck. Rather than her usual designer clothes, she wore a dark blue track suit with neon pink stripes down the sleeves and legs with a pair of white sneakers. When healthy, Julia was a gym rat. In the past few weeks, she'd put on weight in her face and hips. This ordeal, my father's cancer and her own shoulder injury, had aged her. She wasn't the bouncy twenty-something woman I'd remembered.

"Hey, Jason." She waved her left hand and then let it dangle at her side. Since Ryan Cain had stabbed her to hurt me, she'd lost function in her arm. When she used it, like her wave, the hand had little to no sustained strength in it.

"Hey." This must be serious. She never called me Jason, always Junior.

"Heard the sonic boom."

"Sorry."

She signaled with her eyes that I should come inside. "No worries. I closed the draperies upstairs. Nobody would've seen..." she said, waving her right index finger in the air to mimic my landing.

"Thanks."

"Go on in. He's been asking for you. I sent Rosa out for lumpia. She won't be back for a while."

Rosa's absence meant less need for explanation. I hugged Julia, careful not to press too hard.

I climbed the carpeted beige steps to the first floor. In the middle of the family room, Julia had set up a hospital bed in plain view of the front door. From there, Ray could turn his head and see me come up the back exit as well.

Despite my warnings, he'd kept goshenite close to him for so long that he'd contracted Stage Four bone cancer. He'd die the same way Mom had.

The heavy, cold air smelled of ointment and medicine -- enough to gag on. Two at-home care nurses, a large, bald black man and a slender white woman with extra-long brown hair, hovered over Ray's body.

"Hey, Dad," I choked out, trying not to sound awkward. Since I'd turned thirteen I could count the times I'd called him "Dad" on two hands with six fingers missing.

While the woman nurse adjusted the pain medication in his IV drip, the male nurse asked, "This is your son, Ray?"

"Yes, the oldest one," Ray said. "Jesse, every time he calls me 'Dad' it sounds like he's the one in pain."

It didn't shame me. He'd renounced his parental rights to me and kept legal rights to my little brother, Zachary. Not that I wanted him abandoned, too, but it was a good reason not to call him Dad. Back then, Ray had seen me, the troubled, rage blackout, ADHD son, *way* different than his perfect little toddler with chubby arms. Even after he knew about my superpowers. I wished he would have loved me that much and accepted me, too.

I tried not to stare at his swollen, purpled left arm. The veins had collapsed from repeated injections. Every time I visited him since his terminal diagnosis last November, I started our conversations with the same question.

"One to ten?" I asked him.

Ray grimaced and moaned, *"Seventy-five."*

His doctors warned us this moment would come. The medicine's effectiveness would plateau and his pain would just get worse. Mom had gone through this three years ago -- Ray didn't want me to see it. I didn't like his decision back then, but I understood it better now.

"Leave us," he told Jesse and the other nurse. He closed his eyes and licked his lips before adding, "Not you, Honey."

Julia stroked his face with her good hand. "Okay, Baby. Okay."

I knew this might be the last conversation I'd ever have with my father. He looked *that bad.* He'd lost about a third of his body weight and his skin sagged on his bones. It was the worst condition I'd seen him in since. I should've known better than to trust him with goshenite.

It had made him paranoid about life, and its high-level proton radiation was killing him.

"Staring,"

"Huh?"

"You're *staring*, Son."

How did he expect me not to? "Sorry."

I'd visited him once a week for the past six months. My therapist Susan said I should use the time Ray and I had left to heal our relationship. I wasn't so sure something with so many cracks could become whole again. We had become closer, though.

"I wish you hadn't done this to yourself," I said to him.

Ray tensed his dry hands in frustration. "What would you have had me do? I had to protect my family."

After Ryan attacked her, Julia had almost bled to death in Ray's arms. "Nobody blames you for that."

"You do."

"You knew. I told you the risks. What about the lead safe?"

"Super-speeders, teleporters, whatever -- how was I supposed to get them out in time?"

"And the lead shielding?" I'd put him in this position in the first place, but I hadn't kept him there. "No. You had to be in control, didn't you?"

Ray coughed or choked – I couldn't tell. Julia handed him the white Styrofoam cup from the dining room table. He bent the straw into his mouth and sipped it. I'd upset him, kicked a dying man while he was down. Still, I had a point. If Kai and her partner stormed in here right now, they could kill us all without a struggle. I doubted

Ray could even aim the handgun I knew he had underneath his pillow.

Still hacking, Ray dropped the cup onto the floor next to his bed. Julia sighed from exhaustion. "I'll clean that up," she said.

When she stepped to the kitchen for paper towels, my father eyes pleaded with me for help. I knew what he wanted me to do – relieve him of his suffering. He wanted me to do for him what I'd told him I'd done for George and use the green emerald radiation in my blood to invigorate him. When I'd done it for George he returned to his former state. So would Ray – but not for long. In fact, it would *worsen* his condition.

Every time Ray asked me to do something to benefit him my heart burned like I'd eaten a bowl full of ghost peppers. *Why should I make you feel better? How many times have you made excuses for why you couldn't care about me?*

"*Please,*" he insisted. His eyes watered. "Do it."

"For Mom," I said just above a whisper.

I concentrated the emerald energy in my blood and forced it into Ray's body. In an instant, his skin filled out and he almost looked like the Ray I remembered. The mound of bruised flesh on his arm dissolved.

Propping himself up on his elbows, he said, "Thanks, Champ. I needed that. We have to hurry. Jesse and Emily won't stay out for long. I keep switching nurses until I get a set who will."

Julia returned with a roll of paper towels. "You Champion men are all alike," she scowled while cleaning up the mess. "Five minutes, Jason Ray, Jr. Not a second longer. Promise me!"

I almost took offense at her using my entire name. "Deal."

Ray swung his legs over the side of the bed and stood. He relished the movement. He hadn't walked on his own in a pretty long time. With one hand on his IV stand, he pointed toward his study. "Let's go."

While Jesse and Emily milled around in the living room we sneaked into his study and locked the door.

What's this about?

Ray set a black briefcase on his desk and a long bottle of scotch next to it. Scotch was his drink and it had to be top shelf. This bottle had "Macallan 25" written in fancy script on the white label. He'd never opened it.

"Julia gave me this for a wedding present," he said. "I'd planned to do this on your twenty-first birthday, but under the circumstances..."

It's a trap. "I'm good, Dad, thanks. This can't take long. Anyway, it might screw up my concentration."

"It won't. And you can't get drunk."

My father reached into the oak cabinet for a corkscrew and two glasses. It wasn't an invitation I could decline. He opened the bottle and poured brown liquid into the glasses. Then he handed me one and clinked his glass against mine.

"What's the toast?" I asked him.

Ray paused for a beat. "What would I say at your high school graduation? Maybe you go to college? I'd say something there. At your wedding, birth of my first grandchild..."

His eyes welled up with tears. Dabbing at them with his fingers, he took a deep extended breath and fought a cry rising in his throat.

"To long life." When I said it, my own voice cracked.

"*Salud*," Ray said while downing his drink in one swallow. "Good booze,"

It took me a few tries to finish without throwing up. *What's he get out of this stuff?* The "notes," as he called them, were buttery but the instant it hit my throat the hints of sweetness changed to flame. "Yeah...what you said."

He poured himself another round and offered me the same. "Another?"

"Thanks, but..."

"Don't have long, right?" he groaned after taking a sip. "The kind of money we pay these in-home care people. Jesse, Emily -- they won't sit on their hands and let you just die in peace."

The word *die* stuck like a knife in my heart. I pushed past the alcohol's effects and my swelling hurt and confusion to concentrate. Otherwise Ray would drop where he stood.

"All right. What's next?"

Ray took another swig and tapped the top of the briefcase. It looked brand new and smelled of freshly conditioned leather. He keyed the code on the metal dial locks and popped them open.

"This belongs to you."

He twisted it around and showed me its contents. There were stacks of new $100 bills bound in $1,000 increments and a large manila package wrapped in plastic.

I told him, "No, I'm not running these drugs to Colombia for you."

He snickered. "You have your mother's sense of humor."

It was seriously one of the best compliments he'd ever paid me. "What is it?"

He stroked the stacks of cash. "Ever tell you I wanted to be a public defender?"

Any time he'd talked about his profession, or anything else for that matter, I'd tuned him out. "Don't think so."

"One look at the hours and the salary and I knew I couldn't hack it and have things the way I wanted for your mom. So, corporate law it was. I hated every day of it, but you see what it's done for us."

Yeah. Long hours, but the pay was much better. So good in fact that, although Mom and I still didn't get to see him much, there's nothing we wanted that we couldn't have. She drove a BMW with $500-a-piece performance tires Ray always complained about replacing. Every year for Christmas I got the toys I wanted and then some.

Then Mom died, he married and divorced Debra, and it all came to a screeching halt.

He said, "I know Courtney left you enough funds to last you a lifetime, but you deserved your birthright. Half a million dollars. Zachary's is in a trust. It was going to be payable after my…"

I'd seen this much money before so I wasn't shocked. Though I anticipated what he was going to say, I hated hearing him say it.

"I figured, why wait?" He handed me the package next to the cash. "I wanted to see you open it."

I did so and what I found I never would've expected him to give me. There was a bunch of Mom's old jewelry in it, including her engagement ring and wedding band. A wad of sepia toned pictures bound by in a rubber band, a man's gold pocket watch, a white gold crucifix and chain, a package of sealed letters, and the Champion family Bible that smelled like old cheese.

A lump formed in my throat as I returned the objects back to the package. Ray stopped me when I got to the crucifix. "Don't do what I did," he said. His hand touched the chain and my hand at the same time. "This was mine. Your great-grandmother gave it to me after I got baptized. Haven't been to church the way I should. Don't pack God away for a rainy day. You need Him."

I nodded my head and blinked back tears. "He'll be there for me? *Like you were?*"

"Signing over my custody to Debra was the best thing I could've done for you."

"*For* me? You mean *to me.*"

I'd known he'd felt that way ever since I found out he'd done it, and he had my things shipped to Debra's apartment. That moment when he didn't care enough, when he couldn't face me like a man, was when "Dad" became Ray. His acknowledgment of it fired up my anger.

For a quick moment he left it at that. Then he raised his hand in a salute. "Look at you. You've gone from Reject High' to *saving the world.*" His voice broke. "Annie and Deb and...*God*...made you who you are. You're a *Champion,* the kind of man I always wanted to be -- a hero. *My hero.*"

I cried, as well. Ray locked me in an embrace. We hugged for a while until I felt his body sagging in my arms. "Dad?"

He didn't respond. My powers had lost their effect, though I tightened my concentration. He had to get back to bed.

Still hugging him, I asked at his ear. "Can you walk?"

He wheezed out a weak, "No."

I hoisted Ray into my arms and grabbed his IV stand with my left hand. I maneuvered enough to open the door and came out to a full audience.

Julia's worried face said it all. "You said a five minute walk to the study and back," she said with fake anger in her voice. "You've been gone at least ten."

I apologized as I approached the bed. "Sorry," I said. "Lost track of time."

Jesse helped me get Ray back into bed. I didn't need help. I could have lifted them both by my fingers. "Easy," Jesse warned me. "Don't want to dislodge the IV after your little trip. We've had a heck of a time keeping it in."

Just then, a crazy idea popped into my head. "What's my father's blood type?"

"AB negative. Why?"

The same as mine. Maybe a blood transfusion? What about his veins, would they hold long enough? Did we have time to do one, no questions? "No reason."

"Don't get him out of bed again. He needs rest, not vigorous exercise."

I didn't appreciate Jesse's threatening tone. He'd taken one look at my wiry body and thought he could bully me. As much as I wanted to prove him wrong, I said, "Okay."

I let him and Emily tend to Ray and doubled back to the study. Closing the briefcase, I gazed at Ray's unfinished bottle of scotch and the tumblers sitting next to it. My heart thumped with emotion. All those years, all those times I'd hated him for giving me up. He couldn't have raised me before the superpowers, and he used legal ways to make it so that he wouldn't try. For a control freak, admitting how lousy of a father he was in writing must have been hard. It must also be why Debra didn't hate him the way I thought she should.

A hand rested on my shoulder. I could tell by the thinness of the fingers and the expensive scent of perfume that it was Julia. "He planned it this way, you know. To the letter."

I didn't expect anything different from him. "Figures."

Julia touched my elbow and escorted me to the kitchen away from the murmuring nurses working on my father. "He's gone on and on about fixing things with you. Did he?"

I don't know if you can fix years of damage in ten minutes, but it was a step in the right direction. "Kind of."

She blurted out, "You're thinking of giving him some of your blood, aren't you?"

My thoughts come in crashing waves and I never rule them out, which is a problem when you act out on the ones that damage things or people. "He'd be healthy again."

She used the water dispenser on the fridge for a glass of water. "*If* it worked, yes. But, before you make him an immortal god, I'd ask him if that's what he wants."

I faced her. "We're not *immortal gods,* Julia," I said to her. "We can still die. We're still human."

"Rhapsody, Sasha, Esteban and Selby can, but *you?*" Her brow furrowed. "You survived a *nuclear explosion,* Jason. If that can't kill you, I doubt anything else will."

I didn't want to tell her about David King. He'd drunk three vials of my "immortal blood" in front of me and I was still able to kill him.

Briefcase in hand, I followed Julia to where Ray lay. When we saw him, Julia covered her mouth. I dropped the briefcase. Jesse hooked up a machine in a red case to Ray's bare chest and ribs while Emily performed CPR on him. "Julia, call 911!" she shouted.

The wall clock moved forward, but besides its forward ticking, I couldn't tell time moved.

"Stop CPR. Do not touch patient. Analyzing heart rhythm," a mechanical voice said.

After a moment, the machine said. "Shock advised. Charging. Stand clear of patient."

"Stand back," Jesse said.

Emily retreated as Jesse pressed a yellow button. Ray's body jerked with an electric current. Then Emily resumed CPR on the machine's direction.

Julia spoke on the phone with an emergency responder. She gave the operator their address. I knew it was common procedure, and Ray might not die, but the process still set me on edge. After she hung up, Julia yanked on my right arm. I'd been levitating a few inches off of the floor. I got a grip on my nerves and set down on the hardwood before anyone else noticed.

I faced Julia and grabbed her shoulders. "Get me a syringe and a needle. He needs my blood."

She wriggled beneath my grasp. "I don't have one. Let go. You're hurting me."

I'd forgotten about her damaged arm and the pressure I was using on it. "They're nurses. One of them has to have one, right?"

Her eyes darted back and forth. "I don't know!" she shouted in a controlled voice. "You don't know what you're doing. You could put air in your veins or his. Both of you could die."

My throat tightened and burned. "What am I supposed to do? Nothing?"

"Shock advised. Stay clear of patient. Press the orange button now."

Again, the red machine sent electricity through Ray's body. The first jump start on his heart hadn't worked.

The second didn't either. I focused my powers on his body again. No change.

Julia gripped my forearm as Emily resumed CPR. Squeezing my fists, I fought the urge to punch through a wall. Julia closed her tear-filled eyes and prayed in Arabic. I didn't know her to be a person of faith. My lips formed words, but no sound came out.

Not ten feet away my father battled for his life. I could see his body, still as death.

Jesse pressed the orange button a last time. Julia continued to pray, louder this time -- definitely Arabic. I held my breath. Ray's body arced with current and relaxed. I watched his chest and waited. Neither Jesse nor Emily said a word.

That wasn't good enough. I rushed over to Ray's bedside. "Is he dead?"

Jesse ignored me. Emily stopped CPR as emergency personnel rolled a gurney into the room. Julia ceased praying and stood by, answering questions when asked.

After they lifted Ray's body onto the gurney, they strapped him down and attached a clear mask to his face. One of the nurses squeezed the bulb attached to it, while the paramedics rolled him away.

Julia kissed me on the cheek. "I'll call you," she said.

She might be in shock, but she was way too calm for me. My stepmother trailed the paramedics, who had him out of the house in no time.

Whirling around to Jesse, who packed his and Emily's things, I repeated my question. "Is he dead?"

"He has a weak pulse. Let them work," was all he said.

"Is he going to live?"

He gripped my shoulders, which ticked me off. What had been a flicker of anger inside me had spread into wildfire. I felt myself on the edge of raging. Something about Jesse keyed my nerves.

"Calm down! He's…"

"Calm down" was the absolute worst thing to tell someone with anger issues. Without thinking, I sent my hands into Jesse's chest. He flew across the room and crashed against the stone-faced fireplace.

The next thing I knew, I was standing on an unfamiliar street of my father's subdivision. I had no idea how I'd gotten there. My skin was sweaty. I was breathing hard. Livewires slithered and popped on the street.

To my right a sedan had burned down to the chassis with a skeleton in the driver's seat, its skull leaned against the steering wheel. The heat from the flames and the scent of seared flesh was overwhelming. I threw up onto the street.

An electrical pole lay near my feet, wires dangling from it like unkempt hair. It was all the evidence I needed. Since I'd gotten superpowers this was my worst fear.

It happened.

I'd raged and killed someone.

CHAPTER SEVEN

I'm a killer

Oh God, oh God, oh God.

I kept trying to convince myself: *I'm not a murderer.* Except, from the looks of it, the opposite was true. I'd killed someone and didn't even know about it.

The man who'd burned to death in his car might not have seen it that way. I'd caved in his sedan's roof with a utility pole and trapped him inside. Had he pleaded for mercy? Cried for help? Did I flinch? Care even? There was no way to tell. Skeletons don't talk.

I killed King -- a career psychopath who experimented on teenagers with cancer-causing radiation. I'd done the world a favor. *Murder.*

I'd taken heliodor from six of King's men, and then I assumed they'd died from old age. *Murder.* They should have died seventy to eighty years ago, though. They'd outlived all their loved ones. No one would miss them, anyway, right?

Still murder.

This one wasn't anything like King or his lackeys. He could've had a family. I couldn't deliver a proper apology to his relatives or confess to police. I'd done more damage than the eye could see and there was no way to measure it.

I cursed myself. So much for turning over a new leaf. I'd just grown a *tree* of old leaves. To make things worse, at this point, I wasn't sure whether my father was dead or alive. Julia said she'd call me. I hoped it wouldn't be anytime soon.

The sun blazed overhead. In a daze, I surveyed the immediate area. People peeked through their windows to investigate. I masked up and activated my armor's cloaking. The ones who saw me -- I knew what they were thinking. *He's a vigilante like the ones at Union Station.*

Unwilling to stick around and deal with the authorities, I stepped around the utility pole I'd crushed, and I leaped into the air. Except I landed a couple feet from where I started.

"Okay, don't panic," I told myself. "Just relax."

I gave it another go with worse results. My mouth was dry, but not like my powers were on. More like I needed something to drink because it was hot.

My thoughts scattered all over the place. I needed a full dose of ADHD meds now, not the reduced level I was on. *Crap!* A chorus of sirens converged on me. I cursed and jumped over and over again.

I can't fly.

Heart pounding in my chest, I gave in to my lone remaining impulse – *run.*

I sprinted in the opposite direction of the destruction I'd caused, down the hill and around the corner. All the houses looked the same – brick fronts, several levels, picture perfect lawns and trimmed hedges. I turned around, hoping for anything to spark my sense of direction.

In the distance a grove of oak trees surrounded a playground. I headed toward it. As I neared it, I realized that one set of police sirens closed in on my location.

I kept jumping. Nothing happened. Desperate tears mingled with sweat wet my face and neck. *What should I do, climb a tree? There's nowhere to hide!*

"C'mon!" I yelled, cursing at myself. "Work already!"

All I needed was one jump to get me across the city and away from everything. *I blacked out. It wasn't my fault I killed him! I didn't ask to be like this!* No one would believe the truth if I told it to them. With my powers active, I could have at least proved I wasn't insane. What was I supposed to do now?

Three police cars swerved into position – two in front of me and one behind – I didn't have the presence of mind to run anymore. All six policemen trained their guns on me. They shouted commands one over the other – "don't move," "freeze," and "down on the ground." *Déjà vu.* These guys must have trained at the same academy as the officers who tried to arrest me an hour ago.

I wasn't sure which one to do first. I put my hands up to keep them from shooting. My bodysuit could protect me, but I was in no rush to test its bulletproof qualities.

The policeman at my back ran towards me and forced my wrists into metal cuffs. Once he did, I yanked at them. Of course they didn't break. The last time I'd been in handcuffs I couldn't break them because they had goshenite on them. These were a normal set.

While the one who cuffed me read me my Miranda rights, another officer grasped a handful of mask. "Masquerade party's over," he said.

"No!" I begged him. "Please."

In a second, he'd reveal my identity and broadcast it all over the news. Wouldn't matter I was only sixteen – I was a vigilante.

"We got one of 'em," he said to one of the others. "Think the reward will go to us?"

The $20,000 bounty Chicago called a reward for information leading to our arrest? With my identity in their pocket, they'd connect the dots to the others. Then Sasha, Rhapsody and even Esteban would have to go on the run to protect themselves.

"I'm a *human being,*" I argued back. "I have rights."

"You're a *terrorist,*" my arresting officer said. "You have no rights."

I'd been stupid enough to let my stupid emotions trigger a rage blackout. Susan had taught me ways to cope with my anger, and I'd forgotten to use them. I knew better than to let Jesse rile me.

Closing my eyes, I held my breath and waited for the stretching material to finally give and for my mask to come off. Right when it did, nausea hit my stomach. That might distract the cop...*vomit all over his legs.*

I burped and hoped more would come up. No luck. *Why am I sitting and not standing?* Air conditioning and the stench of cigarette and marijuana smoke blew into my face.

I opened my eyes. I'd been teleported into the passenger seat of a speeding car with Kai at the wheel.

As she zipped through local traffic, she waved her hand over my cuffs. "Buckle up. I like it fast," she said as the scent of teleportation sulfur filled the car. Don't mind the weed. Keeps the voices quiet."

Voices? Is she kidding? I did as she said. Without my powers, I had no control in this situation. Rubbing my sore wrists, I said, "Thanks."

The best thing I could do was wait until this weed-smoking criminal hit a stop light. Then I'd make a run for it. But when I tore the utility pole in half, I shorted the traffic lights near Ray's development. She wouldn't have to brake before hitting the highway entryway.

Not like she would have anyway. Kai drove like demons were chasing her. We're on the run, right? Whatever it was, she didn't say.

I couldn't tell much about her car from the inside. Except Kai's a slob. Fossilized French Fries, bunched up yellow fast-food wrappers and crumbs littered the carpet. Dark liquid -- soda pop or coffee -- had dribbled down the side of the car's charcoal gray paneling. Inside the ashtray was a handful of gray cinders and an inch-long dark brown rolled stick.

Wondering how much she'd reveal, I came out and asked her, "Where're we going?"

"To see *him*." She said "him" with reverence, like he was a king or something. "Where else?"

I patted my sweaty palms against my legs. Prickly body armor did little to dry them off. The temperature in the car was ninety degrees. My abilities usually shielded me from weather extremes...when they were on. Even the cooling system in the suit had its limits.

"You make him sound like he's important."

She plucked a cigarette from a pack wedged between her gearbox and her seat. "Important," she said, rolling her eyes as she lit up.

I didn't push further. Didn't want to know any more about her partner. Not yet. He could be worse company than she was, and I could only handle so much more at this point.

I swiped my brow with the back of my hand. "Aren't you hot?"

"Heat doesn't bother me. Air conditioning doesn't work if it did. Windows, either."

I pressed the button for the automatic windows. Nothing. Either Kai had activated the override control or she was telling the truth.

I thought for a moment before asking her something else. "Why'd you save me?"

She let out a stream of cigarette smoke into the sizzling hot air. "You ask a lot of questions."

Rhapsody had once accused me of the same thing. She'd said "asks stupid questions" should be a modification on my IEP. I'd give anything for my ex-girlfriend to make a wisecrack about me now. It'd mean I wasn't alone in this.

"I ask too many questions? Don't answer them," I said, stifling a cough. Nicotine smoke was bad enough without a lingering film.

She chuckled and puffed. "I didn't save you. I secured an asset."

For a moment I'd forgotten I was a hostage. Kai acted more like a mentally unstable, homicidal friend with a death wish than a captor.

"Here's a question for *you*. How'd you get yourself arrested? What'd you have to do to get that much cop attention?"

Did she know what I'd done? Had she seen it? Heavy guilt pangs weighed down my stomach.

I cleared my throat.

"Pegged you for a deontologist. Didn't know you had it in you!"

"Deon—what?"

Kai cut around another car so fast I thought we'd clipped its headlight. *"Deontologist.* Kant? Read much?"

I shrugged. "Can't what?"

She pointed a finger in my direction like I'd done something wrong. "It's philosophy. Whatever is wrong is *wrong*. I'm more of a 'whatever-feels-good-at-the-time' kind of chick."

Her philosophy disgusted me. "I have rage blackouts, and I raged, and…"

"Wait!" She swerved around a creeping red crossover SUV. "You're super strong *and* you have rage blackouts? Ooh…that's not a conflict of interest."

Correction: I *used to be* super strong. "My powers are gone."

She snuffed out the cigarette butt in the overflowing ashtray. "You're joking."

Her tone suggested disappointment. She knew we wouldn't be having this conversation if I had my powers. Now, I wished I'd kept my mouth shut. Maybe I could've bluffed her into freeing me before spilling the beans about no longer being a threat.

"What were you doing out here anyway?" I asked her.

Kai pointed to a black panel with a blue LED display just below her satellite radio control buttons. "Police scanner chatter about vigilantes. I followed the breadcrumbs. Subtlety isn't your thing. Besides I have a thing for mega hot dudes and violent streaks."

No one, not even Sasha, would've called me *mega hot*, which further proved Kai was completely out of her mind. "You've been stalking me?"

"Like I told you, *securing an asset*. I was in North High for weeks before you noticed me."

I didn't feel bad about that. After all, North High was huge and she was a shape-shifter. "I'm an *asset?*"

"The others don't matter to us, Jason. Only *you.*"

Her partner had wanted me for a meeting in less than twenty-four hours and now we've got an earlier face-to-face. *For what?* I was "normal" now. Worthless.

I took a breath. The heat and humidity in the car was oppressive. "Then what was the Multiplex about?"

"Smoking you out," she said.

Wait, what? "But…"

"We're not going to talk for a while."

Miles down the road, my cell phone rang. Even if it was Julia I couldn't handle more bad news right now. I let it go to voicemail and broke the silence. "Calls go straight to my bodysuit mask."

A white lie – they *could* go through to my mask but I hadn't set it up that way. The heads up holographic display flickering so close to my face made my brain crazy.

Her dark eyes wandered over my body like I was a plate of barbecue ribs. "Pretty cool tech, huh?"

Invisible ants crawled across my skin. "So you 'smoked me out'. Your partner won't want me. I'm worthless without my abilities."

She honked her horn and shouted a few choice words at the person driving in front of her. "You undervalue your importance."

"To *you?* You're *murderers.*"

She flashed a wicked smile. "I'm *efficient* at what I do."

That's all it took to shut me up.

In the moments we weren't talking, my phone rang once more. Again I ignored it. Julia could leave me a message about my dead father and I'd listen to it when I was in a better mood. Like July, 2017.

I studied Kai's face for the first time. She was close to Sasha's class of beauty, but I wasn't attracted to her. The last time I saw Kai, she'd worn a white blouse and black slacks. She'd changed into a dark blue tank top and white skinny jeans. A lead ball hung from her neck and dangled just above her chest. *A green emerald.* The lead shielding prevented me from accessing its radiation. Not like I could.

She had a tattoo on her right shoulder. Written in black script under a cross was the name, "Christine." Beads of sweat formed on her forehead. Looks like she'd lied, too. Heat did get to her after all.

Kai popped another cigarette into her mouth and lit up. "You're staring."

My father had said the same thing to me. *Did he make it? Would I be an orphan before the sun set?* I'd finally made him proud of me, and all it had taken was for me to absorb a nuclear blast with my body. I hated myself for craving his acceptance.

"Who's Christine?" I asked her. "Leader of your crime syndicate?"

Kai took a long drag and gave me a cold stare. "My *real* mom."

Hughes and Camuto had given her away. Which made no sense. They didn't know Kai would survive or inherit their powers?

Why would they have put her in a place where she could potentially hurt people? Unless they didn't care.

Or they thought she'd die before it made a difference. *Where are we going? Traveller? Xobai? Walsh?* I couldn't read her mind.

The BAE.AT fortress was in Walsh. The Collective used to operate there. Since Christmas, we'd kept clear of it. Our equipment and reserve cash were there. Maybe she'd figured that and wanted to clean us out. I didn't know or care. I just wanted out.

"Where are we going?"

This time my phone chirped with text messages back-to-back-to-back. The repetitive sounds annoyed Kai. "Turn it off before they ping your location."

Knowing Sasha, she'd already pinged me. "The phone comes through my suit," I lied. "I have to mask up to turn it off."

She waved her hand. "You try anything and I'll drown you in the Pacific."

I donned my mask, cued up the display, and waited for it to pick up my messages. "All right," I said in a distorted voice.

Kai snuffed out her cigarette butt and turned on the car fan. For a second the scent of hot seawater replaced the rancid funk in the air. Thank God my mask filtered most of it.

The onboard system showed seven manila message folders. Julia had sent the first marked urgent. After it, I eyed a series of seven text messages, in caps. All were the same except for the last one.

The repeated text messages from Rhapsody read, "SFEHSE." The final message said, "PINGED UR 20. EXTRACT SOON."

"Safehouse" was a code word for the "Safehouse protocol." Rhapsody, Esteban and I put it into place after we'd rescued Debra from certain death. Last year, Aunt Dee and Zachary were a lucky test run. We hired men armed with goshenite to move them every few hours to mask their whereabouts. Right now, Debra could be a dozen different places. I wouldn't know exactly where she was until she contacted me. With her, Aunt Dee and Zachary in hiding, the only people at risk now were Ray and Julia.

I needed to get them off of Kai's radar.

Wait. Sasha and Rhapsody were going to extract me? *How?* I'd been the strategist in Sasha's absence. I'd been the one making the plans. Who would do it now, Rhapsody *by herself?* I would've told the person I was rescuing, me in this case, to distract the kidnapper. Kai had feelings for me, so I'd have told myself to play on those.

I would have kissed her, though from the looks of it her mouth might taste like a dirty garbage can. *If I can kiss her without throwing up, I'll make a play for her boob but grab her emerald instead. Then, I'll crash through the roof and fly away.*

As I thought about it, that was a pretty dumb idea. My first draft plans usually were a little on the stupid side. Without knowing what was wrong with my body, there was no guarantee my powers would work with an emerald, anyway.

My heart beat faster in my chest. My relatives were safe and an extraction was coming. Now I had *hope.* I tried not to sound excited, but my voice rose in pitch as I said, "Offline."

"What's that?" Kai asked me. Her voice was tight with concern.

I swallowed hard and sold the biggest lie I'd told her so far. I hadn't checked Julia's voicemail. Deep in my heart, I'd hoped what I was about to say wasn't true. "I think my dad is dead," I said.

She placed her right hand on my knee and squeezed, which had the opposite effect that she intended. "Sorry."

Ever since I met her face-to-face, Kai had wanted to jump my bones. Even Captain Obvious understood that. I had to play her attraction to me to my advantage. Along with that train of thought, I tried not to shrink back when she kept rubbing my leg to comfort me.

I'd forgotten to take off my mask. By the time I did, Kai grew suspicious. She cut her eyes at me and lifted her hand from my leg to swipe sweat from her brow. "What was the *real* message? You playing games, *Cap?* I'll…"

Before I could deflect, Kai slammed on the brakes and collided with the tractor trailer in front of us. The driver behind us smashed into our rear bumper and our heads thrashed forward and back with violent force. Another car swerved into the passenger side. The impact closed us in on three sides and shattered all the car's windows.

The driver side air bag deployed and smacked against Kai's face, but mine didn't deploy. White dust swirled around in a cloud and burned my nostrils. I coughed until my lungs hurt.

When I finally breathed clear again I noticed everything had come to a halt. Cars, trucks, SUVs and tractor trailers had collided in a multi-car pileup that made my head spin to think about. Orange and silver barriers blocked all four lanes of the highway. The motorists who weren't unconscious or injured honked their horns in frustration for help.

I maneuvered my limbs. Maybe a bruise on my right side and whiplash or strained ligaments in my neck. There was no way to tell without hospital treatment, and I wasn't doing that.

There was a better way -- continue with my plan and steal Kai's green emerald.

She lay on the airbag, eyes closed, and a trail of blood leaking from a cut at her hairline. I dodged the jagged glass pieces and craned my sore neck through the window. A fishtailed maroon sports car blocked me from opening the door. The sun's rays reflected off of the roofs of the standstill traffic. By straining my eyes past them, I saw a confusing scene. Blue uniformed policemen attending the mess looked bewildered.

I turned my attention to Kai, who hadn't moved. I reached my hand between the airbag and just under her. My fingers wandered around the chain until they reached the green emerald. Radioactive electricity shot up my arm and through my body. My mouth dried, *cotton dry*.

I was back!

Before I could yank the stone from the chain, a hand touched my left shoulder. I froze. *Can't be.* At first I thought Kai woke up, but the hand was coming from the backseat, and it was far too gentle to be hers.

Out of the corner of my eye, I saw the empty backseat. Meaning one thing.

This – the multi-car pileup, *was the extraction plan.*

"C'mon Cap," Rhapsody whispered. I turned intangible. "Time to go. Sasha's parked on the rumble strip a half mile back."

"Just a sec." I readjusted my fingers around the chain and yanked. Kai's neck jerked. *Why isn't it giving?* "I've almost got her emerald."

"Forget her powers. Let's go before she wakes up."

I couldn't go back to being regular *and* powerless. I yanked again. The chain didn't break. Kai mumbled and stirred on the airbag. *No.* The vigor in my veins a minute ago disappeared.

"Rhapsody," Kai said.

At once, Rhapsody and I became visible. Kai had goshenite in the car somewhere. Had I known that, I would've used it against her to get free in the first place. Usually I could feel the presence of high proton radiation tingling in my bloodstream but not now. The white stones must be lead shielded, too.

Rhapsody cursed and tried to open the back door to no avail.

Kai smiled and sucked her teeth. "Things like this happen with *amateurs*. You need a teleporter."

She was right. Of all the things going on right now, I'd forgotten about Esteban. He could've gotten us out of here without breaking a sweat if he wasn't still obsessing over me and Sasha. Instead, the three of us had to fend for ourselves. No doubt we're a better team when we're all together.

"'Amateurs'? We saved the world *twice*," Rhapsody said to her.

She clapped with fake praise. "It's not like you knew what you were doing. You followed directions without knowing why. You're all poorly-trained dogs."

Kai's answer ticked off Rhapsody so much she switched over to Spanish curse words before saying, "Hughes and Camuto didn't hug you enough when you were a kid, so you get a match to burn the world down? You and your boyfriend are going to rule over a pile of ash?"

Kai chewed her lip and closed her eyes. Had Rhapsody made a decent point, given her something to think about? I doubted it. Her brain was churning.

"Nice stall," Kai said.

She teleported away in a cloud of green smoke, leaving Rhapsody and me trapped to stew in the car.

"You were stalling?" I climbed over the gearbox and tried opening the jammed driver's side door.

"Totally," she replied. "Wasn't even my insult 'A' game."

I panicked and pounded the door panel with my fist. No lock button. When I tried using the outside handle, it didn't work either. This wasn't normal. She'd made some sort of safety modification to the vehicle.

"Can you ghost us out?" I asked Rhapsody in frustration.

She shook her head. "Already tried. Climb out. I'll follow you."

I turned my body and kicked out the remaining window shards. "How is she taking away your powers with goshenite if she's not here to use it?" I asked her while easing my body through the opening.

"Don't know, Dude." Once we were out she pointed behind us. "Look."

I whipped my head around. My neck roared with pain, but what I saw held my attention past the agony. Sasha's clones fought Kai at every turn. When Kai got the advantage over one of them, that clone dropped from sight and reappeared to rejoin the fight. Sasha's clones held their own the best they could with Kai teleporting in and out in green blurs. Maybe someone with a good camera angle could've identified Sasha, but the action moved so fast, I doubted it. We masked up to protect ourselves just in case.

"I've got him," Rhapsody said in her headset.

Sasha responded and said a breathless "Copy that" before absorbing her clones at once. I viewed her in the distance through the collage of smashed cars with her hands on her thighs and gasping for breath.

Kai got the worst end of it. She'd fallen to her knees. From the looks of it, she'd be too exhausted to keep me captive or to teleport anywhere for a while.

Now was our chance to escape. The question was *how?*

Rhapsody wrapped her arms around my waist and glued herself to my side. I couldn't see her eyes through her mask but I was sure she wondered why we weren't already in the air. I knew her nonverbal movements. "Punch it, Cap. Pick up Girl Genius on the way out."

I offered the shortest explanation I could think of. "I can't fly anymore," I said. "My powers are gone."

She cursed and couldn't help but to ask. "What? You flew to Ray's like an hour ago."

I kept my anger in check. "That's why I was trying to steal her green emerald."

"None of this makes any sense," she said.

Tell me about it.

Kai got to her feet. Our window of opportunity to escape was closing fast. Even Sasha noticed. "What's the holdup?" she asked in our ears.

I'd never gotten higher than a D in Spanish so I had trouble with translating Rhapsody's rapid-fire Spanish beyond the basics. What I understood was "he," "no" and what I assumed was the word for "fly." In the meantime, she'd turned us invisible to buy me a little time to figure out how to get us in the air.

Kai limped in our direction. Once she had enough energy to cancel our invisibility, we'd be toast.

"You've done it a thousand times, Cap," Rhapsody said, still holding onto me. *"Fly."*

My stomach tightened. "I *can't*."

"I know you can!" Sasha yelled through my earpiece. "Do it."

I swallowed my doubts, bent my knees a little, and jumped. We lifted off from the ground at a slow speed. I heard the wind whistle past my ears as we ascended into the sky. Confidence sparked in my chest. I upped our speed and looped over toward Sasha. *Go faster?* Should my powers flame out, we'd be spots on the pavement.

Right when we reached Sasha we stopped midair -- forty feet above ground. Our limbs froze, too. Kai had a scarlet emerald, too, which gave her control over our bodies. Some of the prisms must have survived the solar storm we'd created. Did she have morganite, heliodor, and aquamarine prisms, too?

Grunting, screaming, I urged my body to break Kai's hold. Sweat covered my body inside of my suit. Her mental grip grew tighter. We had to break it. A drop at this height might kill us.

Our visibility flashed on and off and then it solidified. We were sitting ducks.

Without warning, we plummeted down to street level. Rhapsody screamed. I uttered some sort of roller coaster drop-type yell that I'd later wish I could take back. I crash landed first on the hood of a yellow taxicab and shattered all its windows. Rhapsody landed on my chest. The impact knocked the wind out of me. I couldn't tell Rhapsody to get up, and my arms hurt so badly that waving her away looked like wiggling more than anything else.

Thankfully she got the hint and tenderly moved off of me.

Then our world turned green.

CHAPTER EIGHT

we become inmates

We'd teleported into a space devoid of light. Our rubber soles squeaked against the floor as we moved around. My stomach churned and cramped, way more than usual. We'd traveled far. My gag reflex kicked in, but nothing came up. I doubted I could have vomited even if I wanted to.

I reached out for Rhapsody. Finding her shoulder about a foot to my left, my hand wandered down to hers. Together, we pressed the center of each other's palms.

A purplish glow lit up the room and reflected off the wall surface. Now that we had light, I guessed that the room's walls were about nineteen to twenty feet apart and constructed with thick metal that could contain radiation. Sasha once told me extra thick metal would more than likely keep us from escaping.

This place was built for people like us.

Or more appropriately, for the person I used to be.

She pulled back her mask and brushed her hands through her mussed hair. "There's a vent twenty feet up. Guess that's how we're getting air in here?"

I unmasked as well. "Or that's how they'll pump in poison gas."

"Not really a glass-half-full kind of guy, huh Cap?"

Assuming they wanted us alive, perhaps they'd drop food that way, too. Good thing Sasha wasn't in here. A place this small and enclosed would've sent her claustrophobia into overdrive.

I heard Rhapsody's ragged breathing. She'd taken a front row seat next to me on the I'm-Freaking-Out-Train.

"Cap, what's happen…"

Rhapsody never finished her question. No gunshots. Nobody else was around. *Kai. How'd she have enough juice to teleport us after fighting Sasha? How was she watching us?* I had to know.

My neck still blazing with pain from the car crash, I focused up at the vent. Anger boiled in my gut over everything – Ray's condition, the Multiplex, being dropped half a football field onto a car roof. Everything. I cursed Kai and everyone else involved I could think of.

"What do you want from me?" I screamed until my vocal strings burned.

I wished my powers worked. I'd fly up to the vent, tear it apart, and fight my way to her. Remembering the failure of a few minutes ago, I didn't try jumping again. A case of the dull aches settled into my muscles and bones. It hurt to breathe and to keep my eyes open. The signal wouldn't work on my cell phone, but maybe I could listen to the message Julia had left? At least I'd have a shot at knowing whether my father was alive.

"Play voicemail." I said it as low as I could, but it still gave off a small echo.

First message, marked urgent, said the automated voice.

The recording paused for a second, long enough for me to hear the background voices. *Were there beeps?* Then the sound cut out. Of course. My signal gave out. Ray was still in limbo to me. He could be dead or alive. I chose *alive*. His death meant I'd be without both of my parents. Of course Debra counted as a parent, but there was a little something different about blood relatives.

I clenched my fists and beat my forehead. Something, *anything*, had to work.

I slithered to the ground and laid my face against the cold floor. My breath created a circle of condensation on the surface. Numbness trickled into my limbs, and shooting pains traveled from the hot throbbing in my head down to my toes. Kai and her partner wanted me for some reason. Now they had me a day early.

It had been a full day since I'd been captured. Or an hour. Ten minutes. Who knows? My wristwatch/Geiger counter had broken when I fell onto the cab roof. Checking the display on my bodysuit would drain its solar battery and without it, I'd be in the dark. Besides, finding out how much time had passed would *unravel* me. I'd think about Ray, Julia, and Debra.

What about Rhapsody and Sasha? Had they been captured, too? Where are their cells? I'd been wracked with too much physical pain to explore. I whispered Rhapsody's name. Either she hadn't heard me, she'd passed out, or she had been moved. Either way, she did not answer.

I rolled onto my back and stared at the vent. By using the purple glow from my suit I was able to make out its rectangular shape.

"You're *watching* me? You *want* me? Come and *get me*," I told my captor.

She didn't answer. I didn't expect her to. She was too busy observing. When I got out of here I'd beat her and her partner to within an inch of their lives. Then they'd answer *my* questions.

I glanced at the cell's right corner -- a toilet in the corner, a washbasin, and a towel dispenser. *How had I missed seeing them before? Had it always been there? What kind of shape were they in?* There were no powerful smells. My bladder was full of liquid lead. Peeing on camera was way different than, say, violating guy protocol and not skipping a stall. That's a privacy breach but a forgivable offense. "Nope," I told myself. "Don't have to go quite *that* bad."

Suddenly the brightest white light I'd ever witnessed entered the room. It was blinding even though I closed my eyes and turned over to escape it. I heard something slide a short distance across the floor. Then, just like that, the light disappeared. My bodysuit glowed a little brighter after being exposed to it even for such a short time.

Once my eyes readjusted, I spotted a beige food tray – a bread roll, a lump of something white that could be mashed potatoes, a square piece of meat, a carton of drink and plastic silverware. I didn't know how hungry I was before now, but eating it meant giving in. Kai and her partner wanted me to stay alive, do what they wanted me to do. I'd live, but to spite them.

So I shoveled the food in my mouth, hating every well-seasoned, good-tasting bite. To make myself feel okay about swallowing it, I convinced myself that I needed the energy. *What for?* I didn't have powers anymore. Did I need energy to die more slowly while lying in a room? *Regular human beings can eat a meal a day and survive, right?* I decided then I'd nibble at the next two meals they offered me, as little as possible. Whatever they wanted to do to me, they needed me fit and healthy but mentally unhinged. That's why I was in this horror movie of a cell. I'd work to keep it together and deprive them of something important.

Unable to fight the urge any longer, I low-crawled over to the toilet, unzipped my bodysuit and used the toilet. I waved a one-fingered salute to the ceiling as I flushed. I turned the metal faucet handle to the left – *would the water get hot?* It did. There was a heater, and a heater meant this was a facility or a building, not a movable storage crate.

I returned to my spot on the floor and found myself dozing off. The throbbing in the middle of my spine radiated down my legs and kept me awake. I *wanted* to sleep with no dreams. Most times I envisioned something crazy having to do with my day. Susan called those *filtering dreams*. The context of today so far had been filled with death and violence. I'd rather not see the burning corpse of the man I'd killed or my dying father in my mind's eye if I could help it.

My eyes felt bruised and sore. I repositioned myself, trying to find a position to lessen the agony in my joints and muscles. In desperation I glanced back at the tray. I'd missed the white pill lying next to my empty drink carton. *Am I dreaming? Was the pill there before? Did I wish it there?*

I'd swallowed pills like this most of the past few years for my ADHD. Downing another drug wouldn't matter in the big picture, would it? It didn't look like Adderall. They didn't mean me any good, but I was no good to them dead.

I scooted over to the tray and palmed the pill. *This'll make me feel better.* I placed it in my mouth. The bitter capsule dissolved a bit on my tongue. It tasted like chalk. After I considered forcing it down my throat, I spit the pill out and figured I'd find a way to live with the pain.

They wanted to play with me. I wasn't going to enter the game or abide by their rules. Rule following has never been my thing.

A familiar male voice echoed from above me. "That was stupid," he said.

I crawled to my knees. *Esteban.* Everything was coming into place. Kai hadn't teleported us to this place at all. He did it for her.

"Maybe it was, but I'm not taking it. Watch me pee all you want if it does something for you."

"It's *Vicodin,*" he said. "It'll help with the pain from the accident. No worries. You take Schedule II narcotics every day. Not that big of a difference."

No worries? Didn't this fool see me locked up in a metal room?

I didn't care if his reasoning made sense. Everything hurt like crazy. A painkiller would have helped. I wasn't taking the pill.

"Screw yourself. We *trusted* you and you abandoned us." That's where he'd been all this time. *How much has he told them?* "You told them how much, *everything?* The fortress, our houses, the beach house – what *don't* they know?"

Esteban said nothing, which further ignited my anger.

"You think giving me up will keep them from killing you? Good luck with that."

I needed answers and I'd get them one way or another. It might as well be through him.

"That's not…"

I interrupted him. "You want revenge, right?" That couldn't be the only thing that had him turn on us, so I pushed his buttons on purpose. "You helped lock me in here to get back at me for kissing Sasha? Give it up, dude. She wants me. Not you."

He cleared his throat. His hate for me burned him inside. I could tell by the way his voice rose in pitch, almost screeching over the speaker system. "It's *bigger* than that."

"Really?" I'd done it, gotten under his skin. Now I had to kick it up a couple notches. "It's not because of what we did in the car before you caught us? That's the reason Rhapsody broke up with me, not a kiss. She couldn't deal. You never forget your first love."

My statements lingered with him. He couldn't read my mind because of my ADHD, so my lies stuck. When he didn't respond to me I had him hooked. I stood for the grand finale. "Sorry. I won't say anything else. It's better you don't know *everything*. I wouldn't want to, either."

With a pop of smoke Esteban appeared in the room behind me and locked his arm around my neck. He pointed a sharp object at my top of my kidney in a vulnerable spot of the armor. "You think that's funny, to mess up my relationship." His spittle and hot breath hit the back of my neck. "Tell me what happened, and when you're finished I may not filet you."

Under normal circumstances I might fear for my life. But this was *Esteban* – all emotion and jokes and little action. His threats were empty to me. Even without my powers I intimidated him. The only way he'd stab me was if I pushed him close to the edge.

His forearm tightened around my throat so I rambled to give myself a minute. "We kissed today," I lied. "Not just in the car."

He cleared his throat. "Where?"

"Before then, at a few stop lights."

I stepped my leg back. It burned with fire. While I didn't need super strength to throw him over my shoulder, it'd all go to crap if he teleported out and left me here. I had no idea how to disarm him, other than make it up as I went along.

"She said 'I want you' to me. She pulled the car into a lot and parked, and…you sure you really want to hear the rest?"

I said things I knew would deeply hurt him. He'd made it personal when he switched sides. Sasha hadn't told Esteban the truth. Her health allowed her to be intimate with him. She didn't want to. There was a reason for that, and even I, Captain Obvious, knew it had to do with her feelings for me.

"Talk," he said.

His limbs trembled slightly. I'd broken him. The knife he'd pointed at my back pricked my skin. A quick flick of the wrist and it would cut straight into me. I'd have to make my move right here, right now. "We unzipped our suits, and she put her hand…"

"And…" he interrupted, "a-and…"

"Yeah," I lied. "She just grabbed…"

I tossed Esteban over my shoulder and seized the green emerald around his neck in one motion. Clutching it in my fist, I absorbed its radiation. The inside of my mouth dried, cotton dry. I'd regained my powers. Now I had to find Rhapsody. "Where's the exit?" I asked him.

Still on the ground, he laughed. "There *is* no exit. It's a series of cells fifteen feet underground. The walls are four feet of depleted uranium. You need me to teleport you out."

"No way. I give this back to you and you'll send me into the wall. Call Kai. Get us out of here."

"Who's Kai?"

Esteban genuinely sounded confused. I didn't buy his dumb act. He knew *exactly* who Kai was – even if she didn't use her true form or identity with him.

I crossed the room to the wall and put my fist into it. Like I'd suspected and he said, it was dense metal. I'd buried my hand up to my wrist and still hadn't reached the other side. He was telling the truth. Punching through it wasn't possible.

With that realization I masked up, flew to the top of the room, removed the metal vent cover and tossed it to the ground. The cover clanged when it struck the floor.

The rectangular opening wasn't wide, but I squeezed into it and crawled through a forest of cobwebs down the shaft to the next vent. Someone sat in the center of the room and rocked back and forth. *Sasha*. I listened hard.

Her breaths quickened from the noise. A claustrophobic, she'd been crying for a while. Her captivity must be a living nightmare for her.

She sniffed. "Jason?"

I wanted to go to her, to comfort her. We'd all been there -- a dark place where you don't see a way out. At first you feel trapped. Then you start thinking. *What's the point of all this? Why go on for this?* After that you beg the darkness to surround you and swallow you whole. She wouldn't get to that point. I'd promised to keep her alive. "I'll be right back," I told her. "Hang on."

Past her cell was Rhapsody's. I crushed her grate and chucked it down the vent passage. It never hit a back wall, but it slid until stopping a considerable distance ahead of me.

I descended down to the surface. She threw her arms around my neck and hugged me. "How'd you get your powers back?"

"Long story. Let's get out of here." I handed her Esteban's green emerald necklace. "The walls are too deep for me to punch through."

Rhapsody grunted as she ghosted us across to Sasha's cell. After watching me hobble like an old man, she handed the necklace back to me. "You need this more than I do," she said.

Sasha hadn't moved since I first saw her minutes ago. I gave her my hand and helped her stand. With her help, the three of us would hatch an escape plan.

A thundering roar originated from the ceiling. Our captors were onto us. The machine eliminated one of our options to get out.

"Okay, now there is that." I tried not to sound worried.

Sasha trembled at the sound. She was in no condition to help us. Not yet. Though I didn't feel an immediate rush of air, it was coming.

"They're pumping gas in here. I can smell it."

"No." Rhapsody pointed to the top of her head. "Look!"

In the pale purple light small strands of her black hair stuck up, like static electricity. Kai hadn't added poison gas to the room. She was sucking the oxygen out. My lungs struggled to get air.

Rhapsody spoke fast. "Fly us up. Cut your powers out. Let me ghost us the rest."

That was a lot of timing and guesswork. I'd have to hold onto them both without super strength at a significant rate of speed. Between the two of them, that's three hundred-plus pounds of human being I'd be responsible for besides my own.

"What if I overshoot?" My head pounded. *How fast do I have to go?*

When flying I think about my speed to control it. I'd need at least a ballpark estimate to think about. One wrong move and we'd die a lot more violent death than suffocation. None of us had any idea of what was more than fifteen feet above us, and if Esteban was lying about the depth, we'd die.

"Screw the math, Cap!" Rhapsody coughed out.

"Screwing the math means we die," I yelled back.

Rhapsody almost lost her balance. *"Staying here* means we die, too."

Sasha wavered as she used me to steady herself. "How much do you weigh?"

She'd spoken so softly that I had to read her lips. "A buck fifty or so."

She looked at Rhapsody, who yelled her weight over the sound of the vacuum. For our entire relationship, I'd had super strength, so I never thought about her outweighing me by a couple pounds.

Sasha's ability to do complicated math problems in her head without a calculator or scratch paper amazed me. She turned to Rhapsody and said, "Arms straight."

Rhapsody stiffened her body. Sasha followed suit. I grabbed hold of them around their waists. Rhapsody held my right hand so we could share custody of the green emerald.

The pressure increased tenfold on our brains.

"Seventy miles per hour," Sasha whispered into my ear.

Taking a deep breath, I launched us toward the ceiling.

CHAPTER NINE

evicted from a castle

We reached it far faster than I expected to. I blinked and realized my powers had dropped without my knowing. Rhapsody ghosted us through the ceiling, insulation, and infrastructure. My heart skipped a few beats when we reached terminal velocity halfway through a level. As our arms solidified we helped each other crawl up to lay face down on the floor to rest.

All three of us unmasked and gasped so hard I almost choked. There was plenty of air. Rhapsody had made us invisible, so I scanned the room for the next thing to try to kill us.

Thick maroon draperies with gold fringe hung over a twenty-foot high bay window. Ahead of us stood a massive floor-to-ceiling in-wall bookcase. Every shelf was filled. To our right was an ivory mantle above a large fireplace. Gold paper with maroon flecks in it covered the walls. The bottom floor of Sasha's house would have fit in the humongous space.

Nothing deadly, so far

The plush white carpet felt like a soft cotton towel against my sweaty face. I pulled myself together to a crawling position, which was the best I could do under my own power. Rhapsody sensed my agony and pushed the green emerald over to me. I tied its cord into a knot and put it on over my head. With no other resources available, it would have to do.

I got to my feet and bolted the double doors by backing a high-backed upholstered chair underneath the doorknobs. Who knew? Maybe Kai's partner couldn't teleport and the barricade might delay him?

Being Captain Obvious and all, I asked, "Where are we?"

Sasha stood and walked over to the window. She parted the heavy curtains. From the way her head moved, she had to be eyeing the grid of iron bars lining the length and width of the windows. Behind them, the landscape was pitch black.

I asked her, "How can you see anything?"

She clicked her teeth in thought. "Can't make out much from the topography – trees, no mountains nearby. We're two, maybe three stories up."

That got me thinking. Three stories was too far to jump without my powers. But I had an emerald in my hand. And I'd flown out of the dungeon, sort of. *We'll be safe. As long as it's not too far, I can get us out.*

My stomach tightened. "Ghost us through and I'll fly us out."

Rhapsody panted and made a time-out sign with her hands. "Need a hot minute."

A camera with the flashing red light in the corner of the room swiveled. "Don't have a hot minute. Get it together. Big Brother is watching."

"So?" Sasha argued. "He's *been* watching. And you'll fly us...where exactly?"

Seriously? "Any place where we won't get locked up. Someplace safe. It's *that* simple."

"Haven't you been paying attention? Look at us! Nothing's *that* simple!" Sasha screamed at me.

I wondered if she had a point.

"We hide. And *then* what? How long until they find us? We'll do this again...all over again. Who's to say my parents, yours, and Ruby don't have guns pointed at their heads right now?"

"Safe house," I said to remind her.

"Are they 'safe' with us around? Will they ever be 'safe' if we're not?"

When she repeated the word *safe,* it plucked a tight string inside of my body. Courtney, our old mentor, once told us that "safe" meant we were more powerful than the people after us. Right now, safe house or not, that definitely wasn't the case -- for us or for our loved ones. For all we knew, though we'd set up safe houses, they could already be dead.

"Girl Genius has a point," Rhapsody said to me. "I don't know about you all, but I'm tired of looking over my shoulder, Cap."

Kill or be killed. It was a problem we continually faced. And I didn't want to be a killer.

"You're right," I said. She usually was. We escape and the people we want to protect suffer. Even if I flew at supersonic speeds, flying at night posed a risk. Two of our enemies could teleport, and unlike us, they didn't hesitate to kill. Esteban was one of them now.

Rhapsody raised her voice. "You two wanna stay here and die or go outside and die?"

No one said anything for minutes. What could we say? What could I say? The girls will go with whatever I want to do, *if I can decide.* There was no correct answer. Still, I had to give one.

Sasha crossed her arms in expectation. "Hughes said things would get more complicated," she said.

He wasn't lying. We're doomed if we do, and we're doomed if we don't.

Our indecision lasted long enough for a teleporter to enter the room. Dressed in a black suit with a buttoned-down maroon shirt, loose collar and no tie, he leaned heavily on a polished wooden cane with a black handle. He appeared to be in his early-thirties, though his slicked-back curly brown hair, healthy tan and clean-shaven face gave him a younger look. His eyes, the shape of his eyebrows – they struck me as familiar. Did I know him or his parents?

A dull, sharpness flared in my muscles and bones. I patted around my neck. *Gone.* The carpeting and papered walls blurred and spun around. After a few seconds my balance returned.

Our guest's voice sparkled – surprising for, I assumed, a psychopath. "Welcome to my home."

The silver chain dangled from his slender fingers. He'd stolen Esteban's green emerald from me. Great. I had to deal with *one more thing.*

Rhapsody cracked her neck. "You always toss your guests into a dark hole?"

"Esteban had a bone to pick with all of you -- for one reason or another," he said.

I had to know. "Esteban did this?"

"Makes sense he's pissed at *us*." Sasha pointed at Rhapsody. "Why's he pissed at *you*?"

Her shoulder shrug didn't convince me of her innocence. Rhapsody totally knew why and wasn't revealing it to us.

Before I could poke into her mind, she deflected. "You had nothing to do with it?" she asked our host. "Not buying it on sale."

Our host shook his head. "Believe it or not…"

"Not…"

"…Kai got out of her cage and put you there, Rhapsody. Not me."

My patience burst. "That's crap. You *built* the cells."

"My father had this place constructed after his favorite European castle, brick for brick. Blame him or his architect. Both have a flair for that kind of thing."

A chill fluttered from the base of my neck down my spine. *Was his father David King?*

"I'm not what you think." He waved his right hand toward the brass handled double doors. "Follow me."

What other choice was there? My muscles and tendons ached each time I moved, paused, stood – whatever. When we reached the double doors he turned to me and asked for help. He showed me his hand, which was curled forward and stiff. "Do you mind?"

What's up with him? "You're kidding, right? Can't you teleport us through it?"

He didn't answer.

With great effort for such a small task, I knocked the hand carved chair to the floor and twisted the handles.

Rhapsody and Sasha trailed us into the dining area. He'd laid out a magnificent spread of food – cold cut meats, breads, fine cheeses, colorful fruit, salad greens, and red wine -- across a table covered in a white tablecloth. The table almost spanned the length of the entire room. My stomach rumbled at the sight. The last full meal I'd eaten was the fast food breakfast Sasha had brought to school, and at least half a day had passed since then.

Instead of poison he could've laced it with a drug to knock us unconscious, get what he needed. The food in the dungeon was okay. This could be, too.

I'd broken my one meal vow not long after I'd made it. Wouldn't be the first time. Nearing complete weakness I couldn't help myself. With a white China plate in hand, I loaded it down with everything our host selected – roast beef, white cheese, red grapes, and rolls. Rhapsody followed my lead. Sasha hesitated but did the same. We'd eat what he ate just in case he'd screwed with it.

He eased into the seat at the table's head next to me. Rhapsody and Sasha settled to my right. He prayed over the meal. Funny. "Even demons believe in Jesus," my mom used to say.

"What's your name?" Rhapsody asked him with a mouthful of roll.

He dabbed a white cloth napkin at the corners of his mouth and sipped his red wine. He leaned forward. "Tell me what you know about yourselves first. I'll fill in the blanks."

I pounded my fist against the table hard enough to rattle the plates and silverware. "Or you could answer a simple question first. Who are you?"

Sasha ignored me and told him what he asked to know – about how a solar storm named "Carrington" irradiated six beryl deposits, and how our blood metabolizes high proton radiation into superhuman abilities.

"There are seven hundred of us," I added.

Our host laughed as he chewed a couple red grapes. "That's not a lot to go on."

"And the Collective tried containing the explosion," Rhapsody said.

He repeated "Collective" like he was thinking about what the word meant. "That sounds like a fantastically dumb idea."

"Jason absorbed the energy of the second blast. There's other stuff in King's journal…"

His voiced spiked with interest. "Did he? How did it feel? The absorption?"

How to describe it? "Like being soaked in gasoline and hugging the sun."

Rhapsody clanged her gold fork against her plate. "Story time is over, Mr. Dodge-an-Answer. Who are you? What do you want, and why are we here?"

He folded his good left hand over his fist. "I go by Iain. I'm not much for my first name. The way you three won the genetic lottery – I lost it the same way. Multiple sclerosis. It's the worst on the right side of my body."

Iain's reasons for not wearing a prism might be the same as Sasha's were, which confused me even more. "Put a prism on then."

Iain's neck tensed. "Not that easy. I can't metabolize rads anymore. Jade arranged this meeting, and Kai stepped in and took over in her place."

Sasha finished a bite a ham before asking him, "Her name's *Jade*? Or Jade and Kai are twins?"

"Who she is depends on the time of day."

What? "Why'd she call herself Kai? Is it a nickname or her middle name or something?"

Then Rhapsody suggested something completely ridiculous. "Nah, dude. She's got alternate personalities, like those *telenovela* chicks Ruby used to watch."

Iain snapped his fingers. *"Exactly.* A textbook case of DID. Jade is her given name. There's Amauri…she's the emotional alter. Kai, whom you've met, has a taste for violence. And *Kyla.* You must meet Kyla."

She has alternate personality disorder and she's a shape shifter? I guess it's not any weirder than a kid with rage blackouts having super-strength. "How long ago did you meet…*her?"* I asked before biting into my roast beef sandwich. The spicy mustard against the meat tasted crazy good. I didn't know I could enjoy eating food anymore.

"Your *parents* weren't thought of." Iain polished off his wine and continued. "Jade's sickness emerged as mine did. We had something else in common – a need for a cure. We experimented and failed until a solution presented itself. And that solution is sitting next to me."

No wonder he was being nice to us. I devoured everything else on my plate. I'd need the strength to fight.

"The issue for us is *genetic*, Jason. Jade and I need you, if you are willing."

Of course I was their answer. He didn't mention my blood, but I knew he wanted to. What he said hit home for me. If the tables were turned and his blood could take away my rage blackouts and ADHD, I'd ask for it, too.

I wanted to stand up and leave, but my joints had locked, and it was difficult to move besides chewing, talking, and listening. If I started moving now, I'd be ready to go in another five to ten minutes.

He's not the type to ask. Why didn't he just take whatever he needed from me? "Who says you have to be 'fixed'?"

Iain rested his chin on his left palm. "I'm in constant pain. With your blood gone from Orizaba...I only need a vial of your blood for the Omega antigen. I can't synthesize it."

Omega antigen? And how did he know about King's Mexican fortress?

Esteban.

He didn't tell me King had tried to do a similar thing, and it had nearly killed him? Did he want Iain to figure it out on his own?

"A small request." He emphasized the word *small*. "We've done the genetic mapping. Give me what I want. We've been civilized about this thus far, haven't we?"

I pounded my fist so hard the silverware rattled. "Jade or Kai or whatever her name is blew up the

Multiplex to get to our attention. Is that 'civilized'? What about locking us in your horror movie basement and sucking the air out?"

"Again, your imprisonment was Kai and Esteban's doing. My approach has a softer touch than torture."

I didn't buy his brand of bull. Neither did Sasha.

"Side effects? Risks of seizure, heart attack, stroke? What aren't you telling us about this 'Omega antigen'?"

I blurted out, "I thought *I* was Captain Obvious? There's a whole lot he's not telling us."

"King wanted Jason's blood and 'needed' all six pints in his body." She leaned over the table, eyes narrowed. "Who else dies if you don't get your way?"

"I'm *not* like David," he said. "He tried to kill you and conquer the planet. All I want is life without a cane, no regrets, maybe a family. The antigen in your blood will replicate itself and can cure my illness and Jade's, as well from a holistic standpoint."

"What else is there?" Rhapsody shot back.

Iain's face straightened. "So skeptical for a child. What makes you think there's something else?"

"There's always something else," I said. "You're not getting my blood."

"Fine," he said. "Less civilized."

He pulled out a list of addresses from a drawer underneath the table and tossed it to me.

All of them except one were safe houses – two in our state, one in Pennsylvania – an address in Panama and North Hospital. He knew the whereabouts of Sasha's parents, my father and stepparents, Aunt Dee, Zachary, and Rhapsody's mom. Debra was stashed in a safe house no one knew about, not even me. Still, I'd kill Esteban for his betrayal if I got the chance.

Rhapsody cursed Iain and threw her napkin to the center of the table. "Not like King? You put a gun to the head of everyone we love. That's a King move."

With no crystals or powers, it meant we were in no position to negotiate terms. He held all of the leverage. Like the last time I'd bargained my blood, I had no choice but to do it.

"What happens to us afterward?" I muttered. "Will you leave us all alone?"

"North High reopens next week. Go back to living normal lives."

"Normal life?" Rhapsody asked him. "Really?"

A normal life. It's all I'd wanted to have for the past four years. So did Sasha. Rhapsody, too. Now I wasn't sure it was what I wanted, but I didn't have a choice, did I? I'd be a civilian whether I liked it or not. Ray would die. I'd be an orphan. I'd graduate high school in another year or so, and then what? How is that "normal" to go from the things I know and the things I've done to…*nothing?*

His fingers dawdled across a wrinkle in the tablecloth. "Yes, Rhapsody, you can go back to your shack and live in squalor. Ruby could come out of hiding."

Rhapsody let the insult pass. He'd gotten to her.

"How do we know you'll keep your word to us?" I asked him.

Iain's bright toothy smile made me uncomfortable. "There are few guarantees in life."

Sasha, Rhapsody and I eyed one another. They expected me to do something – trust him, give in, save them all. But, like Sasha said, could it be that simple?

"All right."

"Excellent," he said. "Let's have tiramisu. My chef is Italian, and it's top notch."

After we watched him eat dessert, Iain escorted us to the grand foyer of his home. A ginormous crystal chandelier hung from the vaulted ceiling and reflected off the polished white marble floor. *Is it made of goshenite?* To our left a winding staircase led to the second floor. *What's up there?*

On a table near the wall a black blood pressure sleeve, a pair of rubber gloves, a cotton ball, a brown bottle with a Q-tip sticking out of it, a wrapped bandage, and a plastic tube waited. He'd known I'd say yes all along.

I sat in the cushioned chair next to it, unzipped my bodysuit, and freed my right arm. The sooner this was over, the better. Rhapsody and Sasha looked at me with a mixture of admiration and pity. This was the second time I'd given blood to keep someone from being killed, but this time it wasn't just my loved ones. It was their families, too. That power play was new.

I couldn't fight the ominous feeling rising in my gut. Ray liked to say, "There's no such thing as a free lunch." Could we really go back home and resume our lives? Too easy. The only reason King had left us alone was because I'd killed him.

Iain wasted no time with the preparations. He fastened the black cuff around my bicep and pumped it until my veins stuck out and I could feel my pulse. Then he swabbed the cold dark liquid in the brown bottle in circles on my arm near the bend.

"Make a fist," he said to me.

Iain was so happy his bad hand shook. I half expected him to giggle like a little girl at any moment. I would too, I guess, if I'd get a cure for a major illness.

I looked away as he stuck the needle into my vein and the vial filled up with blood. Once he'd capped it, he placed the cotton ball over the bleeding dot on my skin.

"Hold this," he said.

As I did, he handed me a bandage, which I spread over the puncture site. I zipped my bodysuit back up. He shook the blood in the vial and held it up to the light, like he'd won a first place trophy. I waited for him to drop an aquamarine prism into it and drink it, like King had done, but he did not. All he did was point his cane toward the door and say, "Thank you. You can see yourselves out."

Rhapsody had enough. "Hit it and quit it. That's it? How are we supposed to get home?"

Without turning around, Iain leaned on his cane. "Down the driveway. Take a right on the main road. You can catch transportation from there – use your powers. Hitchhike. Or, Jade could drive you."

Sasha waved her hand to say no thanks. "We're good."

We left the stone-faced castle and started the walk down the macadam driveway, which Iain neglected to mention was at least a quarter mile long. The summer night air felt good against my face. I breathed it in and didn't catch the scent of seawater. We must be inland.

The ache in my limbs let up a little. I'd hate every step of this long walk but it was bearable to me.

The black wrought iron gates swung open as we neared them and closed behind us. Beyond their boundaries lay utter darkness. Unless a car drove past occasionally with its headlights on, we'd have to activate our suits to see anything. We'd look like glowing purple aliens walking down the street. How would we escape being noticed?

"Well, at least he bought us dinner first," Rhapsody joked.

What she said was funny. I wanted to laugh. The thought of what had just happened consumed me. I'd been blackmailed into giving up my blood by a lunatic. *Again.* Our loved ones – as long as we had powers and they were living – they would be leverage against us. *Again.* Nothing would change that, would it?

I donned my mask and cued up the display. It was 1:15 in the morning. The weight of the day's events settled onto my shoulders. I tensed up thinking about it. I'd been shot at, my father had almost died, and I'd blacked out and killed someone. Kai had kidnapped us, put us in a dungeon, and nearly killed us. Then Iain, if that was his real name, claimed my blood was the key to healing his multiple sclerosis and Jade's mental problems.

The thought of everything that happened made me even more tired.

In a moment the geographical map would show our location. On the right side of my face were the message folders. I had two voicemail messages, both marked urgent. The time stamp was wrong since the signal had been blocked underground. I'd check them once our location was clear.

A bubble pop sounded in my earpiece. "We're in Medford," I said through my mask. "About five hours from home, it looks like."

Sasha brushed her hands through her hair. "Medford, Oregon? Dad has a private plane at the airport. It's probably not that far from here. I'll make a few calls."

Rhapsody twirled her finger in the air. "Once again, Sasha and her money to the rescue."

"Haven't we been through enough today?" Sasha shot back. "Charter your own plane if you think mine is too good for you."

"You're not too good for me," she shot back. "It's that you *think* you're too good for me."

While the two of them continued to insult each other, I glanced back at Iain's sprawling house. He hadn't turned off the light in the foyer after we'd left. From far away, it looked welcoming.

I wondered about the underground cells we had been locked in. It was obvious there were more than three cells down there. Were they occupied? Did the prisoners survive the oxygen purge? Without intending to, I stopped walking and gazed back at the castle. *The castle.* The parapets, the way it stretched out – it was the same castle we'd found a picture of in King's safe or identical to it.

Sasha said what I was thinking. "That's the Collective's old castle!"

A sick feeling hit my stomach. Iain had said his methods had "a softer touch" than the torture we'd been through. He'd done more than just locate our safe houses. His father was someone in the Collective. Not Hughes – Iain didn't look a drop like a black man. He could've only been fathered by King, Welker, or Peters. They were the only ones to survive the Carrington event explosion.

After I yanked off my mask and unzipped my suit, I found my cell phone in the top left breast pocket and checked my voicemail that way. The girls continued to argue while I did.

First message, marked urgent, sent at 1:15 a.m.

"Jason. It's Julia."

I braced myself for the worst. My stepmother never called me Jason. Her voice cracked like she'd been screaming or crying or hysterically screaming and crying for hours.

"Ray is in ICU," she continued. "He's on a ventilator. Drop whatever you're doing. Get here as soon as you can. I won't make a move until you see him."

Make a move? Like unplug him? I wanted to hang up and run back home if I had to, but the next call came from the hospital and not Julia.

Second message, marked urgent, from 916-555-7931 sent at 1:15 a.m. The phone receiver on her end fell to the floor. Afterwards, I heard a commotion of mixed voices and alarms.

"What do you mean he's gone?" asked an authoritative male voice. "People just don't disappear, Claudia! Do you have any clue how much losing a terminally cancer patient will cost us? Get a security guard in here!"

My heart sank into my feet.

"Where's the equipment?" the man asked. "Or did that just vanish into thin air, too?"

I could tell Claudia was a young nurse by the sound of voice. "I-I don't know."

"Did you notify his wife? Where is she?"

Then the phone disconnected.

My brain started to hurt with an indescribable pressure. It was only after I got lightheaded that I realized I hadn't been breathing.

The automated voicemail instructions replayed in my ear. Rhapsody wiggled the phone from between my fingers. Sasha said something I didn't hear.

Rhapsody listened to the last voicemail message on my phone and screamed. Sasha, having the cooler head, made phone calls. She paced back and forth in the street and cursed over and over again. I'd assumed she was calling the security team we'd hired for the safe houses. I also assumed they were too dead to answer our calls.

Activity slowly returned to my limbs. My lips trembled. Iain was correct. He was nothing like King. He was far worse in what he'd just done to us.

"He's got them, doesn't he?" I asked them matter-of-factly.

Sasha bobbed her head. "Yes," she sniffed. "He got them all."

CHAPTER TEN

the Jason Champion I know

Numbness. Quiet. What was there to say? Peters had told us. As long as we had loved ones, they'd be used by our enemies to make us do their bidding. Iain had thought I was going to say no and had taken our families as insurance. The problem for us was that now he had my blood *and* the people we cared about most. Maybe I was a pessimist, but I didn't see him throwing the doors open to let them out.

The way he'd let us go – it almost seemed like he was daring us. *Once you figure it out come back and try to save them.*

Without help, there was no way any of them would escape. The choice, for me, was crystal clear. Powers or not, I had to help them. "We've got to go back," I said to them.

Rhapsody agreed without hesitation. "He's got my mom. You don't even have to ask me."

"Wait!" Sasha crossed her arms and resumed pacing -- a terrible sign for the smartest person of the three of us. "It's a suicide mission. How do we get into the cells? When or if we do get in there, how do we get them all out? What's the strategy?"

They were good questions. All of the prisms we had had been destroyed in the last solar storm. I doubted that any were here in Medford, Oregon. "We get our powers back somehow, and...I don't know!" I said.

"Hmm..." Sasha said. "Maybe..."

She had to be plotting our next move. We were wasting time by standing in the middle of the road doing nothing. The gate's pointed bars were high and slick with the evening dew. Each gate end was embedded in a smooth and solid concrete foundation. Climbing it would be ridiculously difficult. But our families were locked up in there. We had to do something.

Think, Jason, think. How do we get in? How do we then get out?

Loud, rapid clicking drowned out the chirping insects -- like a clock's secondhand doing triple time. Rhapsody and I looked around for the source.

Sasha. She held her arm out in our direction and smiled -- her Geiger counter watch.

"It was a hunch," she said. "I'd turned it off. Both of you are giving off .13 rads."

Rhapsody's eyebrows knitted together. "And your point is?"

"You never lost your powers."

What? That didn't make any sense. Why was I still in pain? Sasha's bomb didn't make any sense.

"I know you're supposed to be smarter than I am," Rhapsody said, "but that's *dumb,*"

The insult didn't faze her. Who was she and what did she do with my ex? "Your powers come from your brain. Your adrenal system kicks on your powers. It's wired to your brain. So if your brain is offline, your powers are affected."

When we first discovered our abilities last year, Sasha was the one to tell me the only reason I had been jumping instead of flying. I *thought* I had to land. Our blood was still radioactive. She was right. We hadn't lost our powers. *How do we turn them back on?*

So what took our brains offline? What does that even mean?

"What does that mean?" I asked her.

"She means we're in our heads, Cap," Rhapsody said.

Sasha clapped her hands. *"Exactly.* All we have to do to kick them back on is to get you *out* of your heads. Rhapsody, when did your powers start acting funny?"

Her lips tightened. "After he cheated on me. Again. With *you*. Again. Remember?"

Even in the darkness I could tell by Sasha's tight movements she was *angry*. "Oh, will you get over it already?" She took a deep cleansing breath. "Jason was my first love. Whether you like it or not, he's a part of me forever. I can't stop loving him. I *won't* stop loving him. I'm not gonna apologize for that, but I am sorry I did it the wrong way."

I'd never heard Sasha state her feelings for me out loud. Esteban was right. She'd been hung up on me ever since we'd broken up. To be fair, Selby had manipulated her into cheating on me. I should've given our relationship another chance. I saw that now.

"I didn't try hard enough for you. I'm sorry." I repeated it with feeling. "I'm so sorry."

"No," Rhapsody said softly. "You didn't."

Sasha tagged onto the end of my statement. "They were moments of weakness for me – for both of us. I wasn't thinking straight."

She made it sound like every kiss we'd shared outside of our relationship was a mistake. As I thought back – the near kiss in Sasha's convertible, the kissing in her bedroom, our secret late night phone talks – they were mistakes. I'd kissed Rhapsody while I was with Sasha, as well. A one hundred percent committed boyfriend wouldn't have done that. A good friend wouldn't have taken advantage of an ex-girlfriend, either.

"'Sorry' is all you've got? Truth? I *never* had your full attention." Rhapsody raised her voice and pointed at me. "Never! Even after we…a part of you was always with her, too, wasn't it?"

"I think it still is," Sasha said. Her eyes darted from me to Rhapsody as if to say *look at her*. After a second it sank in why Sasha stayed on the same subject. "It still is, isn't it?"

The truth was hard to face. I thought about my ex every day and never told her. "Yeah."

Rhapsody cursed in Spanish before finally switching back to English. "I'm done. Once we do this and everyone is safe, I'm out. I'm so done with both of you. You're a couple of lying…"

Rhapsody stopped ranting and raving abruptly. My mouth dropped open. Her body was totally invisible. Sasha had egged Rhapsody on to get her mad, which had triggered her adrenaline and her powers.

"Where are you?" I called out.

Rhapsody rematerialized above us. The flying ability she'd inherited from my blood was back, too. "Let's get this over with," she said.

With a wave of her hand, Rhapsody made us intangible. Sasha and I ghosted through the gates and solidified on the other side. There had to be an outside entry to the cells, right?

"Mask up. Be careful," Rhapsody said before she turned invisible. Her voice got softer. "I'll be in touch soon."

In the darkness and shadows it was impossible to tell where the land's boundaries were. Though we stepped softly, the well-mowed grass swooshed as we walked. Out of the corner of my eye, I saw Sasha grab the mask hanging at the back of her neck. I held her hand to stop her. Our skin wasn't touching but the contact shot warmth into my body.

"You meant everything you said?" I asked her.

Sasha continued to walk forward. "I figured if I could piss her off her powers would kick on involuntarily. Let's keep moving."

I caught up with her and the extra movement caused grief for my sore muscles. Right before I was going to ask her my question again, she started to talk. "I've been reading this book lately, and it's got me...you ever read something that describes *exactly* the kind of person you are?"

I didn't read unless I had to for school and not even then most of the time. "Not really."

"Well, this one has got me down to a T. After what I said to Rhapsody – I want to crawl into a hole. Yup, I meant every word."

My heart swelled with excitement. "Why? What book is this? And why are you reading it?"

Her voice lowered to a whisper. "While I was healing my folks did family counseling at home. Not like I could get up and leave." She let some time pass as we walked before she picked up the story. "After a couple sessions I stopped faking trips to the bathroom. Therapist handed me this red book. It said people like me hold on when we should let go because we don't want to be alone."

"Who likes being alone?" I asked her. I sure didn't. *Was I one of these people?*

"Jason, Esteban and I broke up and got back together six times. I chased after you when you were in love with someone else. *That's* not letting go to people like me."

"People like you?" I asked.

"Children of alcoholic parents."

Joyce Anderson, Sasha's mother, was a raging alcoholic. She'd started drinking heavily when her husband announced he was leaving her. Once, I'd actually seen her passed out and face down on her carpet. I'd wondered how Sasha dealt with it. Now I knew.

"First time she drank in front of me...I was four years old. It was reddish brown – brandy, her drink. I took a sip and spat it out. Joyce laughed. I remember the funk of that stuff."

For someone who never talked about her feelings, Sasha had changed from a wall to a rushing river. All I could say was, "That's crazy."

Sasha continued opening up. "Jason, I'm scared we're not going to make it back this time."

I reached for her hand and squeezed it. "I made you a promise. I'll keep you alive."

In the moonlight, I saw a single tear slide down Sasha's face. She wiped it away with her glove and put her mask on. "Then make sure you keep it."

"I need my abilities back."

She continued looking forward. "I agree. What was your trigger emotion?"

The first time I'd used my powers was when Selby tried to cut me. I punched through a concrete wall that time. I'd thrown Ray's Cougar, messed up Selby's ribs, and fought my former principal and Peters. All those times it was the same feeling.

"Anger," I said.

"I'm not going to make you angry," she said. "I don't want you raging out on me."

That made me think of the last time I'd blacked out and the damage I'd done. I'd have to find a different way to activate them. "Let's mask up," I said. "Rhapsody might be calling."

After we put our masks on, we heard Rhapsody's steady stream of cursing. "What are you two doing? Are you two serious, right now? I…"

"We copy," Sasha said. "What's going on?"

"I found the entrance. Castle's southeast corner. What's your 20?"

Sasha pointed at the sky and drew an imaginary line to the earth. "Headed your way."

"Wait! Don't!" Her voice rang with urgency.

I held my hand as a bar across Sasha's midsection. I heard a low rumble like a chorus of angry animals. Before I could think to run, one of them pounced on my back and pinned me to the grass. It blew its hot breath at the back of my neck. As I struggled to get free it bore its crushing weight down on my arms and legs to keep me from moving. Soon, pins and needles from the lack of circulation crept into my limbs.

I screamed for help but with my face mashed against the ground I could barely move my lips enough to breathe. Rhapsody knew about these things before we did. She could fly faster than the speed of sound. Her strength was like mine used to be. Why wasn't she helping us?

The animal tore at the back of my suit with its sharp teeth. The material, which had been crafted to defend against bullets, only delayed this attack. The skin on my back burned from the scrape of the animal's biting. At this rate I'd be a human plate of ribs in another minute or so.

Suddenly a force knocked the thing off of me. I still couldn't move other than to position my chin against the ground to be able to see. Rhapsody grabbed me by the arm and hoisted me into the air. In a final attempt to catch us, one of the things leapt an incredible distance and clamped onto my foot. I yelped and wiggled my leg to shake it off. Instead of falling, it tightened its grip on my ankle. A sharp hot pain ebbed down my foot and wet my socks. It had drawn blood. I'd have to deal with the pain from this for the rest of the mission.

We were so high in the air now that I expected the thing to lose consciousness. This was no ordinary animal. My foot was bleeding and the pain from it led me to believe I wouldn't be able to walk on it, given the thing ever let go. I was close to passing out from hyperventilating.

"Cap!" Rhapsody yelled. "Stay with me! Cap?"

She dropped me and Sasha. With the creature attached to my leg, I fell a lot faster than Sasha did. It positioned itself on my body and met me face-to-face. It looked like a cross between a Doberman and a bear. The thing bore its bloodstained teeth – *was it smiling at me?* Sensing victory, it opened its awful mouth to tear my head off.

This was the end of the line.

Without warning it slipped off of my body. Rhapsody secured her bloody right arm around my chest. Sasha held onto her left arm. The thing plummeted to the ground.

Rhapsody made us invisible to cover our landing at the castle's southeast corner. The two remaining animals circled the perimeter. I thought of them as animals, though I couldn't tell exactly what they were. They were much too large to be that quick and agile. The moonlight reflected off of their sleek black skin as they prowled – their growls rumbled in the darkness.

They knew we were close but could not see us to attack. Still, I knew we'd have to move quickly. I was bleeding and, with highly-developed senses of smell, a regular canine could detect the scent of my blood. Who knew what these things could do?

We ghosted through a manhole cover and into a large tunnel. Sasha went first, then Rhapsody, then I took up the rear. Using the metal rungs sticking out from the passage's side, we climbed down. I tried to use my right foot as little as possible. The pain made me want to puke. We said nothing to each other until we hit the bottom where the tunnel straightened out. It smelled like stale water and mold.

Of the three of us, I was the tallest, and even limping on one foot, I'd have to bend at the neck a little to walk through it.

"Can you put weight on it?" Sasha asked me.

Until she said something, I'd been standing solely on my left leg and used my right toe only for balance. I shifted my stance a little and the extra weight made my knee buckle. "Uh uh."

Sasha slipped under my right arm and let me use her for support. "That complicates the plan a bit. Did you get a good look at those *things*?"

I said, "I wish I hadn't."

Rhapsody circled around me to inspect the back of my bodysuit. Her gloved fingers felt like knives digging into my skin. Her silence spoke volumes. "That bad, huh?" I asked her.

She tried to couch her assessment with enthusiasm, which she was terrible at doing. "Well, some of your suit is left…for the most part."

Even without my powers, at least I considered myself an extra pair of hands. On a bum ankle and with my back torn to shreds, I was a liability. "Go on without me," I said to them.

"There is no 'without you'," Sasha said to me. "We need all three of us to make this work."

Rhapsody blocked our path. "All we need to do is turn his powers back on like mine. What'll piss you off that bad, Cap? Will Selby and Sasha's sex tape do it? I might get internet down here."

Sasha stiffened. "Rhapsody," she said in a flat tone.

"I almost cheated on you with Esteban," she said. "We hooked up while we were dating. I let him head to third base before we stopped."

Sasha was livid. "Are you *serious?* All the crap you gave us and you did worse?"

She was joking...or *was she?* Heat flooded my collar. She was getting to me. "Stop!"

"Why?" she asked in a playful tone. "Are you turning green, getting *angry?"*

I had to let my secret out. "Because I could kill you if I rage."

Silence. A faint drip of water echoed through the tunnel. It was always a possibility that none of us talked about – my lack of control when I black out. I'd raged with super strength twice before – once at my therapist Susan's office and again in the BAE.AT fortress. I'd done a slew of damage both times, but no one ever got hurt because of it. "I *killed* someone," I choked up. "Sent a telephone pole onto his car and it blew up. He...she burned to death."

Sasha took my mask off and hers. She stared straight into my eyes. "I don't believe that."

"For what it's worth, Jason," Rhapsody said in the background, "Neither do I."

I limped away from Sasha and leaned against the curved tunnel's metal wall. The torn skin on my ankle throbbed. "The guy didn't have a chance to escape, and it's *my fault,*" I said. "Believe what you want about me. You didn't see it."

Sasha argued back, "Neither did you. You blacked out. You might not have done anything. You've been set up before. You think it's not a possibility it was someone else?"

I hadn't thought about it. Someone else making me think I'd raged and killed someone. Maybe. But Sasha didn't have a clue about what it felt like to rage. The power of your emotions is a tidal wave like rush – overwhelming, dangerous, and out of control. A speeding truck with no brakes.

Then nothing. No sound. No light. No feeling.

When you come to, all that's left surrounding you is the damage you caused and people to fill in the blanks for you. I'd seen security video of myself once, thrashing and screaming inside of an abandoned classroom. It was an out-of-body experience. That person looked like me and was dressed like me, but it was difficult to believe he and I were the same person. To this day, only Debra has seen that tape, and she tore through a box of tissues watching it. Rage blackouts made me into an animal and now two more people I care about knew the worst of it.

Sasha placed her gloved hands on my cheeks. "Forget all of that. Listen to me. The Jason Champion I know doesn't kill, even when he doesn't mean to. You didn't do it."

"But King...Orizaba..."

"I know what it looks like." Her eyes did not move from me. Our surroundings and Rhapsody faded away. I saw only her. I heard only her voice. "You think you did something awful because you've done awful things before. You're wrong. You didn't do this. King was a killer who surrounded himself with killers."

Her words didn't surprise me, but the sincerity behind them did. Sasha said it like she was there, as if she had seen what really happened. "You weren't there," I said. "You don't know."

She jumped back at me. "I know you. I know your heart. And I believe in you."

Debra had said that once to me, but no one else had ever told me that. I never knew how to take it. It wasn't an "I believe in God" kind of belief. She could see me and touch me.

What does she mean?

"Deep down, I know you're good," she said. "I'll keep telling you until you believe it for yourself. Even if you think you're not. I know you are good, Jason."

My eyes filled with tears. I refused to let them fall. "You do?"

"With all my heart."

She'd lifted my spirits so much that the pain in my ankle had given up a little bit. I looked around for Rhapsody. Far at the end of the corridor, I spotted a moving purple shine. Figuring it was her, Sasha and I headed her way. She ducked under my arm and offered herself as support. Though I felt I could make it on my own I didn't turn her down. Reluctant to put weight on it, I dragged me right foot along with each step. It made the walk excruciatingly long, but we finished.

By the time we got there, Rhapsody had her back against a metal door. I didn't have to ask what was behind it. She'd found the control room for the cells. I wondered why there wasn't a lock on it until I noticed a thick layer of orange rust surrounding the outside.

"You want to ghost us through in case it's a trap or something?" Sasha suggested.

Rhapsody tapped her temple with her finger. "Great minds think alike, Girl Genius," she said. "I did that while you two were…down there."

"And?" I asked. "What's in there?"

I could tell by the change in my body weight that Rhapsody had made us intangible. "You wouldn't believe me if I told you. Come see for yourself."

CHAPTER ELEVEN

we lose someone

Sitting cross-legged in a comfortable looking office chair, a little girl swiveled back and forth. About six- or seven-years-old in a frilly blue nightgown, she had a dark brown fuzz ball of an Afro. She giggled and watched a console of monitors. Each screen emitted small cones of blue light that cast shadows onto the wall behind her. She wiggled her hands in formations to make finger animals. It was a cute scene until she smiled. The eerie sparkle of her white teeth gave me chills. They were smaller but familiar. That's how I knew we were eavesdropping on a shape-shifting serial killer.

Forgetting about my bum ankle, I put my weight on it, lost my balance and almost fell right on my butt. The girls backed out with way more balance than I did, but they had two functional feet, whereas I had one.

"That's *Kai*," I said in a loud whisper.

My ankle throbbed and burned. Meanwhile, Rhapsody's sarcastic comments were operating at a steady hum. "You think?" she asked me.

"Nuh uh. Kai's an *adult* personality," Sasha said. "Kyla's the kid persona, I think."

Kyla? The kid Iain said we just "had" to meet? Sounded like a trap. Especially since the only side I'd seen of this chick was the psychotic one. Unless they all were.

"Check this out. I'll ghost us through," Rhapsody said, her voice just above a whisper. "Then we should…"

Sasha put a finger to her lips, said "shh," and nodded her head at the sealed door.

Kyla might be listening? Could she hear through the metal?

Rhapsody gave her a death stare. "Did you just *shh* me, Girl Genius?"

Sasha shot back, "You don't know who could be listening."

"Like I was saying." Rhapsody spoke even louder than the first time. "We ghost through and take her out."

None of us said a word for a moment. We'd never talked openly about it – *ending someone else's life.* I'd killed King with no explanation to anyone. No one asked for details. I wouldn't tell them if they did. I'd used goshenite to take away his powers. He'd almost murdered my stepmother, and I'd taken it out on him. If I hadn't stopped King, who could have?

His last breath, a moaning rattle, gnawed at my conscience. I swallowed hard and forced myself past it. Personal feelings didn't matter.

Kill Jade or subdue her, whatever, but we had to be on the same page to make this work. Sasha had the swing vote, and from the way her brow wrinkled, she wasn't considering it, either. "*Kill* her?" Sasha's eye widened. "You're serious? She's a *child*!"

Rhapsody wildly shook her head. "No. You're not thinking clearly. She's an animal, like those dogs. How many people did she kill to in the Multiplex to get to Jason? It's her life now or ours later."

More silence passed between us. Dripping water pooled on the passage's floor at an annoyingly slow rate. The unnatural chill in the air was noticeable. I didn't want to kill anybody. I also didn't want to die. Why did I have to pick?

I read Sasha's eyes. The wheels of her brain turned. What other way was there? If one of us would have a plan, she would be the one.

One thing was for sure, she wasn't thinking mind control. When I erased Selby's memories it worked somewhat because I knew what to take out of his mind. Or I thought I did. Even then it was risky. Should that be our only option, I'd be the go-to man.

Sasha's journey into Officer Spivey's mind had left him brain damaged and it eventually ended his life. It'd be too much guesswork to go into Kyla's brain. Who knew what this girl's mental problems were? Could I go in her brain if I wanted to? When I did could I get out? Erasing memories might not even do it.

Our non-answers spoke for us. Satisfied that we had taken her side, Rhapsody walked to the door. Once we went through it there was no turning back. The little girl inside, whether she was a little girl or not, was about to die. I wasn't prepared. Neither was Sasha. Rhapsody, however, had a blankness behind her eyes I hadn't seen before, like something had died inside of her.

I held my breath as she leaned forward to ghost through the door. We hadn't discussed anything, and an assassination wasn't something to freelance.

"Wait!" I shouted to her.

Rhapsody didn't hesitate and walked forward at full speed. Her face smacked with a thud against the metal surface. She rubbed her forehead and cursed in pain.

The whole scene confused us. "Your powers are off?" I asked her.

Her cross look froze the air. All right, it was a dumb question. I admit it.

Sasha stated the even more obvious fact, "Yeah. Or *someone turned them off.*"

The purple lights cast by our body suits showed we were alone in the corridor, from what we could see. Of course, that didn't cover invisible people or teleporters.

Our quick breathing was audible in the enclosed space. All of us were way panicked. *But no one had come down into the corridor, had they?* I had a hard time thinking how we'd defeat an enemy without powers and in this shape.

Suddenly a high-pitched soprano voice sounded from inside the control room chamber. *"I heeeear yoooou!"*

With that, she teleported us into the control room in a swirl of green mist. She had turned on every available light in the room. Amazingly, it wasn't any less spooky. One fluorescent tube flickering overhead made it hard to focus. The control room was narrower than I thought at first glance, and it smelled like a mix of oil, dust and old rotten cheese. Nausea bubbled in the pit of my stomach from the teleporting. I wish I knew how to control my body better. The girls were fine. *How come nobody else but me got nauseous?*

Still perched in the swivel chair, the girl smiled. Every time she turned, the chair's axel squeaked. The light from the monitors cast a bluish tint on her afro. She said, "I was wondering if you were going to come in or not."

The whole scene was awkward and dangerous. I'd never been around a person with whatever kind of mental illness she had, but she didn't strike me as being stable. One wrong word could set her off. One right word might, too. Plus, at any second she could shift to another form and personality. She might have already.

"You're *Kyla?*" I asked.

"I don't know if I should tell you." Though what she said made it sound obvious I couldn't be sure. She playfully twisted a strands of her hair. "Mommy said for me not to talk to strangers. Are you 'strangers'? Do you know her?"

Sasha, Rhapsody, and I looked at one another. We knew her *birth* mother, yes. *Is that the answer she's looking for?* "Yeah," Rhapsody said. "We do."

She tilted her head and asked us, "What's her first name? That's the password. You have to know the password."

Or what? Rhapsody looked at me for confirmation to speak. After all, I'd spent the most time with her. Then an idea hit me. Her arm tattoo had *Christine* on it. Could that be it? "Christine," I said without hesitation. "Her name's Christine."

"Not *her*," she said with disgust. "My *real* mommy."

We knew her as well. "Amauri," I said. Speaking her name made me sad. I remember watching Camuto bleed out and being unable to do something about it.

"I'm Kyla." She paused and turned to Sasha. "Your hair's so pretty!"

Struck by the compliment and the girl's kindness, she blushed. "Thanks. I love your natural look! My name's Sasha." She pointed to me. "This is Jason, and..."

"...and *you're* Rhapsody."

The abrupt way she'd said Rhapsody's name reminded me how dangerous Kyla was. *How did she know? Does she have access to Kai's memories as a different personality?*

I'd already forgotten the plan. We had to kill Kyla. *When's Rhapsody going to make her move? How? What'll it be?* I'd sworn to myself to watch Rhapsody's movements from here on out to prepare myself for the worst. My ex looked like she could smoke a pack of cigarettes by the way she nervously twiddled her fingers.

"Are you here to visit our friends?" Kyla asked us.

She called tortured captives *friends?* "Yes! Where are they?" I asked her.

Kyla pointed her small finger to the circuit television consoles. "Down there."

The three of us circled her and stared at the color displays. A spark of heat ignited in my chest. Rhapsody covered her mouth to hold back the curse words but it didn't do much to muffle her voice. Sasha blinked back angry tears. There, in adjoining cells, were our loved ones. Caged. Like animals about to be put down.

The displays were some sort of technology that allowed us to see perfectly, although I remember the space being devoid of life. The one to the far left monitored the cell with the busted air vent that I'd been in. Ray and Julia were in that one. My father still wore his hospital gown, and she was wearing the same jumpsuit I'd seen her in at the house. Rhapsody sidled up to me and leaned close to my ear.

"Reminds me of Pápa," Rhapsody said to me. "New plan. We get down there."

Ray faced the camera. Around his neck was my old prism necklace – the one the Collective had given me and King had stolen from me. Iain must have given it to him, but how'd Iain gotten it in the first place?

Giving my father, who was dying from bone cancer, a necklace oozing with cancer-causing radiation was a sick game to play with me. They gave him a better quality of life while making his cancer worse. Whether I got to him or not, he'd die soon.

In the next cell over was Ruby, Rhapsody's mom. None of us had seen her since she'd gone into hiding last year.

Rhapsody reached her fingers towards Ruby's pacing image. "Máma."

Ruby's brown hair had grown past the straps of her blue and white flower print sundress. From what I could tell, she looked thinner and more tanned than I remembered. Happier, too. Living in Panama must have treated her well.

The third room held Aunt Dee and Zachary. I felt a tug at my heart. My little brother walked in circles. I'd never seen him walk that well before. Months had passed since he and Aunt Dee had moved to the East Coast, I think. I'd lost track of the time. Where was Debra? I didn't let myself think she was dead, only that she had somehow escaped. It could've been the one time she'd left the house and they couldn't track her.

Sasha cursed at Iain when she realized her parents, Wesley and Joyce, were being held in the fourth cell. According to the way Sasha described their interactions, it was a miracle they were in the same room and not arguing each other to death. Their divorce had recently been finalized, and Joyce was a month or so sober.

Since Sasha's stabbing, they had called somewhat of a truce. Wesley paced the floor while Joyce lay on her stomach and rested her head on her crossed arms. Sasha's eyes met mine. We needed to get in and get them out.

The question was *how?* There were so many things that could go wrong. Where was the detention center in relation to us? Since none of us could teleport, how would we get in? How could we get out?

"See her Kyla?" Rhapsody's voice cracked as she motioned to Ruby's monitor. "That's *my* mommy. I haven't seen her in a long time. I miss her."

"Aww. I miss my mommy, too." Kyla patted Rhapsody's arm. "I miss Daddy more, though."

Her pity for Rhapsody made me think of my family members. *All of them are trapped down there.* We had to get them out, and one thing Kai said was true -- for a good extraction plan, we needed a teleporter on our side.

"Can you bring them here?" she asked.

Kyla sucked her teeth. "Mommy said I'm not supposed to. It's against Iain's rules."

Crap. Now she's talking about another one of her personalities. "What happens if you *break* the rules, just this once?" I asked her. "Will Mommy hurt you?"

Kyla whistled a haunting string of notes. "Nope. But Kai will. She's *mean.*"

None of us wanted that character to resurface. There had to be another way.

Sasha's eyes lit up. "Can you send us in?"

"…and come with us?" I added.

The idea was insane. I'd absorbed nuclear radiation and used an aquamarine to raise my dead mother from the grave. Was going into a cell with a split personality psychopath *that* much worse?

Kyla smirked. "She *didn't* say anything about that. Sure. I wanna come."

I breathed a sigh of relief. "Thanks. Now how fast…"

Without warning, Kyla teleported us into the first cell with Ray. Nausea rumbled deep in my stomach. Thankfully, after I burped nothing else rose into my throat. Kyla fainted from the strain of teleporting herself plus three people, but Sasha and Rhapsody grabbed her arms to keep her from hitting the floor. Transporting over long distances or with too many people wore Esteban out, so it must have happened to her as well.

The girls helped Kyla back against a metal wall for support. She'd need time to recuperate. Then, we'd need Rhapsody to ghost everyone over into the next cell. By the time we got to the end cell with Sasha's parents in it, Kyla would have to teleport eleven people out. That could take all of her strength. She'd need to rest up.

Surprised by my appearance out of thin air, Julia frantically waved me over. "Jason?"

I rushed to my father's side and took Julia's spot by propping Ray's back up against my knee. She knelt at his side. "How'd you get down here?" she asked me.

"Doesn't matter." I took Ray's hand. A dried trail of blood was on his arm from the IV. Then he shook with a violent spasm, I guessed from the coldness in the chamber.

"Here, Baby." Julia removed her cloth jumpsuit top and covered Ray's shoulders with it. With just a black tank top on, her jagged red surgical scars were visible.

My father moaned in pain. I noticed the heliodor crystal from the necklace wasn't as bright as the others. It was the prism that had been keeping him alive. Heliodor slows aging, among other things, but it was also advancing his already-advanced cancer.

I tried not to sound full of pity when I tried to get his attention. "Dad?"

His eyes rolled toward my face. He was slipping away, and he knew it. "A moment, Julia." His voice faltered so he cleared his throat and mouthed. "Please."

A moment, I thought. That's all I have left with him – a moment.

Julia retreated to the cell's corner away from the others. This was the closest to alone Ray and I would get. There was space but absolutely no privacy. The chamber was chilly and noiseless, besides our voices. Even whispering wouldn't have helped contain our conversation. I'd have to become an orphan in front of an audience.

Ray's voice wavered and cracked. He wanted to speak but couldn't quite make out the words. Since he wasn't using it anyway, I focused on the scarlet emerald's energy, which would allow me to read his mind. "Don't talk. Just think what you want to say."

"I'm dying," he said in his mind.

"I thought I was supposed to be Captain Obvious."

My joke failed to lighten the mood. "Do something for me."

After seeing him in this condition and knowing how I'd contributed to it, I'd agree to do almost anything. "All right. What's up?"

His eyes flashed down to the prims fastened around his neck. "Take it. You need it."

Clearly, he'd lost it. I shook my head. "No. You need it. You'll *die.*"

"I'll die anyway," he thought. "You know that."

My father erupted into a coughing fit that lasted a minute. Julia wandered over. I thought she'd come quicker than that. She unbuttoned and untied his hospital gown on the side. Using the loose fabric, she covered his mouth as he hacked. Several small spots of blood dotted the gown where he'd coughed into it.

Julia stroked his forehead with her good hand until Ray stared at her to stop. Even with the crystals around his neck, his condition grew worse by the minute. His pale skin was dry and wrinkled. At his healthiest, he weighed a little over two hundred pounds. Now, he'd be lucky to step on a scale and move it half that much. His brown eyes had a milky film on them. He smelled like medicinal rub.

I hated to admit it. Ray was right. Prisms or not, he didn't have long.

My heart dropped. *Why should I feel bad about him dying?* Everything that went wrong in my life could be traced back to him. The times Debra couldn't pay the light bill and we spent hot summer nights in the dark – he could've thrown money at it. The last three times I filled out a first day of school contact form I skipped the "father" blank because he always had Julia make excuses for him. The first time I lost a fight after school it was on him, too. He could've taught me how to fight back.

When Mom died, Ray *left me.* Wasn't it my right to be *angry?*

But right before I got my powers, and I'd almost written him off for good, something changed. He came around us more. For my sixteenth birthday, he bought me a fire engine red '64 Mustang and promised me stick shift driving lessons. He'd paid Debra's medical bills.

Up until now I hadn't questioned the shift in character. Deep down maybe he *knew* he was going to die. Was he trying to get himself right with God? I couldn't let him go out like this. He was my father. Like it or not, I did love him.

He groaned and thought, "Not your fault, Champ."

But it *was.* A part of him must think that. Had I not given him goshenite to protect himself against my enemies, he wouldn't have gotten sick. *See, even when I try to do the right thing, I screw up.* Hanging my head I blinked back tears. "I did this."

Ray must've sensed it and he gently squeezed my hand. He didn't blame me.

"You don't get it!" The guilt piled inside of me. "I-I can't do anything right. I never could. You told me that once, remember?"

He paused and took a heavy breath. Ray's eyes teared up. "What do I know? You saved the world. You're a Champion. A hero. My hero."

I flashed back in my mind to lying across six provenance crystals during a solar storm. Because of it radioactivity flowed through my blood without harming me. If I could do that, couldn't I save my dad? Couldn't I save them all?

I looked down at him. I didn't know how I did it, but I felt his emotions. He was proud of me. Finally.

"I'm not leaving you," I said. With my arms underneath his legs and at his back, I shifted myself forward. I don't know what I was thinking. Without my powers, lifting barbells was hard for me and that was with two healthy feet. Six months ago I would've left him there, taken the crystals, and not thought twice about it. Not now.

I got to my knees with his body close to mine. A surge of energy zipped through my body. *The prisms.* I wanted to reject the green emerald radiation, but it felt too good to resist. My muscles and bones drank in the power. The pain in my ankle subsided and I exhaled.

Suddenly, a flurry of images flashed into my brain. I saw Ray and my mother, Anna, in a doctor's office. They were looking at a blank sonogram. Both of them cried. My mother whispered the name, "Zachary." That's why Mom was upset Ray had named my little brother

Zachary – it was their baby's name first but she had miscarried.

Then I saw his law office. He laid papers on his desk with my name on them. I had a feeling they must have been how he legally got out of raising me.

The last one was of him embracing my mom. She was wearing her burial dress. I suspected she'd visited him after I used aquamarines to raise her from the dead. She reached out her arms to hug him and they embraced.

Right then it hit me. I'd been viewing his biggest regrets.

With that, Ray's body shivered against me. He sighed once, a brief, shallow gasp. His body fell limp. And then, nothing.

CHAPTER TWELVE

four personalities and counting

When the realization that I was holding my father's lifeless body struck me I had to fight the urge to drop it.

I slumped to my knees and gently set him down.

He's gone.

An incredible force rose in my chest. *Was I gonna throw up?* I fought the pressure but it didn't work. Heavy, terrible wails came out. No stopping them. Pain and loss weighted me to the metal floor.

Both my birth parents were dead. Radioactive prisms had killed them. The same radioactive prisms that gave me superpowers. The irony wasn't lost on me.

While the others kept their distance, Julia squatted next to me. She and Ray just got married last year. They'd put off their honeymoon until I regained consciousness after the explosion. Then he'd started paying Debra's medical bills and put it off again. Around the holidays last year, Ray's cancer diagnosis came. He had to leave his law practice.

I'd ruined their marriage because I was *different.*

Julia brushed a hand through her honey brown and blonde hair and softly said my name. Not "Junior," the nickname she loved and I hated, but my name.

"Jason."

She wants to talk to me? Why? Why doesn't she hate me? I'd hate me if I were her. I didn't want to exist right about now.

From the corner of my eyes, I could tell Julia's eyes burrowed holes into my face. She wanted me to look back at her, to say something, *anything*. No. Not after this.

My stepmother said my name as a question. "Jason?"

She squeezed my gloved hand. In two years we'd rarely touched beyond an occasional halfhearted hug. For me, she was unusually hot for a stepmother and it made me uncomfortable. Besides, I wasn't the cute, chubby, lovable stepson. I'm the one with the disciplinary record and mental issues – the one she *tolerated*.

She took the hint and dropped my hand.

My eyes burned. I forced myself to glance in her direction. *What does she want?*

"Wait." I felt like a jerk. Ray stared off into space. Even without much light around, I got creeped out by my father's unblinking brown eyes. Julia asked for my help and I'd basically told her to screw off.

With her trembling right hand, Julia closed Ray's eyelids herself. Until then, she'd kept her emotions in check. Touching her husband's body broke her. She collapsed over him, her back jerking in spasms with each scream. Debra had thought my father married a younger woman for sex and that she wanted his money. From the looks of it, their relationship was so much more than that.

This entire scene was surreal. I was watching a movie about my life through someone else's eyes. I couldn't feel the padded inside of my bodysuit or its cooling system anymore. My entire body was blazing hot and numb from the inside out.

Julia unfastened the necklace from around Ray's neck and handed it to me. "Here." she said as she pressed the prisms into my hand. "He'd want you to have this."

I couldn't take it, but I had to. My fingers folded around it. With the security catch broken, I tied the titanium chain into a knot. Energy pulsed through my veins. Physically, at least, I felt like myself again.

"Thanks," I said. "You can call me Junior. You know, if you want. It's not *that* bad."

She sniffed and gave a small chuckle. "No," she said with a smile. "Nobody who can do what you do is a 'junior' anything."

Julia brushed her hands off on her pants and stood. I got to my feet as well.

Throughout this whole thing, Sasha and Rhapsody had kept their distance. Now that it was over, they approached us with Kyla, who had awakened from fainting.

Sasha put a hand on my shoulder to comfort me. "I don't know what to say besides I'm here for you."

I expected Rhapsody to give the best advice. Her father, George, had died of radioactive prism bone cancer. He and Mom worked on top of the burial site for the provenance aquamarine. Of anyone near this messed up situation, I figured she'd have the most to say. She'd always had my back.

Why isn't she saying something?

Rhapsody bit her lip and shrugged. "I'm here if you need it, too, you know."

That's all she said.

Seeing this happen had to have reminded her of George. I'm not sure what else there was to do in this moment, but I needed *more*.

Suddenly the purple aura given off by our bodysuits dimmed to a mild, throbbing glow. Then a series of flickers. A second later all that remained of the light was what amounted to three birthday candles.

Julia's voice cracked as she wagged a finger at us. "What's happening to you?"

Rhapsody gave the quickest explanation possible. "Solar powered suits and no sun."

"I'm afraid of the dark," Kyla said with a twinge of fear. "Turn on the lights, please."

We'd forgotten about her. She was the only way we were getting out of here. I squinted to see her location. She wasn't next to Sasha and Rhapsody. If she teleported out, we'd be screwed even more.

"No worries. It's okay," I said, halfway trying to convince myself and her at the same time.

Sasha added, "Nothing will happen to you. Here. Take my hand."

"No!" She screamed as if someone were after her. "Christine used to say that…"

Her adoptive mom? What happened to her? We were treading in dangerous waters here. I didn't ask so as not to push Kyla to shapeshift into a different, worse personality.

"Lights, please! Turn on the lights!" Her voice quaked with fear. "He's coming!"

My pulse raced. Who was she talking about? Iain? Someone else?

"Where are you?" Rhapsody shouted from the left side of the room.

Julia yelled back. "She's over here!"

Her voice sounded a yard or so away, to my right, I thought. All I saw were moving shadows. "Get her to calm down!" I yelled back. "And where is 'over here'?"

"I think she's at your twelve o' clock," Rhapsody said. "Start walking."

And trip over my father's dead body because I couldn't see it? No way. I stayed put.

Kyla's shrill voice heightened in pitch by the minute. "No. No! Don't touch me!"

Our suits barely lit up anymore. I felt my lungs heaving. Was our air running out?

A painful moan filled the room. Kyla's, I guessed. It was impossible to tell until she started talking again.

"Don't let him hurt me," was the last thing she said.

As our eyes adjusted to the lack of light, we called out Kyla's name and waited for her to respond. She'd stopped making noise, and none of us could positively pin down a location. Nobody else would die today if I had anything to do with it.

I became aware of my heartbeat and how fast it was racing. *She's our exit strategy. I'm not an idiot. She's a mentally disturbed woman. Not a scared little girl. Right?*

The solar batteries in our suits gave out one after another. By the rapid squeak and thump of our rubber soles against the floor I could tell everyone else was moving as frantically as I was. Kyla made no sound at all and wouldn't respond to her name.

A square of bright light cut through the darkness at the other end of the room. Sasha's voice rang out. "Here I am."

I retrieved my cell phone from the inside of my suit and did the same. "This is me."

Julia joined in, and Rhapsody used hers, as well. We'd created a circle. Ray's body was close to the center, along with someone tall enough to be an adult. She'd changed clothes from the nightgown she had been wearing to a pair of dark fitted jeans, a button-down shirt and boots.

Crap. Kyla had switched personalities. If it was "Kai," we'd better be prepared to fight her, but she dressed a little differently than this.

I looked down at the prisms on my necklace and removed the heliodor. Sasha would need it, but I knew better than to chuck it over to her in the dark. Once my cell phone's backlight timed out, I started moving in her direction to hand it to her personally.

"Freeze."

The voice sounded like Kai's, but instead of her harsh edge, it had a touch of softness to it. Maybe this was one we hadn't seen yet. "Jade?" I said with hesitation.

"How do you know my name?" she asked.

This was the fourth personality we'd encountered, first Amauri – the one Kyla called "Mommy," then Kai, Kyla, and now, Jade. How many were there? Who was the main one? The whole thing was a mind trip. No way was I going to tell her the truth and risk another face change. "Umm..."

Rhapsody interrupted me. "We worked with the Collective. Eris Stafford, Jeff Peters, Vivienne Coker, Belinda King, Solomon Hughes – they were...*friends.* They told us."

They'd manipulated and misled us, kept secrets from us. I'd call the Collective members a lot of things, but "friends" was not one of them. No wonder she hesitated, and when she said "friends" it sounded forced.

The mention of Hughes caught Jade's attention. He was her father, and telling from the energy in her movements in the dark, she didn't know much about him.

"What do you know about *Solomon Hughes?*" she asked with sudden curiosity.

Sasha came up with an ingenious plan. "Take us into the other cells, Help us free the others, get them to the surface. We'll tell you everything we know."

"*All* of them?" She sounded incredulous. "You're lying. You know nothing about my father."

"He used to be a slave," I told her. "And he liked to drink expensive scotch."

She bought it. Jade relished the information like it was good food. If she went this wild over something that small, I imagined what she'd say when I told her about how he'd saved my life. "Fourteen-year-old Oban," she said. "His breath stunk of it. Even now I can't forget the smell."

They've met? When? How?

Jade continued. "When Iain finds us, he'll kill everyone. Maybe even me."

Still lying on its back, Ray's unmoving body served as a reminder that my father could've died at home in peace if Iain hadn't moved him. I owed him one for that. I wasn't afraid of what he could do. Ron Welker tried to kill us. Peters and King each had tried more than once. I almost *wished* he'd find us so I could beat him.

"Yeah, we've heard that before," I said. "Let him try."

Julia disagreed. "Hold on. You want him to try?"

Satisfied, Jade motioned toward us with her hands. "Moving targets are harder to hit. We'll be quick. Come close, and focus on going to the next cell."

"*Focus,*" Julia repeated. "Got it."

That was the secret to keep from throwing up. *Focus?* No wonder I sucked at it.

I took one last look at Ray. "One more thing," I said as Jade prepared to teleport the five of us. "When this is over – we come back for him. He deserves better than this."

Jade frowned. "You're on your own for that."

Sasha eased to my right side. Her hand found my bicep and squeezed it. She was with me. When the time came to bury my dad properly, I wouldn't do it on my own. No one would convince me otherwise.

I handed Sasha the heliodor prism from my necklace. "You'll need this."

She slipped it into her inner bodysuit pocket, inhaled deeply and said, "I forgot how good this felt."

Rhapsody and Julia followed Jade over to us. Once we had gathered into a five-member group, she said, "We stay long enough to find them and go. No longer."

Before anyone could ask questions Jade teleported us. We landed in Ruby's cell in a dark cloud of mist. I'd never noticed it before, but the teleportation after mist smelled like sulfur mixed with dust. *The closer the quarters, the stronger the stench, I guess.*

Next to me, Julia moaned. "Is it always like this?"

"Like an acid trip on a roller coaster?" Sasha asked her. "Pretty much."

"Who's there?" Ruby's voice was quick and agitated. "Who's there?"

Once my cell phone was on, I used the flashlight app and shined it in the direction the sound had come from. A couple yards away Ruby shielded her face with her hand. Rhapsody ran toward her mother, and we trailed after her.

As she reached her, Rhapsody shouted, "Mom!"

"Rana?" Ruby called out in a weary voice. "Rana" was Spanish for "frog." Unsure of Rhapsody's gender before she was born, George and Ruby had decorated her nursery with frogs.

The two tearfully hugged and exchanged words in Spanish. I wanted to let them catch up for a minute, but Jade wasn't having it. Again, she didn't warn us. With another *pop* we'd moved into the next cell. The nausea was okay the last time we'd teleported, but my stomach was beginning to revolt.

No one talked. I shined my phone all over the chamber. Zachary and Aunt Dee lay on the floor on the far side of the room. My little brother's back rose and fell in quick movements. He'd been crying – probably for a while. Since they'd been abducted on the East Coast, he'd be starving by now. That and he definitely needed a diaper change. I stopped breathing through my nose because of the stench of stale urine.

Next to him, Aunt Dee snored. She was barefoot and wearing a faded purple dress. I slowed my walk to a leisurely pace to give my body a break. Being transported across space felt like being unraveled and then wound back up. I'd tried to focus, but some random though kept getting in the way. For an ADHD kid, this was my daily life.

Aunt Dee was a heavy sleeper so I shook her shoulder hard. I whispered her name. "Aunt Dee. Wake up."

She stopped snoring and mumbled my name. "Jason?"

Jade teleported us into the last cell, which held Sasha's parents. The movement woke Zachary up and he started to whimper. Aunt Dee got to her knees and coughed. She was a goner unless someone got her to the toilet. Using her phone to do just that, Sasha guided Aunt Dee to the corner of the room and they made it just in time.

At the sight of her daughter, Joyce held out an accusing finger. "What is this?" she asked Sasha. "*He* had something to do with this, didn't he? This is his fault!"

"He" meant me. Sasha's mom had it out for me ever since the flimsy robbery story we'd made up to explain how Sasha got stabbed. I'd gotten everyone, including the police, into believing the story. Joyce still distrusted me, which was why she wouldn't let me see Sasha in the hospital or at home.

Confused, Wesley held up his hands. "Sasha, who are all these people?"

Jade moved ahead of us. Her eyes counted the number of people in the room. There were nine people to teleport, and the strain showed on her sweaty face. This was the last stop. In a moment, we'd be above ground.

"I said no time for introductions," she said out of breath.

I picked up my smelly little brother, who nuzzled against my chest and ran his hand over my suit's small metal plates. "We can surface now. That's everyone," I said.

Jade shook her head no as the familiar sulfur smell whirled around us. "No, it's not," she said as we disappeared.

CHAPTER THIRTEEN

a horror movie of a hospital

"I don't believe my eyes" didn't quite cover it.

Everyone was queasy after this teleportation trip. Hard to focus when you don't know where you're going. We could be at ground level or have gone lower into the earth. Jade hadn't told us. She'd misinterpreted Sasha when she said "free the others." Sasha meant our family members. Not these people.

While everyone else rubbed their eyes I painfully adjusted to the buzzing overhead lights a little faster. Everything was blurry at first besides the bright red lumps of gauze, tan bodies, and dark green sheets. I held Zachary's face against my chest. No human being, especially so tiny, should see anything near this gruesome.

"Oh God," Julia waved her hand in front of her face. "What's that sme--"

Her gagging fit cut off the end of her question. Rhapsody, Sasha, and I recognized the scent of bodily fluids and said nothing. It was a one of the scene's many grisly details I'd not soon forget.

We had to get out of here fast. "Jade!"

Of course she didn't answer. She'd abandoned us.

Speaking nasally to avoid inhaling the stench, Wesley fired off a stream of difficult-to-answer questions. "Who's 'Jade'? That weird little girl, Kyla, where'd she go? We're stuck here? Where are we? How did we even get down here in the first place? I was at home..."

"With *her?*"

He stopped her with his hand. "Not now, Joyce."

"Don't talk to Mom like that," Sasha said to him. "Forget Jade, Dad. We'll find our own way out."

"How, Sasha? How do you intend to do that? You're injured. You should be resting, not dressed in a scaly morph suit and running around with Jason. And –"

Sasha shut him up by splitting off into two clones – Sasha's default clone, "Clone Sasha," which she controlled through her brain's pleasure spots, and "Angry Sasha," whom she commanded through her amygdala.

Wesley recovered from seeing three versions of his daughter in time to keep his ex-wife from hitting the ground. Ruby, Aunt Dee, and Julia had seen us use our powers before, so it didn't shock them.

They'd all have to take care of themselves until we figured this out. I handed off my frightened little brother to Aunt Dee, and she covered his eyes with her hand. "Lord have mercy" was all she would say.

At the same time, Ruby scooted over to Rhapsody and held her by the arm. "Are you sure about all this, *hija*? You trust him? He got us into all this."

Her eyes softened. "Actually, I got *him* into all this, Máma, but he'll get us out."

Pride surged in my chest. In her own way, she believed in me, too.

"Be careful," Ruby warned her after the two shared a quick hug.

Then Original Sasha, the clones, Rhapsody, and I masked up. With our suits out of power, however, their automated air circulation system didn't work. Having fabric over our faces helped dampen the stale air's stench.

Together, we rounded the makeshift stretchers and assessed what we'd mistakenly gotten ourselves into. The place was *big*. Sterile. I had no idea how to measure square footage, but Sasha once told me her house's bottom floor was two thousand square feet plus some. This was at least that size. More.

We walked to investigate. Our boots stuck to the white tile. Could be any substance on the floor. I'd be better off not knowing.

Rhapsody shuddered at the sickening peel of her boot sole from the floor's surface. "Cap, for real dude -- if you know what it is, don't tell me," Rhapsody said.

We were in a laboratory. Iain had admitted he'd experimented to cure his MS. Should've known *human testing* was part of it. The humans he'd worked on were people we knew – Selby, Ryan Cain and the Hernandez triplets -- Luis, Julio, and Esteban.

Luis and Julio had been here the longest. Jagged black veins and puncture wounds covered their bodies, neck to waist – the effects of swallowing my blood and an aquamarine. Their bodies had a violent reaction to it instead of making them immortal. Apparently, the types still had to match for a transfusion to work. Mine was an extremely rare AB negative like Rhapsody's.

"So much for untested science," I said, repeating something Peters had told us.

Esteban sustained no injuries save for a quarter-sized pink scar on his chest where Ryan Cain had shot him. Selby had a dent in his left side from where I'd crushed his ribs.

"Not over here," Original Sasha said. Her eyes lingered on our former friends. "He hasn't touched these guys."

Why not? With everything going on around us, I couldn't tell if Ryan's, Esteban's and Selby's torsos actually moved. Was I imagining it? Steadying my vision required a focus I didn't have. *At this point, I'm not sure I care either way.*

"Are they even alive?" I asked out loud.

Original Sasha plucked a silver backed mirror from a nearby table and held it first underneath Julio's nose, then Luis'. No condensation. "They're dead. Have been for half a day, I think."

Those two were a long shot in the first place. They were the rotting bodies we smelled.

As she moved on to check Ryan and Selby, I heard audible gasps and dry heaving. For a moment, I'd forgotten our families who'd tagged along with us. Their sight had returned and they were disgusted by what they were seeing. Aunt Dee rocked a squirming Zachary, but he screamed full blast. Wesley, Joyce, Julia and Ruby covered their faces with whatever clothes they could to help settle their stomachs.

I looked around the room for Jade and shouted over my little brother's wails. "Seriously?" I yelled at the ceiling. "We had a *deal*, Jade."

"Psychopaths these days just aren't reliable, I guess," Rhapsody said.

"Sarcasm is not helping!" I said back.

She clapped her hands. "I meant we need a new plan, Cap. That's all."

Sasha had checked Selby last. Her voice had a hint of concern. "Selby, Ryan, and Esteban are barely hanging on. I mean, like, a good guess? Maybe a couple minutes."

Okay, Iain *had* done something to them. Fine. Why did she care? She'd dated Selby and Esteban, but to worry about them after all they'd done? Way insulting considering all three had tried to off me at various points last year.

"I have an idea," she continued. "One of my clones found a –"

Sasha continued to explain her ideas, but I zoned out to where I didn't hear her or our family members who talked about how weird everything was. Fixed to the nearest wall was a chrome cabinet. There was something important inside – I know it. It might be surrounded by a baboon heart or something crazy, but whatever. I stepped around Selby and approached it. Once I got close enough, I sensed the familiar sizzle of high proton radiation in my veins. *Had to be prisms or something like it.*

With two fingers, I smashed the lock and pulled the door open. On its shelves was a collection of prisms – brilliant, sparkling green emeralds, goshenite, heliodor, and scarlet emeralds. *How'd these things survive the solar storms that made the others explode? Lead shielding?* At least the two most dangerous ones – morganite and aquamarine – weren't present. Morganite releases inner desires. Aquamarines raise the dead. Believe it or not, the effects of those two were way worse than superpowers.

"Jason?" Rhapsody used my name and dragged it out.

I eyed the jewel collection. "We can use these."

Why waste them? We could give our family members temporary powers, just to escape. *They won't get cancer that fast, right?* My thoughts ran wild. *Ray.* He'd grown addicted to goshenite. Bad idea.

Rhapsody became a warning label. "We can, but we shouldn't. Think."

"You think I'm not thinking?" For a successful extraction plan, we needed a teleporter.

Somehow Original Sasha figured out what I'd been thinking. "Not even a little bit, Jason. Don't do it."

I brushed the prisms into my palm and closed my fist. Too many to pocket in my suit, but not if we split the load. Esteban needed one plus a real good reason to rescue us. Revenge might be it.

"Jade's gone." I dropped equal amounts of the mixed colored jewels into their gloved palms. "Extraction plan for ten people. Kai said every good extraction plan needs a teleporter. I'm up for ideas if you have a better one."

Rhapsody rarely cursed in earshot of Ruby, so she kept mouthing the f-words. "She also left us in a --- horror movie. You're talking about *that* -- teleporter?" She pointed at Esteban. "Are you -- serious? You -- trust Esteban to not -- kill us all?"

I pointed at the stretchers. "Look around. See what Iain did to Esteban and his brothers? He'll want revenge on *him* not us. Okay, maybe me, but not you two."

"Yeah. Well, I could give two –"

Sasha interrupted her. "It's our only good option. A ten person extraction."

A shot of pain hit my heart. I'd counted Aunt Dee and Zachary, Wesley and Joyce, Ruby, the three of us plus Esteban. I'd said *ten* not nine. I was still counting my father. The second time I'd thought about him in the past couple minutes. With all we'd been through with one another, I still couldn't believe he was *dead*.

Rhapsody's eyes narrowed. Ten instead of nine meant Sasha was counting on leaving Selby behind. *Sasha wanted to let him die.* He'd embarrassed Sasha publicly, nearly stabbed her to death, and murdered dozens of innocent people, including his parents. I could understand not wanting to save him, but I'm not sure I agreed with it. Deciding who lives and dies on a whim. *We're as bad as Iain is. No, we're not. Yeah. Totally are.*

"You want to save Ryan? What for?" Rhapsody's nostrils flared. "Remember when he stabbed Julia? *Three* blood transfusions, Sasha. She'll never use her arm the same way again."

"Yeah?" Sasha's lip quivered. "Like I won't use my womb in any way because of Selby? Forget him."

A gut punch with a lead fist. The announcement silenced us all. Just by reading expressions alone nobody but Wesley and Joyce knew Sasha couldn't have kids anymore. A day ago she'd mentioned babies and a normal life. Was she lying, wishing, or being hopeful?

Couldn't surgery fix it? If it could, wouldn't she have had it already?

We'd lost so much of our present in the past year. Were we going to start losing our dreams and futures, too? Or had we already been robbed of them and I didn't know it?

Before I could say something stupid that didn't help, Clone Sasha and Angry Sasha appeared behind us, out of breath. After Original Sasha absorbed them, she said to us, "There's a metal door bolted from the outside, no hinges. It's gray, real thick, maybe dense lead or even depleted uranium. You couldn't punch through that. Rhapsody couldn't ghost through either."

I glanced over at our suffering families. They looked our way. Aunt Dee had a small spot of drool with bits of orange food on her shoulder from Zachary. He wiggled uncontrollably and she struggled to hold herself together. Julia's face flushed a tint of green. Wesley tended to Joyce and Ruby – both who were chain vomiting over trash cans.

Physics, logic, good sense – they could be against us. But they usually were.

I cracked my knuckles. "Hitting it or ghosting through aren't the answers. Esteban helps us escape. We take Ryan *and* Selby."

Both girls disagreed with me. Didn't matter – it had to be done. Besides, with the shape the guys were in, there was no guarantee they'd survive long anyway.

Sasha held her hand up. "There's something else besides the door. I saw bags of bl—"

A concussive force struck the back of my neck so hard that my teeth rattled. The blow didn't hurt, but it muted the end of Sasha's sentence in my ears and sent them throbbing. Or was that my heartbeat? I couldn't tell the difference.

Green, white, gold, and red brilliant sparkles flew all over the place. I'd opened my hand on reflex and lost control of the prisms. Great, now there was *that*. Esteban only needed one. Should be pretty easy to find *one*.

"Save them!" Though I yelled at Rhapsody and Sasha, I couldn't hear the sound of my own voice anymore outside of my body. Had anything even come out of it?

Our family members gasped and pointed in my direction. *What was behind me that was so bad?*

Whatever. I turned around and punched with all my might.

I'd hit Iain in the chest. He fell backwards into Esteban's stretcher, and the two men collapsed to the floor. Iain cursed and kicked Esteban's prone body so hard it rolled several times.

Standing straight up without the use of a cane, Iain's physical build was imposing. He was taller, more muscular than I was, and the steel in his eyes shocked me. Raised black veins rippled along his forehead, down his neck, and beneath the collar of his maroon button-down silk shirt. They connected and made his face look like a giant living jigsaw puzzle. His skin had turned a pale gray. We'd seen this before on David King, when he'd drank my blood in an attempt to become immortal. *Won't the substance kill him before he could finish me off?*

Iain's eyes drifted downward to my feet and then traveled back up to my face. "And I considered you a *threat.*" His body language, his walk towards me, and the way he said *considered* like I was a bothersome flea – he wanted me to move out of his way.

I stared him down, hoping I communicated without speaking that he could screw himself. He'd have to go through me if he wanted to leave here in one piece.

Iain rolled his neck and cracked it. *Through me* was exactly where he intended to go.

It would go down like this: we'd punch the mess out of one another. In the end, the punching wouldn't matter. I'd have to get the upper hand, like I had with King, to end his life. That's what I'd have to do here. Though I had no desire to kill – he had to be stopped.

"I *am* a threat." My statement sounded a lot more convincing in my head. "Otherwise our families wouldn't be here."

Iain uttered a low, rumbling growl. "We'll see what you become...*after* I start killing them."

He shoved me across the laboratory. I zoomed a dozen yards, whipped around and tumbled over a table. Tools and trays clanged against the floor. Somehow I landed back onto my feet.

Iain was every bit as strong as I was, maybe more so. But his body rejected my AB negative blood. Why wasn't he dead?

He stared me down and strode across the scattered prisms. They crunched beneath his feet. Awesome. Prism dust was useless. Now my last ditch crappy backup plan to use Esteban to teleport everyone out had even failed.

"Your blood's a *step* in my plan." Iain wagged his finger. "The veins are a nuisance, a side effect I haven't cracked yet. But don't be confused. I'm quite healthy, and I'll live *eons*. Thanks to you…"

What else was there? "Wait, let me guess…"

"…you'll see a planet ruled by *us* – government, financial markets, and entertainment – cleansed from inferior life and repopulated. It's the logical progression of Carrington: the next step in human evolution. Besides, what greater ambition is there than world domination?"

"I don't remember King's notes saying anything about large-scale genocide."

"They were shortsighted, Sasha" Iain said. "A superior race living with an inferior one in peace is flawed logic. Can't put super humans and a fry cook in the same cereal bowl can you?"

Yeah, he's one of those. We expected that, and I didn't care why or what for – nothing else mattered but stopping him from testing his hypothesis.

Rhapsody balled her fists and parted her legs. "World domination, huh? Good luck with that."

Then, Jade emerged from a green mist cloud. Or was it Kai?

"Don't need luck," she said with bravado. "I have her."

Definitely Kai, which was bad news for us. The thing in my brain that made me *not* want to murder people on impulse – she didn't have that.

Aunt Dee sat on the floor to my right and held Zachary from running to us. With my mask on, he couldn't tell which one of us was which. Joyce, Ruby and

Julia had slumped down against the white wall to my left. Wesley guarded them.

Then, in a second, they were all gone in a wisp of green smoke. I held my breath, waiting.

Where were they?

A moment later Kai teleported in next to Iain. She dusted off her hands, like snuffing out five people's lives was something to be proud of. I clenched my jaw to keep the rage and tears under control. "Where are they?" I screamed. "Bring them back!"

"Don't worry, Jason, they're back in their cells," Sasha said with confidence. "That many people – it had to be a close teleportation."

Kai shrugged. She breathed hard. I could tell she didn't like being figured out that easily.

Rhapsody called Kai a few nasty names before finishing off with, "We had a deal."

"Not with me."

Kyla, Jade, Amauri, Kai…they're all of the same freaking person! What was the difference? Had Iain promised Kai anything we hadn't thought of?

Sasha had it all figured out before I did. "Jason brought Anna back," she said. "He had to wear an aquamarine to keep his mom alive, and it almost killed him. It'll do the same for you, Kai."

She cleared her throat. "Tell me where my father's body is, and I'll teleport them back."

That was easy. Rhapsody, Esteban, and I had put what was left of Hughes' body into a casket and said our respects over it – the closest thing to a wake we could up with on the fly. Much of his body was dust. Whatever. "The graveyard behind the old asylum in Traveller."

Iain thought over what I'd said. "Jeff Peters. He's there, too?"

The question caught us off guard. Peters? Who cares? He was still alive, as far as I knew. Why did Iain want to know? Was it a test? I always failed tests, no matter what the subject was.

That had to be what Sasha was talking about when I zoned out. There was no winning this, so I just gave him an honest answer. "*Hughes* is buried there. Peters could be anywhere -- with an underage girl, who knows?"

My joke made Iain even angrier. "Tell the *truth,* Jason."

He wouldn't know the truth if it hit him in the face with a bag of nickels. "That *is* 'the truth'. Bring them back. Now."

He turned to Kai. "He dug up the graves and moved the bodies."

Kai parroted what he'd just said. "You dug up the graves and moved the bodies."

Iain nodded with approval at his new mind control abilities. "Good. Take his necklace. Then make him tell you everything."

CHAPTER FOURTEEN

killing is on the table

The muscles in my ankle gave, and I dropped to my left knee. Iain mistook it as a sign of submission. In one motion, he pulled a gun from behind his back, pointed it at me and fired.

I squinted my eyes. Raging fire ripped through my shoulder.

"Didn't have much use for these around here before you," he said. "A little something I mined from the Orizaba fort."

The bullet had entered below my collarbone and exited through my shoulder. My brain scrambled. The throbbing, the bloody gush beneath my suit – I couldn't think. The round had to be goshenite. I tried controlling my breathing so as not to hyperventilate.

Iain waved his weapon at the others. "Hurts, huh?"

Like having my muscles yanked apart with a fishing hook. "Nope," I groaned. "Tickles."

Rhapsody and Sasha stood by, watching. It's all they could do. Iain had scarlet emerald radiation in his blood now, so in addition to freezing them in place, he could hear their thoughts and control their minds. Except for mine. Being immune to mind reading and control while off my Adderall might be the only benefits of my ADHD.

Kai pronounced each word of her question carefully. *"Where is my father buried?"*

I bit my lip hard and couldn't feel the skin. Shivers ran up and down my body. Before long I'd collapse in shock and be unable to answer anyone's questions. *"Assss...s-sylum."*

Kai bent over, hands covering her ears like she'd suffered the worst migraine ever. She straightened up and shape-shifted into a different, *older* face. She'd shifted personalities like changing socks. My eyelids fluttered, but I recognized it: Amauri – the protector.

She opened her hand and displayed two quarter-sized aquamarine stones. "We'll see," she said before teleporting away.

We were alone with Iain and his goshenite gun, unable to stop him. He'd frozen the girls in place right in front of me, but I was bleeding to death and powerless. Keeping me still wasn't necessary. I'd be really still once I ran out of blood.

Sasha's eyes panicked. She screamed my name through her teeth.

With his back to the girls, Iain knelt in front of me and yanked the mask off my head. Without a piece of fabric covering my mouth, my breathing wasn't quite as labored. The smell of death didn't matter anymore. My world spun around. I didn't have much longer.

"Don't you get it?" Rhapsody mumbled. "How much is he worth to you *dead?*"

Without turning to face her, Iain replied over his shoulder. "No worries. There's more of us out there, Rhapsody, and him dying is kind of the point."

"He's gonna kill you and your shapeshifting friend."

"No," he chuckled. "He won't. Not his thing."

"Say he doesn't," Sasha said. "Dead men don't answer questions, do they?"

She had a point.

He turned his attention back to me and steadied my chin in his hand. "Where is he?"

White stars of pain sparkled in my eyesight. I wished with everything I had left that Peters was on the grid. He chose this life or death moment to be out of touch. I'd give up his whereabouts in a second to save everyone else. He'd lived more than two hundred years – a full two or three lives by anyone's standards. Exchanging whatever life force he had left for the survival of ten people seemed like a fair trade.

Annoyed with my inability to answer, Iain stood. "Tell you what." He waved his hand. Suddenly, my energy returned but I still couldn't move. The inside of my suit was soaked with blood on the left side but the wound had sealed and stopped throbbing. I felt so good that it was hard to believe I had even been shot.

My powers were back. I'd broken out of mind control once when Reject High's old principal, Ron Welker, had done it to me. I started to try by moving my toes like before – something he couldn't possibly notice.

He said, "Life's about making choices, Jason. I'll give you another shot at it. Tell me where I can find him, and I won't kill everybody you know and their families."

More than most people, I hated being asked the same question over and over again after I'd given an appropriate answer. Being threatened was right below that. I'd spent my teenage years so far lying my way in and out of things and being threatened. In this case, the truth wasn't working. Debra always reminds me that the Bible says *the truth makes you free*. Not when a psychopath is holding the key to your chains. I'd lie my way to the bottom of hell if it saved everyone.

His promises weren't worth the air he used to make them. There was a loophole. He wouldn't kill everyone I knew? Right. That meant he'd kill most of them not all.

Rhapsody pleaded me with her eyes, as if to say *don't do it, Cap*. What choice did she think I had? Stand here and let us die? Not an option.

Iain whipped out his pistol and released its safety. I couldn't move my head or my eyes away from the girls. He stepped between both girls, unmasked Rhapsody, and pressed the barrel against her chest. I could barely see her face as it was blocked by his shoulder, but I imagined it was inexpressive. He'd kill her first if she made him angry enough, and if there's one thing she excelled at it was ticking people off.

"From your point-of-view, how does it feel to be the *default option?*" he asked her. "He'll choose you only if she's not available. You know that, right?"

Rhapsody grunted and groaned in Spanish words I didn't understand. The last time someone threatened her with a gun it was Welker. She'd had a green emerald hidden underneath her boot and when I thought he'd shot her in the head and she'd died, she'd actually turned invisible and intangible. No hope of that happening here. Iain had stomped all of the prisms I saw into dust. I doubted if any remained but I couldn't be sure.

I held my breath as Iain clicked his tongue like a gunshot and said *bam* mid-chuckle. "I wonder -- which one of you will he miss more? *You?* Hurts when someone you care for doesn't want you anymore, doesn't it? Don't worry, he won't regret his choice." He nodded towards Sasha. "Especially if he has *her*."

That wasn't true. I've always wanted Rhapsody in my life. Though we'd known each other a short time, she was my first friend at Reject High. We'd protected the planet together. She was the first girl to whom I'd said "I love you" and meant it – my first for a couple other things. She was the best friend I'd ever had. Her insecurities and whatever I had going on with Sasha made our relationship impossible to sustain but our friendship was solid.

He hadn't gotten quite the reaction he wanted from her, so he turned to Sasha. Tears rolled down her cheeks in streams. He performed by the same script as he had with Rhapsody. He first unmasked her and then pressed the end of the handgun's barrel to her left breast inches away from her heart. When she whimpered, I knew he had her.

"Stop crying, Sasha," I would've said to her. "It's what he wants." I fooled myself into thinking he'd leave her alone if she did it. She didn't want to die and it showed. Though her sobbing slowed down, he chose to terrorize her anyway.

He aimed the gun at Sasha's breast. "Time's up."

My arms moved a hair forward. "Wait!"

I'd promised Sasha months ago that I'd keep her alive. But he'd kill us if I didn't answer right, and he'd kill us if I did. To sell the lie I needed to pause for a moment to make it dramatic – nothing too long, or else it'd seem like I was thinking hard about it, which I wasn't.

"He has a house in the Heights." I gave him Peters' address and his cell phone number. Hopefully he would find him there to give us time to regroup. "Ping his location if you can't find him there."

"Good boy," he said before pulling the trigger.

I saw an orange blast flash in front of Iain. I held my breath until I realized Sasha hadn't moved. The bullet had passed through her and pierced the wall behind her.

With a move I didn't know she had, Sasha whipped her arm around Iain's elbow and twisted it. He dropped the gun and it clattered to the floor. "Thanks, girl."

"No problem, girl."

My blood. She still had her powers.

Rhapsody circled Iain and stomped forcefully on the back of his right knee. Once he knelt, she aimed the nozzle at his temple. "Let's do a little Q and A session before I blow your brains out."

Iain cursed her and said, "Blow my brains out? Like Cherish did? Let's not."

His mention of her old best friend wouldn't do him any favors. "How many bullets does this thing have in its clip anyway? Fifteen? Twelve?" In a quick motion, she shot Iain in the foot. "Ten, I guess. Why do you want Peters so bad?"

Iain grimaced from the pain. "Dead men don't answer questions," he said.

She fired another goshenite round into his other foot. He wobbled on his knees.

"Living ones do. That's why I shot you in the feet. Try again."

He grunted. "I'm a Collective legacy. Peters, or whatever he calls himself, is my *father*."

I should have known or guessed he and Peters were related. I bet whatever Kai whispered to him at the asylum had something to do with his abandoned son being out for blood. No wonder he gave up resurrecting his wife Diane when Kai arrived. Iain could've wanted to revenge kill her, too, though she was already technically dead.

Iain's face tightened into a smile. Then he laughed. Happy for a guy about to receive a bullet in the head. Small puddles of blood formed under his loafers.

Rhapsody smacked him hard with the pistol's handle. "Shut up."

His laughter waned to snickers. Deep in my gut I had a bad feeling. Debra called it my "spirit," the way God talked to people. I don't know about that, but even though I couldn't put my finger on it, I knew something was wrong.

Sasha waved her hand. "Forget him. Let's find a way out of here and get our families out."

"You're smarter than that. Where can they go where they can't find them? Who protects them from wackos like him and Jade – whoever else is out there? They'll come for those we love when they feel like it. Like with Ray and what happened to him. Debra and her neck. Our parents are prisoners. We have to get rid of these people, starting with him. Otherwise, we have no shot at ever having people we love."

Rhapsody was right. I thought about my dad and the guy I'd trapped in his car who burned to death – the blackness of the burnt skeleton and the car chassis. The screams of the running people from the Multiplex. What were the odds he'd planned another incident bigger and worse? All those bodies, their blood and his, would be on our heads. If I stand by and do nothing I might as well pull the trigger on all of them myself. And yet, I didn't blame her for wanting to off him.

"What if he set up another explosion? You shoot him before we find out and we'll never know. Don't..."

She retrained the gun against Iain's temple. "Done talking, Cap. Not your call."

Rhapsody's brown eyes narrowed. I couldn't look away. She'd never intentionally crossed this line before, which explained why the gun shook in her hand.

"*Do it*," Iain said. "This is what Jason already is, what you're meant to become – *all of you*. Superiors. Pull the trigger Rhapsody."

Her brief moment of hesitation was long enough for a gun to go off twice behind us. One of the shots grazed her left bicep. She winced and examined the cut in her suit.

Kai. She was back, and she had shape-shifted again.

Time slowed down for me. People who have had a life or death situation would understand. When Mom died. My first rage blackout where I'd charged Ray with a butcher knife in my hand. The car accident with Debra where I discovered my powers, the nuclear explosion of the provenance crystals, and the desert with King – one action, one decision could've turned each situation a different, deadly way.

Rhapsody whirled around and returned fire around the room, hitting nothing. "Stay down, both of you," she yelled over the blasts. "I got this."

Though we couldn't see Kai, the sound of return fire was unmistakable. The distraction was long enough for Iain to teleport out, I guessed, to go after his father and kill him. I don't think I ever rooted for Peters before, but I did now.

Rhapsody turned invisible and fired several more times in random directions. I detected a breeze – were there air vents in here I hadn't noticed before?

On her knees, Sasha slid a rolling table in front of us for cover. I ducked behind it with her and pulled at Rhapsody's leg.

"Save it!" Sasha yelled. "Concentrate on taking away her powers!"

Too late. The gun clicked. Rhapsody had run out of ammunition and had nothing to show for it.

She clumsily flopped to the floor behind the table and discarded the gun. Her quick, ragged breaths hissed through her teeth. Her gloved hand reached for mine and held it to her chest, where two bullets had entered her body. "Rip them out," she growled, "like a Band-Aid."

"Band-Aid," I repeated.

"Quick." She licked her dry lips and sucked in air.

Sasha didn't have a scarlet emerald. I had to be the one to do it. I focused the best I could. Bloody particles shot out between my fingers and into the ceiling. Her bleeding continued. I could've pulled one of her arteries or worse, and I'd have to disarm our attacker for her body to heal itself. That meant leaving her here.

"Go," she said, pushing me away with the little strength she had left. "Get the other one."

Desperation filled my voice. "Let me do what I do best."

I risked it and stood to my feet. Nobody was there. Nothing except for the bodies. It didn't make sense. "Where is she?"

Sasha peeked over the table and confirmed what I'd seen. "I don't know."

Rhapsody continued to groan and writhe on the crimson-streaked floor. "Don't…" she said in between her short breaths. "…let them…use…*Anibel.*"

Anibel? "Who's Anibel?"

"*Me.* First name…" she managed before a short coughing spell. "Birth name."

She was giving up. "All this time, I knew Rhapsody wasn't your first name."

My joke made her crack a smile even as she bled.

Sasha hushed her. "Save your strength. We're getting you out of here."

She'd lied. We didn't have an exit. She knew as well as I did that Rhapsody's life would end here soon no matter what. Still, I couldn't have anticipated what she did next. Using me for leverage, her arm tensed. She wanted my help to stand. I held her as she struggled.

With great effort, she said, "Face me…Leslie."

Selby sat upright on his stretcher, a wicked grin stretched across his lips.

CHAPTER FIFTEEN

Showdown with Selby

After Selby revealed himself, Rhapsody stopped moving. I read her mind. Last words? Something profane or funny? Did she love me?

What am I supposed to do? Be my freaking tour guide one last time.

Eight words came across my mind's eye in Rhapsody's voice. They weren't what I'd thought they'd be. But they were *everything*, and I think I understood what she wanted me to do.

I whispered over her face. "I promise not..." My chest ached. I couldn't finish my sentence.

I'd likely never hear her voice again, and I knew I'd think about breaking my promise to her, but I wouldn't, – even if it'd *kill me*.

In this moment, one thing mattered.

I lowered her body to the ground. "I'll stop this, make it right." My insides were on fire.

Selby zoomed to the other side of the metal table we'd been using for cover. I sprang to my feet and smashed a gaping hole through the center of it. Prying the jagged pieces apart, I tossed them to opposite sides of the room. "You're not leaving this room alive."

"Think so?" Selby zipped close to me. The full blast of his hot, stale breath fell on my face. "I can be...on the other side of the world by breakfast."

"Do it. I'll find you."

"You screwed up my brain, *Freak*. No way we're even. Took my folks, too!"

Technically I stopped him from murdering his parents twice – I didn't "take" them from him. I'd wiped away anything in his mind I thought triggered his homicidal tendencies. Obviously I missed a few things.

I cursed and swung a punch he easily dodged.

"Jason spared your life. He could've killed you!" Sasha cried. "Rhapsody was your friend."

He clawed at the mess of short red hair atop of his head. *"He* took my brain apart Sasha – my *brain*. He put back – parts, missing pieces. He..."

I swung again, this time for his face, with intent to knock his head off his body. Even though he talked and moved much slower, I hit nothing but air. He'd sped away to a corner of the room and then lapped the laboratory so fast it blew Iain's silver instruments to the floor and hurt my eyes. His brain might be watered down scrambled eggs but he had superpowers, and a fraction of what he used to be was still way faster than I was.

"You know the feeling...no matter what you do, you're always too slow." His speech stopped and staggered like there was a scratch on the DVD of his mind.

"It's not like I had a manual." My pulse quickened. "I had two choices: fix you or end you."

His voice built in volume. "Not broken. Not yours to 'fix' or 'end'."

"You murdered thirty people," Sasha screamed at him. "You ruined my life, my body! I can't have kids!"

Selby paused before he responded to Sasha, "Should've taken the chance to end me then."

Nothing else he said could have been truer. Altering his brain didn't work.

He had to be *eliminated*.

Selby turned to me. "Taking me out is a lot harder than it looks." He cracked his neck. "Iain couldn't do it. You can?"

Angry and tired of all his halting speech, I flew directly at Selby and missed him by a mile. I crashed headfirst into the wall and hit the metal foundation behind it. People act like it's so easy for an ADHD kid to control impulses, but it was torture to try.

In a blur, he yanked me free and threw me to the floor. What followed was a flurry of solid, extremely fast punches into my face and midsection. I didn't feel the first ones. The armor in the bodysuit was strong, after all. But the last dozen shook my insides until my abdomen and lungs ached.

Hunched over in the fetal position, I couldn't catch a breath. Invisible knives stabbed at my chest and my right side. I needed a break. What was Sasha doing? Standing there and watching me get my butt handed to me?

Breathing hard from exhaustion himself, Selby hit me with a kick to the face. My jaw crunched against his foot. A copper taste trickled inside my mouth. I had enough awareness left to pull off my mask and spit, surprised that a broken tooth didn't follow.

"You can't kill me either."

He kicked me in the gut for good measure, which didn't help. A normal kick.

A headache raged across my brain, too much for me to concentrate. The pounding and burning in my ankle returned. My powers had dropped out at the worst possible time. Apparently, so had his. From the arch of his eyebrows he'd been caught off guard by it as well.

Favoring his left side, Selby dragged me through piles of crumbled drywall and white powder. "Don't need powers for this, Sasha." He pulled me to a sitting position and positioned himself behind me with his right hand clamped down on my forehead.

He wanted to snap my neck. Like King had done to Debra, I imagined.

We faced Sasha. Her expression was a mix of pity, fear and terror for me. She reached out her hand and offered to drop the goshenite she'd used to remove his powers.

"Don't!" she yelled. "Let him go."

"Gimme a good reason."

"I'll do…whatever. Just let him live."

His voice raised in pitch. *"Anything?"*

My stomach turned. The same offer she'd given him when he'd stabbed her before, except he didn't remember it. I'd wiped that memory away. Now, there's no telling what he'd do to her without restrictions. I wouldn't let her sacrifice herself for *me.* Again. Not to him or anyone else. Sasha gave up her fertility. Debra almost died. I'd find a way out of this.

"No," I groaned.

Sasha's shoulders dropped. "Don't kill him."

In the back of my mind, I'd always questioned Sasha's affection for me. At first I thought it was a dare from Asia Jackson or a joke. After that, it could have been the green emerald she'd wanted me to give her. I'd never have a doubt after today.

He chuckled and licked his lips. "You and me – we'll have fun...*after.*"

This was the end. I wouldn't have to remember my parents, Courtney, Camuto, and Hughes. I'd see them soon. There were questions I wanted the answers to – like why me?

Why did I get these powers in the first place?

My heart thumped double time. I *had* to do this on my own, whatever it took.

Selby whipped my neck to the side.

But I wasn't dead.

To convince him I'd died, I fell facedown onto the tile. The warm, slick wetness covering the tile soaked my cheek. I ignored it to make the sell. In reality, vitality roared throughout my veins and limbs. My body, including my ankle and shoulder, had never felt better than it did right now.

Sasha exploded into sobs. "You promised..." was all she said about me.

My heart swelled. Any response would blow my cover.

Selby's weight pressed between my shoulder blades – *did he just step on me?* Fighting not to react, I cracked my left eyelid. He'd grabbed Sasha by the forearm and yanked her over to the metal door – the one she'd found a while ago. I'd suspected it was the only way out of here. She'd said it was made of thick metal. Punching through it wasn't the answer. I'd have to fight every natural instinct I had, but that's what it would take to do this – *to win.* Control. All this time it's what Peters had been telling me to learn.

Timing was everything. Once I got Sasha to safety he'd have his powers back – *I couldn't take away his powers and keep mine, could I?* A wrong move by either one of us and she could get hurt or worse. And I'd promised to keep her alive. *Whatever it cost.*

In a fit of anger, Sasha yelled "I hate you!" and elbowed Selby in his bad ribs. As he recovered, a metallic glint sparked in the far left corner of my eye. *A sharp metal instrument – his calling card.*

That was my opening.

Before he could stab her, I sprung up from the floor and slammed into his back. The blade tumbled from his hand. We crashed flush against the exit door. I pried my face and left shoulder away from the dent I'd created.

Selby's body from the head to the knees was imprinted in the metal. I grabbed him by the waist of his shorts, whipped him into the closest wall and followed it with several punches to the face. His body had a degree of invulnerability which explained why my first punch hadn't caved his face in. Even with that going for him, smashing into such a dense surface and getting beaten up by a superhuman had to hurt.

Hitting him felt *good*. I pummeled him, thinking of his mother, who must've been too scared to protect him from his abusive father, and the group of cemetery mourners whose necks he'd broken. He didn't fight me off. Or he couldn't. Made no difference to me.

I thought about Rhapsody, and I swung at him again and again to show him the same amount of mercy he'd given her.

The picture of the burnt skeleton, the innocent man I'd killed inside of his car, popped into my head. I stopped hitting him, and I secured my left hand at Selby's throat. Cocking my right arm, I wiggled my gloved fingers. Heat flowed to my fist. My glove was covered with his blood. I'd been pounding on Selby for a while, but I hadn't focused my energy on delivering a killing blow. My next punch would end his life.

Since we'd gotten superpowers, when and when not to take lives had been an issue for us. Before I killed King, none of us had taken another person's life. He was close to two hundred years old – all I did was remove his ability to live long. In my mind, that was different from murdering someone in the prime of life.

What other choice did we have? Eventually we'd have to make this call on our enemies. Eventually was today, right now.

"You have to die," I said out loud.

"After all that, he's still alive?" The end of Sasha's question lingered from over my shoulder.

I could hear it in the tremor of her voice. He'd embarrassed her and assaulted her. She'd never achieve her dream of living a normal life and becoming a mother, at least not the way that she wanted to be.

Because of *him*.

She *wanted* him to be dead, for *me* to have killed him. I answered her. "Yes."

"What are you waiting for?"

I didn't want to admit it out loud, but I'd executed enough people as it was – David King, six people in Orizaba and the stranger in the car. I'd only tried to commit one of those. The others were accidents but on my hands regardless. "He's slaughtered so many people."

Selby's eyes rolled, as if to say, "So what? I'll slaughter more."

"You don't deserve to live," I said. Was it my call to make?

My hesitation gave Selby enough time to recover. He vibrated his body so much that I almost lost my grip. The first thing he'd do is eliminate Sasha since he couldn't get rid of me.

That wasn't going to happen. I'd promised her.

I yelled and squeezed his neck with my last bit of strength until I heard a *crack.*

Then Sasha put a bullet into his forehead.

CHAPTER SIXTEEN

I'm really sick of the ground moving

After it was done Sasha dropped the smoking firearm. I crushed it beneath the heel of my boot and stomped its remaining goshenite rounds into dust.

We'd lost more people in the past hour than I wanted to count because of Iain. Because of the gun I'd just pulverized. I wanted to be alone, by myself, to sit on top of a downtown building somewhere.

No way. Not yet. Not while our families were MIA while Iain was still alive and breathing with my blood in his veins.

"Got an idea," I said to Sasha. "Set your Geiger counter down a few rads and follow my lead."

We searched the room for leftover prisms. When I found some, I smashed them with my foot. Sasha knelt down and collected goshenite, scarlet emerald and heliodor in addition to the green emerald she'd already had for herself.

Once her hands were full of multicolored jewels she handed them over to be destroyed. "Here."

I crushed them into dust with my hands. We followed this unspoken system until we'd found them all including the last two – a green emerald and a morganite. A year and a half ago it had all started with these. Cherish Watkins, Rhapsody's schizophrenic best friend, had stolen a bracelet with a pink morganite jewel.

Together, the girls discovered the provenance green emerald in Reject High's basement. Then Rhapsody showed it to me. The rest was history, and here we were.

I clenched my fist over them, preparing to squeeze the gems into nothing, when the room shook.

"Earthquake?" she asked me.

The lab instruments rattled a discordant tune. Being raised on the west coast, our instincts told us to dive under a table. We held out our arms to steady ourselves instead until the tremor stopped.

We paused, breathing, waiting. The earth moved again. *I'm really sick of it doing that.* The flickering fluorescent lights distracted me. I'd been in an earthquake before. I chain cursed, my pulse pounded, all of that. But the weird thing was the shifting came from *above* us, not beneath us.

This wasn't an earthquake. "Not an earthquake. Something is shaking the house."

Sasha peeled back my fingers and took the green emerald. I smashed the morganite – there's no good that could have come from that. She dropped the prism into Esteban's pocket.

"Are you nuts?" I asked her.

A third tremor almost knocked Esteban and his brothers from their tables. "Wasn't this your original plan?" she shot back.

Was he dead? Brain damaged? Did Iain remove Esteban's adrenal gland? I wasn't around when the aquamarine exploded, so bringing him back to life wasn't an option, even as a last resort. The earth quaked again. The ceiling cracked end to end. Pieces of ceiling dropped around us.

Another strong tremor or two and we'd be buried alive. I eyed the spot where Rhapsody lay. Her body was gone. I'd wondered if Sasha had noticed.

"Hey!" I finally said. "We've gotta go!"

"Not yet!"

She turned her back towards me and started messing with whatever was on the chrome table next to the stretcher. In a swift move, she jammed a thin needle into Esteban's left thigh. A second later he shot up to a sitting position and teleported out then back to where he was. The sulfur cloud's residue smelled awful but not any worse than the air we'd been inhaling.

Wild-eyed and breathing hard, he gripped the metal rails on the edge of his stretcher. He swung his legs over the side, set foot on the tile and eased back into the top of his bodysuit.

"You. How?"

Sasha's lips curled into a sly smile. She held up the hypodermic needle. "Iain wanted you to live through it. Makes sense he'd have Epi pens and prisms nearby to bring you back."

"But not to revive my brothers." Esteban called Iain a three syllable name in Spanish Rhapsody used when she'd gotten hurt, which is how I knew it was a curse word.

Sasha clasped her hand around his forearm. "We need your help to get out of here."

Refusing to look at his brothers' dead bodies, he zipped up. "Iain got the drop on me, knocked me out, put me in the control room. I can pop out there or to the cells. I don't even know what state we're in to teleport out."

I jumped in. "Oregon. A city called Medford."

"Never been to Oregon. Besides, Jason, I'd teleport myself into a wall before I'd help you."

I zapped his powers just enough so that he stayed upright long enough to hear me. "You'd kill us all because you got dumped? You don't get it, do you?"

He bared his teeth and leaned in. Spit particles flew out of his mouth. "No, *you* don't get it. My brothers are dead. Your blood killed them, right? Doesn't that mean you killed them? What don't I understand about that?"

I blurted out the truth, "No one ever told them to drink my blood."

He cursed at me. The next tremor brought down more ceiling. White plaster, tan wood fragments, and tufts of pink insulation thundered onto the floor surface.

Sasha pleaded with him. "Help us, Esteban. Save our families. Please."

Esteban clenched his jaw. He was unconvinced. "What about my family? I've lost everything."

Tears brimmed my eyes. I let go of him and eyed a pile of rubble where Rhapsody's body had been. "Rhapsody's dead."

From the erratic way his eyes moved, he'd didn't know. "No. No, no, no, no. That wasn't supposed to happen."

Shoving him in the arm, Sasha yelled, "What'd you think, huh?"

"I don't know." He dropped his chin to his chest.

Enraged and shaking, Sasha screamed at him. "How was drawing him a map to our parents going to turn out, Esteban? He'd become immortal, you'd do your little passive aggressive pouty whining thing and hurt us all, then we'd all go home and play Xbox together? Are you serious right now?"

"Nobody's coming out of this clean," I said in a calm, steady voice – one that even amazed me. "Not Sasha, not *me*. We have to stop him. Or they'll be no one left. We can argue about this later, all right? Do the right thing."

The laboratory rumbled. We didn't have much time, but then again, we never did.

Sasha replicated herself once, and Original Sasha took charge. "There." She motioned to the metal door she said I shouldn't be able to punch through. "It's dense not thick. Open it. He'll need to see wherever it leads to extract them."

How does she know there's something on the other side? There was no time to analyze. I rushed over to it and started punching. For me, it was like everything else I shouldn't have been able to do. I shouldn't have passed seventh grade, shouldn't have avoided jail or juvenile detention, or shouldn't have survived a nuclear explosion. *But I did.*

I remembered that and swung at the metal with everything I had. The entire laboratory shook from wall to wall – this time because of me. I'd done that. I did it again and again, over and over in the same spot. The metal clanged against my hand and gave way in the center. Sasha and Esteban knew better than to stop me or tell me to hurry up. I had this.

I grabbed a handful of dented metal and pulled. It scraped against the floor setting until I'd pulled it free and propped it against the wall. A gust of cool wind rushed into the chamber. The fresh air relieved my lungs and dried my damp skin.

As we suspected, the laboratory was deep underground. The tunnel leading away from it opened at the end into the night.

Sasha ran over to me as the world crumbled around us. "Proper funerals and flowers," I said in no particular direction. "Once the dust settles, and this is all over."

I looked back at Esteban, and we made the sign of the cross over our chests. I pointed to where Rhapsody had been. "And don't forget my father's body down there," I reminded him.

He keyed the light on his bodysuit and vanished in a puff of green sulfur smoke.

Esteban still held a grudge against me. *Did that mean he wouldn't save Aunt Dee and Zachary? Would he leave Ray's body down there?* I didn't trust him – it was a gamble on my part – but Sasha did. When they were dating she must've seen a part of him that I hadn't.

She and I entered the tunnel, which tilted on a slight curve at first and then became steeper going up the further we'd traveled it. The tremors became less violent as we jogged it. Whatever was rocking it didn't move and we'd been distancing ourselves from it.

Iain didn't know we were still alive, our families were on their way to being safe, and we were on the move. A wave of dank mud landed on our heads. After the second time it happened, I brushed off my head and face and masked up.

"I'm gonna need a good wash and perm after this," Sasha said before masking up herself.

The passage had to be a half mile long or more – I hadn't kept track. We stopped once the tunnel curved straight up. I tilted my head back. White stars twinkled in the midnight black sky. Now that I had light, I placed my hands on Sasha's waist, flew out into the open, and set us down on the grass. We were on the flat back side of Iain's expansive property, so far back that the mansion would've been a spot in the distance – if it weren't on fire.

"You're going to kill him," was the first thing Sasha said to me.

Numbness crept inside of my gut. She hadn't said it as a question or left room for doubt – it was a statement of fact.

Goes without saying, I thought to myself. "Yeah."

This is what Hughes meant when he'd told me about my concept of right and wrong changing. Capital punishment wasn't my bag. Now it had to be. Letting Iain live meant far more people would pay the price, like Ray had. He'd said he's wanted a cure for his MS, but he'd left out mass genocide and the revenge on his father.

I knew it had to be done. Regardless of whether or not I wanted to be involved. I might be the only one to do it. I held out my hand, and if she took it, I'd know she'd be joining me. My father died in an empty room because of Iain. And Esteban's brothers were gone – he'd want in on it, too.

How many other deaths was he responsible for?

Sasha slowly reached forward and placed her fingers into mine. They trembled enough for me to notice. Just as I started to let them go and leave her behind, she squeezed my hand. *"Wait."*

My body language must have said what I was thinking, which was *wait for what?*

She pulled her mask away and played with the hair dangling in front of her face. "The Laundry List says that I have trouble expressing my emotions...*feeling* my emotions, really...because it hurts so much. It's true. At least for me, it is."

I had no idea what she was talking about or what "The Laundry List" was or why she was talking about it now. Sounded important. Must be important considering the way her voice kept trailing off as she talked about it.

"Okay," I said. My stomach churned. I was mindful of the inferno in the distance.

Sasha bit her bottom lip. "Thing is...I've loved you from a distance for a *long time*...I didn't say anything not for any other reason other than...I was afraid...afraid of what my feelings meant.

"I didn't think you'd accept me for me," she continued. "I thought you'd want a girl who hadn't had...was a vir...I don't know. It's stupid. But I had to say something now. I had to let you know before we go in there. In case we don't come out."

Weird. Rhapsody, too, had revealed her feelings for me under the threat of imminent death. It was understandable. I had feelings for Sasha, too, and my thoughts froze every time I tried to describe them, even to myself. Different from what I'd experienced being in love with Rhapsody. Powerful just the same but confusing and impossible for me to talk about.

"Okay."

"Basically…for what it's worth, I love you, Jason Champion. I'm ride or die," she said before pausing a beat. "Too soon?"

I shook my head. Not too soon.

CHAPTER SEVENTEEN

it burns

I'd taken Rhapsody's invisibility and ghosting powers for granted while she had them. We'd slip in and out of places without anyone knowing we were coming or had been there.

Without them, Sasha and I had to be more creative about our flying and landing.

Sasha pinched my arm hard enough to get my attention. "Quick," she shouted in the whipping wind. "Trees."

Right. Land behind the flaming trees that look like giant burning stalks of broccoli. Made sense. The clouds of choking blackness helped mask our approach. I set us down in a clearing...if you could call it that anymore. Orange crackling flames formed random patterns in the well-landscaped blackened grass.

Iain had set this fire, and he didn't plan for anything to be left.

My insides tightened as I kicked away the torched branches littering our path. Flakes of gray ash popped and kicked up into the air. I waved away what I could to keep it away from Sasha, but there was no shielding her from this level of destruction. The heat seared the outside of my suits and cooked the padding. Meaning we had to get out of here for Sasha's sake. She wasn't invincible, and I could still suffocate from the smoke.

"Jason!" Her shrill tone said she was hurt and scared. I needed to get her to safety soon.

Easing forward, I focused my concentration on shielding her from falling tree limbs and removing the powers of anyone in the area besides us at the same time. Every once in a while, I'd trip over a bundle of flaming wood and leaves. The rear of the stone-faced mansion came into view. Things were moving fast – I had to think, see everything. A momentary lapse in concentration and he'd have an opening to attack us.

The humid air heavy with the scent of burning wood kept us from detecting sulfur. *Where is he?* Off my powers, my chest would've hurt from my quickening heartbeat. I strained to hear past the rustle of the flames licking at the trees.

He'd gotten the drop on me in the laboratory, but this time, even if he teleported next to me, we'd disable him as soon as he appeared.

Then, I'd *have* to kill him. Selby had shown me that – we'd have no other option.

"You escaped. Impressive." His voice came from behind us.

I turned around to attack Iain. He clocked me in the chin with a solid, heavy object I'd never seen coming.

My head violently whipped backwards and the impact sent me crashing through the back of the house. I rolled across the floor and into an empty room. I'd landed face down onto the plush dark red carpet next to burnt bodies.

The one closest to me had small flickers of yellow light decorating his burnt skin. His back rose and fell in an irregular pattern. *Still alive.* The lids of his green eyes were beet red.

Peters.

I hadn't landed here by accident. Iain had put me here to see. He'd found his father, taken his heliodor, and tortured him to an unrecognizable state.

I'd be next.

Suffering leading to a painful end -- this is exactly his brand of inflicting death. Lifting my head, I saw others lined up next to one another. No way to tell their identities. I didn't want to ask or to think about it. To guess meant to admit in my brain that more people I'd cared about had fallen victim to this clown -- a man whom I'd given my blood and made invincible.

Iain appeared at the doorway just as I'd gotten to my feet. "Welcome to the house that Jeffrey Peters built," he said.

I sapped his powers. Without them, his multiple sclerosis should've drained his mobility but didn't. He didn't sink to both knees like I thought he would. Weird. I froze him in place anyway. Small wisps of emerald smoke trailed from his body as he tried teleporting.

Breathing heavily, he huffed, "Can't hold it forever, *Cap*. Pointless to try."

I hadn't had a low dose Adderall pill in forever. It was all I could do not to be distracted by the heat, the biting scent of sulfur and wood smoke and a dying Peters. Since he'd knocked me off my feet, I'd lost track of Sasha, too. She was on her own out there. Would her brain and cloning abilities be enough? Had to be. Hoping for the best was all I could do at this point.

"You're right." I approached him and grabbed his throat. With one squeeze, I'd snap it like I'd done to Selby. I'd regretted it right after letting go but not for a second since.

"Going to *murder* me?" he sneered. "Like the man in the Jupiter? We're *killers*. Embrace it."

I replayed what I remembered about the man. *Burning body inside of a charred sedan.* The next thing I knew, I'd squeezed my fingers around thin air.

Iain was gone.

Back on my knees the air was somewhat breathable. Peters' eyes communicated his thoughts. "Go," he'd managed to growl.

Time was running out. "You," I coughed out. *"Them."*

His look said it all. They're all dead. He'd be dead soon. Stopping Iain was all that mattered.

I'd have to find him first. No easy task when it's a teleporter.

A blizzard of emerald colored teleportation clouds formed around me. The sulfur fumes combined with the hot air and smoke were overwhelming. Standing to confront him, I choked again. My throat tightened. *Gotta get out of here.*

Iain solidified long enough to hit me. I'd struck at him, too – or of where he *had* been -- and I missed. To disable his abilities, I had to concentrate. My head ached from trying. I couldn't do it with him vanishing every couple half seconds.

Iain swore with his next few swings. "Give up and die!" he sneered.

Not much time passed before I got tired of missing, and I gave up to let him land free shots. I didn't even try to block him – it was pointless.

He wanted me to die. I was tired of *fighting* but not tired of *living*.

Peters charged me with stopping his son. Trouble was I had no idea *how*. How do you defeat someone you can't catch or depower? Brute force wouldn't do it. He didn't have ADHD like I did. I'd lose focus and he wouldn't. He'd use my lapses in concentration to do away with me and then murder everyone else.

Frustrated, I asked Peters out loud. Every other breath I took was interrupted by a cough. "How?"

Peters groaned and stared straight ahead, his eyelids fluttering every few seconds.

In the movies, the guy who gives the advice gives a piece of key information before he dies. All I got from Peters was a phlegm-filled breath. The least he could have done is advise me by saying, *"Control,* Mr. Champion" one last time.

Control was the opposite strategy I'd used in most of my fights. I'd given in to my anger and let the rage I had inside of me take over. The first time I'd fought Selby, I blacked out. The next thing I knew, he was bleeding on the ground. And Ryan Cain -- Principal Rush made me watch the black and white surveillance footage of that battle. He landed more blows than I did, but once I blacked out, it became totally one sided. Like a wild animal, I tore at him. I'd ripped his shirt at the collar, scratched at his skin and then finally, I broke his jaw.

Rage and chaos were my best tools. Staying in control meant the opposite of that. Defeat Iain *without raging?* Couldn't happen. Everything he did was to push me.

I screamed myself hoarse, repeating it as if he could've heard me. "Show yourself!"

He reappeared across from me in the burning room with Sasha. Parts of the ceiling dropped down sending red cinders floating through the boiling hot air. He didn't need a weapon, but Sasha's stiff body language communicated he'd had something at her back. She wasn't helpless by any means, but he was invulnerable and she wasn't. He'd have been smart enough to take away her prisms. That explained why she hadn't used the goshenite crystal to remove his powers.

She had her mask on, but I could read her mind.

"What are you doing?" I didn't say it out loud, but I rambled on the inside.

"Don't," she'd said to me through her thoughts. "I've got this."

"I'll figure it out. He'll kill you."

"Trust me."

Whatever her plan was, she didn't want to share. The last plan failed, and Selby stabbed her.

Not this time.

There had to be something to counteract him. Hughes had once said something about the blood, *my blood...* no, that wasn't it, was it? He'd laid against a tree and withered, he and Courtney. He'd sung a hymn. Hughes used to be a slave and slaves sang in code to send

messages and warnings, right? What was it about –
power? Blood? My blood and its power? Strength?

Whatever. I forgot.

Courtney had the ability to see the future, and her last
words were "It'll all work out" in the end. We'd lost too
much so far not to make an attempt.

The mask did one thing well – shield my eyes from
the smoke. With a flourish of his arm, Iain yelled over the
ruckus. "Have to burn it down!"

I didn't want to know, and I didn't care, but I needed
time to figure it out. "Why?"

He coughed. Invulnerability wasn't all it was cracked
up to be. "Foundation is rotten. Have to tear
down...rebuild...with us. This world can be great..."

"You rehearse that every night?" I yelled back at him.

When we'd unearthed the provenance emerald, I'd
told Peters, "Power corrupts and absolute power
corrupts absolutely." Iain started off wanting to cure his
MS, but it all changed. The ability to do anything you
want anytime you want to will do that.

"You're in my way."

"What do you want to do? Tear down, rebuild,
whatever – you're nuts."

He thrust the object in his hand into Sasha's back. I
held my breath, waiting for her to drop.

Sasha didn't flinch, collapse, or scream.

The next thing I knew, she'd tossed Iain past me and
rolling into the backyard.

How'd she do that?

She pointed down. "Grab his pops. Don't think Peters
is dead yet."

I knelt down and threw Peters over my shoulder. Taking one last glance at the other bodies to make sure they wasn't people we knew, I followed her out of the building and hopped down out of the makeshift exit – a pile of burnt debris, bricks and wood framing.

Two red Medford fire department trucks, one to my left, the other at our right, and a white ambulance had been totaled and turned upside down. Still in their uniforms, firefighters and paramedics lay motionless on the grass with their hoses strewn around them. I didn't see any police cars. Didn't mean there weren't any. No telling what was at the front of the house or the sides.

Helicopter blades steadily chopped overhead. Spotlights shined wide swaths of light on the ground near us. *News helicopters.* I could see more in the distance. *Great, now there's that.* We'd have an audience soon.

"So you took my…"

Sasha briefly showed me her face. Thick black scars covered her once beautiful complexion "Yep," she said before covering up again. "Nevermind that. Don't lose track of Iain."

I'd already lost him until I saw a figure move out of the light. "When did you…?"

She unfastened her suit and reached inside of its pocket. Iain had left her with a heliodor crystal – he knew she couldn't harm him with it. She placed it in Peters' blackened pants pocket. "Two vials of blood water next to the Epi pen. Thought I might need 'em."

And you didn't think you'd die because of it? "Why aren't you…?"

"No time."

Iain would recover soon, and he'd be coming for us.

Sasha replicated herself more times than I'd ever seen before. There had to be close to twenty clones at the ready. Iain downed a vial of blood water and moaned as it took effect.

The army of clones converged on him. Original Sasha and I ran over to assist. When he'd hit one clone, two or three more would swarm him. He teleported further away to thin out the herd and while some of them fell for it, most of the others did not.

Original Sasha held me back when I wanted to step in. "Not yet."

My eyebrows raised. *Wait? What for? Didn't she hear the sirens?*

I watched the fight continue for about a minute more underneath the choppers' spotlights. Original Sasha leaned over and panted like she'd run a long distance marathon though she hadn't moved an inch. Iain hadn't been teleporting with the same frequency, either. Soon, neither of them moved much.

Original Sasha let me go. "Now!"

CHAPTER EIGHTEEN

what might have been

In a blur I attacked Iain. When my fists didn't make contact with his face or body, they struck the earth around us hard enough to shake it. Thanks to the overhead spotlights, my head cast a shadow over his. No way to tell if he was bleeding so I kept punching.

"To your knees!" a man said over a loudspeaker. "Hands in the air."

Not the first time I'd heard a policeman say that to me, so I sank to my knees. Iain rolled from beneath me and stood. Sasha held her hands up in surrender, but she kept Iain from using his abilities. Armed men had surrounded us in a circle. A constellation of red laser beams dotted our chests and, I guessed, our backs, too. They didn't know bullets wouldn't hurt me.

Reminding myself not to be afraid of being shot – though I hated being shot – I warned them.

"Cut it out!" I screamed until my lungs burned. Then I remembered what I'd meant to say – a phrase I'd heard cops yell to one another, at least on TV. "Stand down!"

They acted as if we were on a movie set and somebody other than the director called "cut." What did a sixteen-year-old kid in an armored morph suit know about this? Plenty, it turned out. I'd flown across America and helped save the world. *Twice.*

How can I do it again?

I had green emerald, scarlet emerald, goshenite, heliodor, and morganite radiation in my blood. I'd found with proper focus I was able to channel the abilities each gem gave me. Meaning morganite forces its wearer to obey his/her deepest desires, so couldn't I do that to them by *thinking it?* Most red-blooded men on earth would sprint away from the level twenty crap going on out here, wouldn't they?

Whatever the arresting officers' deepest desire was at the moment, I willed them to do it. All except one ran from the scene. I turned my attention to the news helicopter pilots and forced them to land near the tunnel to the cells, far away from the fire.

Iain winked and pointed a finger gun at the lone officer remaining. "Billy," he said as if he was singing lyrics to a song. "Don't be a hero. Don't be a fool with your life."

Unamused, the officer fired a cluster of rounds at Iain's midsection.

The shells zipped from their original trajectory and flew deep into the middle of the shooter's chest. Busy with redirecting the helicopters to safety, I couldn't stop them all. Neither could Sasha.

He dropped into a heap on a patch of grass.

"*This's* how it'll be," he said to me. "You'll always be a step behind. You'll stop. Hesitate to do what's necessary in the moment. That's why you're so easy to defeat."

I wasn't a soldier, trained killer, or psychopath. "King couldn't do it."

He chuckled. "His mistake. He used Debra like a poker chip. Should've killed her."

Sasha chimed in. "What about Peters? He couldn't do it, either."

The mention of his father drove him over the edge. He broke Sasha's hold, teleported behind her, and he twisted her head at a sick angle.

In response, Sasha rolled her neck, which should've broken but didn't, thanks to my blood. She stepped back and flung him over her back onto the ground. With her boot at his throat, she said. "He's not teleporting anywhere. It's now or never."

Iain gurgled and choked from the pressure she'd put on his neck. We'd beat him a little too easily, hadn't we? *Shouldn't it be way harder than this?* "Something's wrong."

"This is it," she said to me. "We have the advantage. Like he said, don't hesitate."

I felt a warning, or a sign, deep in my belly.

There was someone behind us.

"Castling."

It was Peters, the elderly version, with skin blackened by soot not burns and wrinkled beyond recognition. His torched denim shirt and khaki pants hung from his slender frame. He hobbled forward at a slow but steady pace. "Castling," he'd repeated. "Whatever that is, it's not my son."

Welker had said that word "castling" to me once, I had no idea what it meant. One day, when it popped up in my brain again, I google searched it – it's a move in chess where the king, the most important piece in the game, trades places with a rook, one of the less important players.

I pointed down. "Jade."

"What?" Sasha increased the intensity of her powers to strip Jade of the ability to shapeshift. Sure enough, "Iain" morphed into Jade. *When did they switch places?*

I had to know. "You didn't find Hughes, did you?"

Jade grabbed Sasha's boot and croaked, "Grave was dug up. You lied to me."

Iain had moved Hughes' body from its grave. Wouldn't surprise me if he'd cremated it and spread the ashes.

Sasha locked her foot down on Jade's neck. "He let you go because he'd moved Hughes before you even thought about digging him up. He's playing us all."

"Where is he?" I asked her.

She pointed up and to the far right of the compound. "There. Over the trees. He's waiting for you."

I nodded to Peters – he'd have to take care of Jade – and we flew in the direction she'd indicated.

Over the trees was an open area. We landed in the midst of scattered bodies. *Esteban. Joyce.* Aunt Dee, Zachary, Ruby, and Wesley were unaccounted for. There was no time for us to grieve. Sasha unmasked and knelt over Joyce's body to kiss her face. "When he shows up..." Sasha steadied her shaking voice. "I want a piece of him."

Of course Iain showed up to take credit for his work. Before he could say something ridiculous, I attacked him. With every swing, rage overwhelmed my brain.

He'd teleport behind me, beside me...it didn't matter. I'd lost it. My inability to hone in on one thought, one action at a time – actually *helped me* adjust to his movements. He fought back, but his punches were like annoying flies to me. I knew they wouldn't hurt. I stayed still when he hit me. One punch caused the bones of his right hand to shatter against my face. He screamed and hunched over in pain. My blood's effects were wearing off.

Control. All this time, I'd thought Peters meant I was supposed to *stay* in control. He meant I had to *lose it,* and by losing it, get it? ADHD was a strength not a weakness?

I couldn't waste time or hesitate. Once the powers my blood gave her completely drained out or his invulnerability wore off, whichever came first – I'd have to kill him.

That moment had arrived.

Thick trails of crimson oozed from the corner of Iain's mouth and dribbled down his chin. He hadn't suffered enough for everything. I didn't know how to make him pay other than to stop him, and the one method to ensure it was to snuff out his life.

Iain curled on the ground still nursing his broken hand. "You know how this ends!"

Sasha wound up her leg and delivered a kick to his right side. From this angle it was impossible to tell for sure – she'd probably bruised his ribs. "Not stalling," she said matter-of-factly while sending another kick to the same spot. "Not today."

He resorted to threats. "Esteban's *dead*," he gasped. "I won't tell. Go ahead, get rid of me. You'll *never* find them. *Ever.*"

My heart dropped, but I steeled myself. I'd search every inch of this state, every state, top to bottom from alley to homes and storefronts if I had to. No more innocent blood would flow if I could help it. "Whatever. You're done."

Green wisps rose from his body as he writhed in agony. Sasha's hold on him was slipping. I had to make a move soon.

"Killing me isn't a black and white issue, is it? You're a boy, ill-suited for *godhood*."

I didn't remember much from the night I'd spent drinking with Hughes, but he'd warned me. Regular people laws don't really apply to me anymore. I had to rely on my own sense of right and wrong. Killing him might be wrong in one sense, but I'd done far more good with the year or so I'd had powers than he had in his entire life.

"Jason." Sasha said my name like it hurt her to pronounce it.

"*You don't deserve to be this,*" he rambled. "You don't even *want* it. You want to be 'normal'. Marry a nice girl, Rhapsody even, settle down and have kids and a dog. That's what you deserve. That's what you want."

My head ached. He was right. A part of me craved normalcy because it'd been years since I had it. I don't know about marriage or kids, and I hated most breeds of dogs.

But the mention of Rhapsody made my chest tighten. Memories came flooding back. *The scent of her flowery perfume. Her sarcasm. No, the way she touched me. How her skin felt against mine, and the touch of her lips, and the way she said my name, and she loved me.*

"Kill me, and you'll *become* me," he warned. "Everything you want will slip from your reach! You won't..."

I ignored Iain's words and struck him as hard as I could, instantly killing him.

He didn't have a chance to survive – I'd left no doubt about that. Only my heartbeat and the hiss of my own breathing echoed in my ears. Sasha rushed to my side, shouting and pointing. A field full of vests with "POLICE" emblazoned in white capital letters swarmed around us in riot gear. The circle grew tighter. She yelled again, wrapped her arms around my waist and squeezed.

Without much thought for a final destination, we escaped into the sky.

By morning, the remains of Iain's entire mansion were cordoned off as a crime scene. The bodies would have to be identified before we'd receive phone calls about Joyce. I dropped Sasha off at her house and waited for her to shower and get dressed. Too self-conscious to sit on the furniture, I stood up the whole hour it took her, nodding off every once in a while. In the corner of the room, a half full bottled water sat on a table next to the lamp. I'd seen Joyce's brandy on the same table. I took it as a sign she'd managed to kick the habit before she died.

Sasha came downstairs in a pair of black yoga pants and a multicolored top. "Sorry," she said. Her eyes were fatigued and full of sorrow. "Had trouble getting clean."

I understood and said nothing else.

Before the sun rose we swung by my place. After digging out the extra keys from beneath the mat, in the flower pot on the porch, and taped to the back of the mailbox, I opened the door and keyed the alarm. Debra was curled up in her recliner with a tan quilt draped over her. Even with her bulky black neck brace, she looked peaceful and rested. Relief washed over me. She'd made it back from one of the safe houses and didn't even know about her missing son and best friend.

For today, right now, it had to be enough.

I washed my body until no more black water pooled at my feet and the scent of death disappeared. The aroma of the soap overtook the stink of death on my body, but I still smelled it. I'd remember its awful stench for as long as I lived. Because of the radiation I'd absorbed, my lifespan might be a lot longer than I'd thought it would be.

I dressed, set the alarm, snuck back out of my house and met Sasha in the backyard.

Hungry and exhausted, we flew back to Medford and stopped at a nearby coffeehouse for a dozen bagels and a jolt of caffeine. Then we took a yellow cab to the mansion's street and walked up to the back of the field near the end of the tunnel. We were far enough away from the scorched building to avoid detection.

Blackened trunks stuck up from the ground as reminders of what was once there.

We hid behind one of the largest ones and took turns sneaking peeks at the action.

Sasha stared down at the white lid of her coffee cup. "Miss her yelling at me already."

In a way, I'd miss Joyce, too. "I know."

"Your parents get married, have a kid, stay together long enough to screw you up, and – she could've at least stuck around to finish the job."

Both of my parents were now dead. "Sounds like something..." I choked on my words. "Rhapsody would've said something like that."

"I kept thinking," Sasha said, crossing her arms. "Why was Aunt Dee last? Where was Esteban taking her and the others?"

I'd simply thought they'd come back to try and help us, and when that didn't make any sense, Esteban hadn't gotten them out in time. Either way, it really didn't matter. They weren't coming back.

At such a far distance from the mansion we could only distinguish colors. The large black jagged blob was the castle's remains. The white spots belonged to the bodies they found: Joyce, Esteban, Iain. The thin yellow and black lines were warning tape. The black and blue and tan dots were policemen or officials. A few blue dots broke off from the crowd and approached the entrance to the tunnel.

We'd have to move, soon.

They'd have fun making sense of this one, unless they planned to pin it on the "vigilantes" they couldn't identify, like what had been done with the Chicago train derailment. A convenient excuse, but not one the public put up with for long.

I sipped from my cup. The bitter sweetness did nothing to spike my energy or my mood. "I don't know," I said. "Look at what we've become. We're not criminals. We're not heroes. Why did any of this happen in the first place? There's a reason, *right?*"

Though she was smarter than I was, the question confused even her. "There's a reason. We might not understand it."

That was code for she didn't know what it was either. I wasn't interested in asking any more questions when I couldn't find the answer.

"We'll find them," I said, reassuring myself.

Her eyes moistened. Wesley, Julia, and Ruby were still in the wind, too. She licked her lips and repeated me with a little less confidence than I had. "We'll find them."

"Excuse me. Can I have a word?"

We'd let our guard down. One of the cops investigating the scene exited the tunnel from the back end, not far from where we were standing. He wore a tan suede jacket, navy blue Polo shirt, black slacks, belt, and square-toed shoes. Way more stylish than an official uniform. His jacket bulged on the right side. Definitely a cop.

A familiar-looking cop.

Flashing a badge, he announced himself. "My name's Antwaan McCoy. I'm an officer with Xobai County. Detective, actually, I just got my test results back."

A lump formed in my throat. *The cop from Sasha's beach house.* I'd had my mask on, but he'd seen his Taser have no effect on my body and somehow traced it back to us.

I stated the obvious. "This isn't your case."

"No," he said with a smile. "It's not. It's not *yours* either, is it?"

I wasn't admitting to anything. Neither was Sasha. "Are you here to arrest us? Because that's not going to happen."

"No, Miss Anderson, I'm not, though I'd give anything for some answers that make sense."

She wasn't as naturally distrustful of cops as I was. Debra taught me to be respectful to policemen, especially since trouble followed me around. A lot of good that did me. "Why should we trust you?"

McCoy stuck his hands in his pockets. "I used to know your mother, Anna."

Cops played dirty tricks to get you to admit things, but the way his eyes brightened when he said my mother's name made me think he was sincere. "Prove it."

"Your mother went to Girls' High in Philly." He pulled a worn photograph from his wallet. "Here's her senior graduation picture."

The picture was definitely Mom's. I flipped it over. In her handwriting, she'd written about how much she'd loved him. At the bottom, she'd signed it, "Yours, Annie."

"Tell you what," he said after reclaiming his picture. "Fill in some blanks for me, and I'll tell you about the breadcrumbs you left behind. That way, my curiosity is satisfied and you can make sure your secrets are safe."

Sasha and I looked at each other. Our only other ally was Peters, and his alliance could switch at any moment. I didn't trust him. Sasha didn't trust him. But I believed in my mom. It's not like if he told the truth to his coworkers they'd believe him. He'd more than likely lose his badge.

"Deal," I said. "After we find our families."

Early in the afternoon, Julia, Wesley, Aunt Dee, Zachary, and Ruby were found. Esteban had teleported them to the most obvious spot they could have been found – a hospital. A final act of heroism. All of them were treated for dehydration and the adults had been given mild sleep sedatives. We had to wait until the morning until they'd be released, so we stayed in a nearby hotel in adjoining rooms.

The next day, before they were released, we visited with each of them. Julia already knew Ray was gone, so she had more time to process the loss. Sasha informed her father about his ex-wife, and he embraced his daughter as she wept. He failed at shedding a tear himself. Meanwhile, I comforted Ruby, who was hysterical over losing her only child. Zachary was none the wiser about his father and wouldn't be for a while, I imagined.

After we arrived home, I told Debra everything, leading with Ray's and Joyce's deaths. She fingered the gold cross around her neck and hugged me and Zachary like she'd never seen us before. Sasha and her dad came over, and we spent the night eating pizza and watching videos that made my baby brother laugh.

I stayed up longer than anyone else. Sasha rested her head on my chest and fell asleep. When I couldn't fight off fatigue any longer, I drifted off, too.

I dreamed of what might've been and my heart ached.

CHAPTER NINETEEN

immortality at a price

That weekend we made good on our promise and met Detective McCoy for breakfast downtown. He tipped the waitress fifty dollars to close down a portioned section of the restaurant so we could talk privately. She didn't ask any more questions once he showed her his badge.

Over coffee he asked us about the Union Station derailment. "So, how about it? I have to know."

With a hand brushing her hair back, Sasha told him, "The security cameras are already scrambled. Your phone goes on the table. No recording us. We do it mask on to distort our voices just in case."

He did as he was asked. "Geez. You guys have more trust issues than my ex-wife, and she was nuts."

"Anything we tell you about it won't make sense," I told him. "You'll have to accept that."

"Agreed. Tell me anyway."

He placed his order. We placed ours. His eyes bulged at the long list of food. When the waitress disappeared, Sasha explained our metabolisms.

"I bet you twenty dollars each you don't finish that much food," he said.

No, we hadn't caused the train to jump the tracks. That was our enemies. Yes, I'd stopped it. We'd lost a good friend there, Amauri Camuto. She was about two hundred years old.

He sipped his coffee and huffed in disbelief.

Sasha explained the 1859 Carrington solar flare event, where X-class flares irradiated large deposits of green emerald, scarlet emerald, goshenite, morganite, and aquamarine.

"The radiation from the storm gave us superpowers because of an antigen in our blood," she said. "That's where the Collective came from: Courtney Stafford, Camuto, Solomon Hughes, Ron Welker, Vivienne Coker, Jeff Peters, Belinda King, and David King."

He sipped his coffee. "And these people were your mentors?"

"Half of them," I admitted. "The other half wanted to wipe us off the planet and rule it."

He nearly choked. "Are there any more of you?"

Sasha and I shared a look.

"Probably," I said.

As we shoveled food down into our mouths, McCoy explained how he tracked us down. He told Joyce not to report the stolen card. Then he'd found us by our food orders. "You were hiding from someone – that much was obvious," he said. "Mrs. Anderson blamed the theft on you, which gave me a name – Jason Champion."

With a mouthful of eggs, he continued, "Once I found out your last name was Champion, I made the connection to your mom, and I had to know more."

He called in a favor and pulled our school records, attendance, and discipline. From there, he connected dots between our unexcused absences and the events going on in town that nobody could explain.

"Here's my advice. I'm a regular guy and it took me six months to hazard a good guess." He paid the bill and handed us both twenty dollar bills for losing the bet on us finishing our food. "You have two choices. Live regular lives or be abnormal and disappear."

On Monday, North High reopened. It seemed like we'd been out forever. Sasha and I were excused the first five days back, not to save the world, but to pay our respects to those we lost. The Hernandez triplets' funeral was today. Joyce's was Tuesday, my father's Wednesday, and Rhapsody's Friday. Rhapsody's was last because her family needed the most time to fly in. A great deal of them were coming from Panama.

I'd lost the fight with Ruby and Catholic tradition over Rhapsody's last wishes. *Anibel Cristela Rhapsody Martinez Lowe* was printed on her obituary with her birthdate, death date, and her sixth grade school picture before she went Goth. She'd have been furious. I'd wished she was here to yell and curse at me about it.

Our families had agreed to coordinate them all in the same week. Better to get it all out in one shot than mourn for a month. It made sense.

I attended Esteban's out of gratefulness and respect. He'd lost his brothers to Iain's experimentation, and he had still sacrificed his life to save our family members. No one except for us would ever know what he did. All his mother knew was that they'd been tortured and kidnapped, she was alone, and all three of her sons were dead. She was inconsolable and wailed from beginning to end, mumbling and praying in Spanish.

After the service, Wesley pulled me aside. "Come over for dinner tonight, Jason. There's something we need to talk about."

"Okay."

A few hours later, I flew over to make sure I had an appetite to satisfy. I hadn't eaten much since everything had happened except when I had to.

There, in their luxurious dining room with a mouthful of prime rib and garlic mashed potatoes, he asked me, "Jason, have you given any thought to your future?"

Future? Beyond staying alive? Julia mentioned the reading of Ray's will – to everyone's shock, including mine, he'd left me millions in a trust. I wouldn't get it until I turned twenty-one four plus years from now, but he made Debra the trustee so she could give me an allowance. I'd let her have it, and I could live off the Collective's stash. She'd never have to work another day in her life.

What's Wesley getting at? I dropped my gold fork onto the fine china plate. *Where's he going with this? Has he talked to McCoy?* "Like college or something? Not really."

He placed his hand on Sasha's forearm and rubbed it. "I hate to uproot Sasha so soon after her mother's death, but the school year just started, and my headquarters is in Oregon. She'll be leaving with me after we settle Joyce's matters."

With my eyes trained on him, I asked her, "Is that what *you* want?"

She yanked her arm away, avoided eye contact with Wesley and said, *"Hardly."*

I made an impulsive suggestion. "Stay with us. We have the room."

Her face softened. "You'd do that for me?"

Wesley gave her a hard stare. "Doesn't matter. This science fiction fantasy lifestyle you've been living is over. You're still a minor, Sasha Nicole. You're going."

"Over? There's always another psycho out there, Daddy. What about Jade?"

She had a point. We hadn't heard or seen anything from her. She could still be searching for Hughes, but she had no leads and neither did we. Revenge could be on her mind, though we'd told her everything we knew.

"It's not your job to stop her, Sasha," he said still chewing. "It's not Jason's, either."

I waved my hand. "Hello? I am sitting *right here."*

"And *this* is how you want to rebuild our relationship?" she added. "Force me away from everything I know and everyone I love?"

From there, it became a full-fledged argument. They yelled and cursed out of their frustration with one another and their grief over Joyce.

Whatever my future held, it held. I didn't want to fight about it. I didn't want to fight about *anything*. Not anymore.

◇◇◇

The next day, Joyce's funeral came and went without much fanfare. Wesley did an about face and invited me to ride in the family limousine with him and Sasha. I hadn't been to many funerals, but I knew it was a big deal. We sat together and held hands, though her palm was clammy and she self-consciously dried it over and over again. She'd limited her tears enough to salvage her picture perfect makeup, which included enough to cover the hair-thin scars left on her face from drinking blood water.

She leaned over and whispered in my ear, "He's going to emancipate me. Can you believe it?"

I was shocked. "Why?"

"I promised to live on my own, do some therapy and to visit every other weekend." She paused. "And I added that if he moved me to Portland, you and I would run away together and have a lot of sex."

I was putting on my black suit for the third time this week and realized that I was out of clean white button down shirts. There was a knitted shirt I could wear, but I needed a necktie. In the middle of my panic, Debra walked into my room with a freshly ironed shirt. "Thought you could use this."

I put it on over my undershirt and buttoned it from the bottom. "Thanks."

Debra smoothed a section of my blue and black comforter and sat on it. "I see being a superhero hasn't made you any neater."

I smiled for the first time in a week. "No neck brace today?"

"Nope. I've been good." She craned her neck a little and patted the mattress. "Sit."

"Don't we have to go?"

"If the limousine leaves without me Deidra Lee will raise hell. Sit."

"Yes, ma'am." I did as she asked.

Debra played with my comforter fabric. "Do you remember the first night you spent with me and Zachary?"

"It was cold and we had mac and cheese and hot dogs for dinner."

She smiled. "It was December 19, 2012. I'd rented this awful one bedroom a half mile from Everwood. There was a fire escape, and…"

"…you nailed the windows shut to keep from getting robbed. I remember."

She closed her eyes. "You'd been suspended from school, right before Christmas break. Ray sent you to me, said he didn't know how to raise you without me. He pulled up to the curb, tried to flash his money at me, and said it was for a day.

"You were so angry he'd dumped you off with me." She waved a finger in the air. "You kicked the bars out of one of my two wooden chairs. I offered you mac and cheese and hot dogs for dinner…" She stopped talking to keep herself from crying. "With the bills…it's all I could afford. I was saving up for our second crappy apartment."

Why is she telling me this? I placed a hand on her lap. "Why didn't you take Dad to court for child support?"

She patted my hand and told me the truth. "Family is everything to me, and back then, your dad was vindictive. He wanted to sleep with Julia, so I let him have her. I wanted Zachary and I wanted you, no strings attached. The money wasn't that important."

She continued her story. "So, Zachary was crying, and you picked him up. You rocked him to sleep and laid him down in his crib. That's when I knew you were more than the discipline record and what people thought you were."

"And what am I?" I asked her.

"The boy who ate macaroni and cut up hot dogs like the world owed him something wouldn't have sacrificed his life to save other people. Thank you for bringing *both* of my sons home safely."

I squeezed my eyes to keep from crying. Even at my worst she'd believed in me.

My dad's funeral was the shortest of the three I'd been to. According to both Debra and Julia, it's what he what have wanted. He believed in God. He just didn't believe in long services. It's why he joined a nondenominational church and rarely attended. Unlike Mom's church, which was old school and long, the church service lasted an hour, tops.

I rode with Julia, who insisted on holding my hand. Her parents, her Black father and Egyptian mother, sat across from us. They spoke Arabic more often than not and largely ignored me. I'd never met them before now. They didn't seem overly interested in meeting the son of the man who'd cheated on his faithful wife with their daughter.

Julia turned to me. "I'm going back home."

"Egypt? When?"

She nodded and patted my knee. "Soon. There's nothing left for me here, no offense."

We didn't have the best relationship in the world. "None taken."

"You're welcome to visit. I'll always think of you as my stepson, Zachary, too. Just..." She winked at me and whispered. "Fly out the conventional way, all right?"

"All right."

I gazed out of the window. *Why were we pulling up to Mom's cemetery?* The car slowly rolled over the gravel and grass up to almost the exact spot where Mom was buried. A green tent with silver poles was erected next to it. Ray's plot was right next to hers. After the pastor read a few scriptures, we said goodbye. I laid a white rose on top of his dark brown and gold casket.

"Goodbye Dad," I said. "I'll miss you." And I meant it.

Later I stood outside in the church's parking lot, I stared at the setting sun, its orange and red ribbons wrapping the landscape in its glory. It was beautiful. I fought the urge to fly home or anywhere where I didn't have to celebrate the end of someone else's life. At least this was the second to last one.

Sasha came from behind me and snatched my hand. "Let's go. I sent McCoy a text to let him know we're in the air."

Detective McCoy had been a valuable resource. Ever since we'd told him everything, he'd acted as sort of a guardian angel to us. I'd never thought I'd say I trusted a cop, considering our history with Spivey and my discipline record, but I was getting there.

Picking her up in my arms, I leapt for the horizon. Mid-air, I turned on my suit's cloaking and masked up. To my surprise, Sasha did the same. She'd been prepared to ditch, too. Seeing that, I went supersonic and the sound in my ears dropped out for a split second.

Soon, we were in Xobai on the mountaintop, watching the sun finish setting. I inhaled the saltwater breeze coming off the Pacific.

"You know, Ruby wouldn't hear me on the obituary." I made a bracket with my hands. *"Anibel Cristela Rhapsody Martinez-Lowe.* 'It's Catholic tradition', she said. Rhapsody would've been *so pissed."*

"Yeah, she would've." Sasha brushed her hair behind her ears. *"This* is what she would've wanted. We'd have cremated her and spread her out on the beach, and right as the tide came in, she'd wash away with it."

She loved the ocean. Sasha was right about that much.

She changed the subject. "So, you're not thinking college. Does that mean you're *not* hanging up the cape?"

My stomach tightened when I thought about more than the present moment. For a long time, I had to concern myself with *survival.* "Have you seen my GPA? Discipline record? My guidance counselor thinks I should cut my losses, drop out next year, and then take the GED until I pass it."

Sasha crossed her arms and said, "You're better than that. You could get into college if you tried, Jason."

"What about your cape? You still have your prism."

Sasha smacked her thigh. "Yeah, but I have to get to a place where I'm not facing death every day. I could get a car accident tomorrow, go down in a plane crash, or just go, you know? That's a far more random way to go than having a speedster stab me."

I knew what she meant. None of the people we'd buried so far had died of anything remotely natural. "Yeah."

"I'm not invincible anymore. You *are*. Do we even know if you and I can be around each other without the world crashing down around us?"

I knew that if the world crashed down around me, I didn't want to be without her when it did.

I forced myself to go to Rhapsody's funeral. In my mind, I'd already honored her life enough by sitting on her favorite overlook in Xobai and watching the sun set. To me, the way the sun settled at the end of the ocean meant Rhapsody was finally at peace, comfortable in her own skin, and she was enjoying the new view of wherever she was. My heart ached thinking about her. I tried distracting myself by looking at the gigantic statue of crucified Jesus hanging from the ceiling, but I didn't have time. Ruby snatched my hand, ushered me to the front of the cathedral, and introduced me to family members. I had to assume the people with brown skin were Ruby's side and the browner ones were George's, but I couldn't truly tell until they began to talk to one another.

She introduced me in front of the closed casket the same way every time so I memorized it.

"¡Mira! Esta es Jason Campeón."

I'd gotten D's in Spanish, but even I could've figured that out.

Ruby excitedly waved her hands. "Él y Anibel estaban enamorados . Él salvó su vida y la mía!"

They proceeded to ask me questions that she answered. When one of them engaged her in conversation, I slipped away and found Sasha, who translated for me.

"She's telling them that you and Rhapsody were in love, and that you'd saved her life."

The rest of the service was a blur. We stood up and sat down, sang hymns, said prayers, got up again, sat down again. Communion was served. I took the bread the priest put into my mouth and drank from the cup everyone had drunk from, though it grossed me out. I didn't want to do it, but right before that part of the service, Ruby looked back at me with expectancy in her eyes. I wouldn't refuse her on this day. Plus, I was black, Rhapsody was Panamanian, and Ruby might've wanted them to think I was a good Catholic boy.

The end of the service was awful. Everyone passed by the closed casket to say their final goodbyes. When our row stood, my heart thumped in my chest. I let go of Sasha's hand for fear I'd get emotional and crush her bones. Instead, she rested a hand on my shoulder and walked close to me so that she didn't have to let go. We approached the casket. I imagined her in head-to-toe Goth garb with headphones in her ears and a sarcastic remark at the ready.

She was gone. Forever. Hot knives stuck into my heart. My defenses threatened to break but I held them up. We'd killed Selby. It didn't make me feel any better. His death didn't mean she'd come back. My hands over my face, I cried in the pew. I cried because I'd had to say goodbye to my first love who may or may not be dead. The casket was empty. I had no closure. I'd saved the world for the third time and failed to save people. My father. Sasha's mother. Esteban. What good was having powers to save lives if you couldn't save them all?

Of course, Sasha stayed with me. She sat to my right. I stopped sobbing when a heavy weight smacked onto the pew at my left. Trying my best to compose myself without a tissue, I removed my hands from my face.

It was Peters, dressed in a pinstriped gray suit, walking with a cane. On top of the cane was a golden jewel that looked suspiciously like a piece of heliodor.

"*Ransom,*" he said to us.

I was confused. "What?"

"My real last name is *Ransom.* When you get past – a certain age – you have to create aliases in able to function in society. Social security numbers, IDs and what not."

Yet another lie he'd told us, but I suppose it was necessary to an extent.

"Here." He tossed me a handkerchief and groaned. "I'd like to tell you this – saying goodbye -- is the worst of it, but it's not. People die, walk away. It is what it is."

Sasha sounded interested. "The worst of *what?*"

He ignored her question and repositioned his body to face us as they closed the casket, locked it, and rolled it to the hearse. "I did you a solid and tied up a few loose ends you'd be interested in knowing about."

We mouthed *Jade* to him at the same time. Great, he'd killed her, too.

His smile was full of stained teeth. "No," he said waving a wrinkled hand. "Nothing like that. I took her to that shrink doctor Susan of yours and she started to get her puzzle put back together somehow. With my supervision, of course."

I suppose that meant she wasn't crazy anymore. "She's a *legacy*," I said, recalling Iain's name for Collective children. "She's still out there."

"Yeah," he sighed. He must have been thinking about his son, Iain, and what he'd become. "She's not the only living one. That's why you're still needed. *Both of you.*"

Anger built up inside of me. For *one day* I wanted to walk away from this life. Sasha had surely had enough – she'd lost as much as I had, if not more.

Peters used his cane to leverage himself to his feet. "Stop by the fortress sometime. I'm staying there now. I've planned some improvements you two might be interested in. When you're ready, that is. And I changed your password. Two words."

The last time he'd set it, it was *Rhapsody*. "Changed it to what?"

Peters hobbled his way to the back of the church without answering me. I had a feeling it was the last time we'd see him for a while.

CHAPTER TWENTY

ABOUT THREE YEARS LATER

I inhaled and exhaled, a steady, cleansing breath. Susan didn't have to prompt me. I did it on my own.

She eased back in her leather office chair. "Okay. After this, I think we're done."

I couldn't believe it. "No more EMDR? Forever?"

"You haven't blacked out in more than a year, Jason. You're closing in on two. You haven't had a PTSD episode in a few months, either. Not a cure, but progress."

My shoulders were loose. I wasn't sweating. Yeah, I was relaxed. After all this time I knew how to cope without alcohol or by being medicated beyond Adderall.

"Talk to me about the explosion."

I described the moments one-by-one, opening the pit and getting inside on top of the provenance crystals. The heat...I remembered the searing heat and the humming, the buzzing. My temperature rose a little as I recounted the memory enough for me to notice, but I took a breath and finished the story.

From there, I named each person whose life I took that I knew of. The ones in the Orizaba fortress where I stole heliodor – we gave them names together based on my spotty memory of their appearances. Dinar Patel, Jin

Tao, Paz Luca, Arella Brooks, Tatia Gabriel, Orla Scott. Then, David King, Leslie Selby, and Iain Ransom. And the ones I felt guilt over: Ray and Joyce.

I didn't name Larry Dozier because his death wasn't my fault after all. The police ran forensics on Dozier, and they found he'd long been dead and had somehow been planted in the car. Iain had set the whole thing up to screw with me. *Figures.* He'd deserved to have all of the deaths at his mansion pinned on him.

Then my transition into Rhapsody's last moments was quick and unprompted. I described how she'd lain on her back, bleeding to death. Her glove touched my cheek. The armor was rough against my skin. For the first time since we'd started these EMDR treatment sessions, I didn't stop talking. If I did, she'd tap on her desk with her pen and like a kick-started stalled car, I'd start talking again.

"The only thing left," Susan said, the end of her pen in her mouth, "is what she said to you. What were Rhapsody's last words to you?"

"She told me to remember my humanity." I paused to gather my thoughts. "That I'm human, and I'll still make mistakes. Not to be too hard on myself when I do. It wasn't my fault it was her time to go. No matter what it looks like, God always has a plan. She asked me never to forget her. And she wanted me to love again."

"She said all of that?"

I folded my hands across my stomach and remembered what she'd actually told me. *I love you. Please don't look for me.* "More or less," I lied.

Satisfied, Susan smiled and said, "All right. What's our positive belief?"

She said it along with me. "I'm healthy and whole, not 'normal'."

Susan rounded her desk and gave me a full-bodied hug. We'd been down a long road together, from my first session with her seven years ago until now. She'd insist on once-in-a-while checkups and schedule a session if I had a relapse. Beyond that, my regular visits were over. Finally.

"Big celebration tonight?" she asked me.

I bent over and wrote her a check for the session. "Yup."

"With Amber?"

I shook my head. "Nope. Broke up last month."

"That was quick! Has to be Nia?"

"Uh uh. She stopped returning my texts."

She ran through a list of the girls I'd been talking to over the past six months: Tee, Jessica, Mariah, Wendy? No, no, no, and heck no.

"I might do this one solo," I said.

"You could do that." She peeked out of her office blinds. A mischievous look crossed her face. "Or you could entertain a young lady who skipped her last college class and drove more than two hours to see you cross the finish line."

I looked for myself. Sure enough, Sasha Nicole Anderson was in the parking lot in a pair of cut-off blue jean shorts, a white and blue athletic wear top with red baseball sleeves, matching blue sneakers and sunglasses. She'd wrapped up her hair tight and the top to her purple convertible was down. "You did this?" I asked her.

"You chucked a door through my window," she said with an honest laugh.

"Which I paid for," I pointed out.

She playfully smacked my shoulder. "It's okay to share this moment."

"What, I don't get the 'tell her how you feel' speech?"

Susan bit her lip. "Too late. I kind of sent her screenshots of your journal."

That wasn't even remotely funny. Part of this therapy was to journal anything that caused me emotional distress. A couple pages were dedicated to my feelings for Sasha – all of them, including the ones I'd never want Debra to see. I could calm myself through them, but coping with the guilt I felt about feeling them was the worst.

"Thanks," I said. "Tell Andy I said hi. And hey, how's Jade?"

The lines in her face deepened. "Remember that whole doctor-patient confidentiality thing we talked about? The fundamental rule I can't jeopardize, not even for you."

"Did I mention Jade helped Iain collapse the Multiplex in Vegas and I held it up on my back?"

"You might've mentioned that, yeah." She thought a moment. "Kai is an alternate personality – she did that, and…she's integrated and harmless."

I waved goodbye to Susan and left her office. Sasha met me at the bottom of the stairs and hugged me like it hadn't been six months since we'd touched each other.

"Hey, Cap." Her ruby red lips never looked better. "Congrats."

"Thanks. I'm surprised Football Player didn't mind."

Hand on hip, she keyed the alarm. "I'm sure he'd mind if he knew. Let's go."

I got into the passenger side. The car flew up I-48 and we took a familiar route. I sure could use a Pudgy Burger. The turnoff was a couple more exits down.

She tilted her sunglasses up into her hair. "How's Amber?" she asked me.

"We broke up. How's Football Player?"

Hurt registered on her face. "He's sleeping with a cheerleader, so I'm sure he's fine."

"Sorry."

"Don't be," she said. "His loss. He couldn't wait."

I had to ask. "Wait for what?"

"Wait to turn into somebody else."

My heart thumped. We passed the exit, and soon we were stuck in rush hour traffic, I got curious. "Where are we going?"

She slapped the steering wheel. "Nowhere, now. Got any ideas?"

This was my chance. "One, yeah."

I leaned over to Sasha's side of the car to kiss her. My face had gotten so close to hers that I could smell the spearmint gum on her breath. She kept still, not moving forward or away. She was thinking about it too much. Right when I was about to back off, she dove in and we kissed – long, and hard, and passionately. The drivers behind her honked until it was clear we weren't going to move.

The horns, yelling, and cursing continued for minutes until she pulled back from the kiss and pressed the accelerator. "About time. Are we doing this?" she asked me.

I'd kissed Sasha on impulse after we graduated from North High. She'd asked me then, "Are we doing this?" I hesitated too long. I was surprised I'd actually done enough to walk across a stage and I wasn't sure then. The following week she left for a summer internship in Portland near Wesley. She wouldn't take my calls and he wouldn't let me visit her for three months. Then she was off to Stanford.

So, when she asked "Are we doing this?" again, I almost cut her off and said, "Yes."

The way I answered made her laugh. She reached out for my hand and I held it. Electricity sparked in my veins. "Turns out you're a normal boy, after all," she said. "Except that stuff I've seen online. You've gotta be more careful when you suit up."

I'd hit YouTube a couple of times when I saved people from disasters and didn't get out quick enough not to be snapped with a camera phone. I couldn't let those people die. It wasn't a big deal until the police put out a search warrant for me, the "Vigilante."

Traffic slowed down again. We'd already gone past Pudgy Burger, Debra and Freeman's house, and the cemetery, I asked her, "Are we going to Walsh?"

I expected her to say a different destination. "Yup."

"Why?" I asked.

"I'm ready," she said. "Aren't you?"

I didn't even have to think about it. Pointing to the next exit, I said, "You're going to need to pull off, then. We'll get there tomorrow at this rate."

She did and we parked on a residential street in front of a house. A family of four – a man, his wife, and their toddler twins – walked up the steps to their home. I imagined they'd go in, eat something wholesome and homemade like pot roast and baby potatoes with steamed broccoli, play a family game and put the kids to bed. Then the two of them would watch a movie in the living room or spend time in bed.

Sasha squeezed my hand. "I want this, Jason."

I did, too. "Can we have this?"

"I don't know," she said with a smile. "I've never tried. You?"

"No. It's untested science."

She didn't have to say anything. It needed a test.

Hand-in-hand, we walked down the block and turned the corner to a dead end. There was a completely dark house. Nobody was home. I rang the bell to check. When no one answered, we knew it was safe. No surveillance cameras or open windows. I pressed the inside of my palm and my body suit became visible. To my surprise, Sasha did the same.

We lifted off for Walsh and landed there in minutes. I'm sure the sonic boom we'd made in the air would be added to my collection of appearances on YouTube. McCoy used to be able to get them down but after the last few, he stopped trying. "Keep your face covered and be careful," was all said to me. It was the least I could do.

The fortress opening was covered in weeds, as usual. Peters was down there, watching, waiting. He wanted me to play his game, where I guessed my password. Fun for him but torture for me. I hated guessing games. My last password was "Rhapsody" while I was dating Sasha at the time. His idea of a joke.

"Any guesses?" I asked her. "He said it was two words."

With her finger at her chin, she said, "Has to be something important to you. You'd both know it. I'm pretty sure it's not my name, or yours."

"You'd think he'd put me through enough – hitting me with his car, shooting at me, trying to kill me for the provenance crystal – to at least give me a better hint than 'two words'. Movie? TV show? Animal, vegetable, mineral?"

I blurted out a stream of consciousness of guesses. Sasha laughed at most of them, especially the profane ones.

Then something popped into my head.

Debra would've said it was "God's intervention" if it worked. After all, I'd seen and done in nineteen years, I was beginning to believe someone was watching over me. Sasha squeezed my arm and stroked it. This was a new beginning, with her, the rest of my life. Who knew where it would go and when it would end. Who cared?

One thing I knew – I wouldn't do it alone.

I said it my new password with confidence. "Champion Immortal."

THE END

Discover more by Brian Thompson

Months after absorbing a nuclear explosion, Jason Champion is recuperating in a hospital when he is attacked by a shape-shifter with an agenda. She wants to harvest Jason's radioactive blood to keep his enemy alive.

Following a narrow escape, Jason is joined by his new girlfriend Rhapsody, his ex Sasha, and a new friend, Esteban. While the provenance emerald, scarlet emerald, goshenite, heliodor, and morganite crystals that grant them mysterious powers are safe, there is a new threat.

ISBN: 978-0989105644* Paperback * 300 pages
Available in electronic format at www.amazon.com;
www.bn.com

www.greatnationpublishing.com

The school year ending with Reject High's destruction was enough for Jason Champion.

That is until a mysterious new enemy is possessed with the belief that whoever absorbs the radiation will become immortal.

With no other options and their enemies drawing closer to their goal, Jason and a group that has guarded the origin of their power for a century. Its members think the storm will cause an explosion killing millions.

ISBN: 978-0-989-10563-7 * Paperback *258 pages
Available in electronic format at www.amazon.com;
www.bn.com

After his latest fight, Jason Champion is sent to a rundown alternative school, nicknamed "Reject High."

Rhapsody Lowe shows Jason a crystal that turns her invisible. Jason tries one on and he jumps over a city.

With eleven days until Reject High is destroyed, Jason and his friends must dodge their pursuers and save their power source from falling into the wrong hands.

ISBN: 978-0-989-10560-6 * Paperback * 270 pages
Available in electronic format at www.amazon.com;
www.bn.com

www.greatnationpublishing.com

After a failed coup, a revolutionary named Noor is exiled to earth and sentenced to death. He vows to rule the inferior planet.

In the year 2050, tragedy strikes Harper Lowe, Damario Coley, Quinne Ruiz, and Teanna Kirkwood. Through the Genesis Institute, they are all offered the chance to "begin again."

When the project's true motives are revealed, the group is sent hurtling toward an uncertain future with unpredictable consequences.

ISBN: 978-0-615-60216-1 * Paperback * 264 pages
Available in electronic format at www.amazon.com